Landing on Her Feet

by

Kim Janine Ligon

Landing on Her Feet

Cover Art by *Tina Lynn Stout*

The Wild Rose Press, Inc.
PO Box 708
Adams Basin, NY 14410-0708
Visit us at www.thewildrosepress.com

Publishing History
First Edition, 2023
Trade Paperback ISBN 978-1-5092-4973-2
Digital ISBN 978-1-5092-4974-9

Published in the United States of America

The unmistakable roar of a motorcycle echoed through the diner. Kat stopped where she stood. Her lungs wouldn't refill. She gripped the counter to steady her trembling legs. Out the front window she saw a red-helmeted rider atop a motorcycle pull out of a space in front of the diner and drive away.

Impossible. Not here. He couldn't know she's gone. Not yet. *Other people with red helmets ride motorcycles. Get a grip, girl! People are staring. Stop scowling.* She wiped away the tear that slipped down her cheek, plastered on what she hoped was a pleasant smile, and resumed pouring coffee. She needed to make a good impression. She had to keep *this* job.

Dedication

To the man who holds my hand crossing parking lots; rarely says "no, stop, don't"; always has a good idea about what to make for supper; finds a way to love and support me—even when the endeavor is not one of his choosing; and reads, rereads, and reads again the stories that flow out of my head. You picked another great title. Thank you especially for 'saving' Chase. You were the only one who could do it. *Sine qua non.*

Special thanks to:

*Beverly, Sue, Pam, Lisa, Scott, Jean, Herb, and Cynthia. Parts of this book may look familiar because you read one of its former incarnations.

*Millie for your patient assistance as my in-house editor.

*Susie and Doris (RIP) whose namesakes are in this story.

*Lori and Lisa for your medical knowledge.

*My relatives and in-laws who encouraged me by buying my debut novel and asking for the next one.

*My growing list of blog followers who comment on my posts, bought my debut novel, and loved it.

*My fellow supportive, nurturing Roses who signed up to follow me, hosted me on their blogs, reviewed my book, helped me navigate the unknown world of marketing, and welcomed me with open arms to this garden that Rhonda and RJ tend with loving care. It's a great place to grow and bloom.

*Dianne Rich, the incomparable editor I am blessed to have once again.

*The good Lord who creates a way to get the stories of my heart onto paper and into your hands.

To one and all, although it remains woefully inadequate, I can only say Thank You again from a heart bursting with gratitude!

Chapter One

Kat Russell captured her waist-length blonde hair into a rope-like braid, then pulled it through the hole in the back of her brimmed hat, grabbed her gardening gloves and trowel, and almost skipped out the front door. Spring's siren call echoed in her ears. But she was the only one in the house who heard it. Jocelyn was curled up in her recliner reading, as usual. Pop and Timmy snuggled together on the couch watching an early season Sunday afternoon Phillies game. Seemed unlikely they'd be able to give a play by play when it was over. She'd heard snoring.

The tulips and daffodils struggled to push their way through the winter's accumulation of leaves and yard debris covering their heads. The first order of business was to clean them out, then add some growth enhanced potting soil to revitalize the tired old dirt. She planned to spread the vivid yellow bursts of joy to the backyard using some of the bulbs she thinned out of the front flower beds.

It wouldn't be spring without getting to dig in the dirt. She'd missed only one year. The bulbs forgave her and came out on schedule despite the unavoidable temporary neglect. Good thing. She needed a happy constant in her universe, especially that year.

The bright blue bachelor's buttons made their first appearance the year Kat turned eight. Every year since they'd reseeded themselves and come back brighter and thicker than ever. The tall, delicate freesia with its sweet scent was planted when she was nine. And the bright, cheerful Gerbera daisies peeked out of the ground on the tenth anniversary of their inaugural appearance. Neighbors knew it was spring when they saw mother and daughter with dirty knees and broad smiles, working side by side.

The sun gently warmed her back, slowly melting away the lingering chill of winter. Kat worked the trowel deep into the dirt around the plants, loosened it, and removed unwelcome weeds. She hummed. Cheerful tunes. Uplifting songs. From all those years of planting bulbs and memories that both still bloomed. It was a life affirming ritual. Mom gave her that gene.

A shadow fell across her. She shivered. Must be a really big cloud. Wait. Nothing she planted had that sickening, sweet, musky smell. A hand gripped her shoulder squeezing hard. Another pulled her braid to the side forcing her head to turn. Her eyes unwillingly confirmed what her heart feared.

It *is* him. Her danger antenna hadn't activated. His sentence was twenty years. She'd stopped listening for the roar of his motorcycle long ago.

Prison had not dulled the cruel hardness shining in those steely-gray eyes. His biceps bulged larger than ever. What else did he have to do behind bars? With one quick motion he jerked her to her feet.

Kat found her voice. Soft at first, then roaring. "You're not welcome. Get back on your bike and leave! *Now!*"

Thin lips stretched across crooked, yellowing teeth in what almost passed for a smile. Shivers rocketed up and down her spine. "Babe, is that any way to greet your lover finally come home? I was expecting something a whole lot friendlier, you know?" The syrupy voice dripped with false affection.

Instinctively, she tried to step away from him. He held her in a vise-like grip. Her chest tightened. Her gut tied itself into a triple knot. She had to concentrate just to keep breathing. "I have no reason to be friendly." Icicles encased every word.

"C'mon, little darling. All I want to do is talk, maybe go for a ride. It's been almost six years. We can get reacquainted. Know what I mean?"

"I know *exactly* what you mean. Never again." Kat looked at the front door, willing it to open. It was no use. Pop would never hear over the ball game. *If* he was awake. No one had expected this demon's return. Not yet.

"I think you're gonna change your mind. *Now*!" He grabbed her left arm and pulled hard. Suddenly she was airborne, then landed with a thud on the concrete sidewalk.

A familiar flame of searing pain shot through her fingers and arm. She dropped to her knees, reflexively getting into the safety of the fetal position. He wasn't going to hurt her ever again.

He dragged her across the sidewalk. Knees scraped against the cement. She curled into a tighter ball. A piece of glass split open her right shin. Blood ran down her leg. She refused to cooperate. He struggled against her dead weight past the curb where his motorcycle was parked, to the red car, her car. "Unlock it. You're driving," he demanded.

"No! I won't. *Someone help me!*"

Her screams grew louder. More frequent. Neighbors opened front doors. No one stepped forward to help. They stood in their own yards enthralled and paralyzed by the spectacle on the Russell front lawn.

She yelled, flailed her free arm, and stabbed at his shins with the trowel. He kicked her hand until the metal tool clattered to the sidewalk out of reach. How could she escape?

"Call the cops! He's hurting me!"

He reached into her pockets searching for car keys. She flipped momentarily out of his grasp. He grabbed the braid hanging down her back and yanked hard. Why didn't anyone help? Then he twisted her arm until the elbow bent unnaturally. A sickening pop, then intense pain. A wave of nausea flooded her. She ignored it. She would not stand. If she didn't get to her feet, he'd leave without her. He had to.

The screen door flew open banging loudly against the brick wall. Pop charged down the steps, two at a time, wielding an aluminum baseball bat. "Get out of here, slime bucket, before I take batting practice on your head!" Jim Russell advanced toward them until he was close enough to smell her attacker's fetid breath.

The beast dropped her arm and rapidly retreated from the only person brave enough to challenge him. "I just wanted to talk, old man, chill. No reason to go all nuclear on me. I'm leaving *now,* but I'll be back for what's mine. No one steals from Dirk Crowe and survives." He leapt on the waiting motorcycle and sped away from the curb, narrowly missing a SUV coming down the street. His red helmet remained anchored on the back of the seat.

Jocelyn stopped on the top porch step, arms folded

across her chest, and shook her head with an "I told you so" smirk covering her face. Timmy tried to get past her, but she held him back. Good. He didn't need to be in the middle of this. For once, Jocelyn was actually being helpful.

Kat couldn't move. Pop reached down to help her stand. "Let's go in and get you cleaned up." Her left arm hung limply at her side. The pain magnified. She grasped Pop's hand with the right one.

"I didn't know he was out. He *will* be back. Dirk never makes idle threats."

Kat linked arms with her father. Pop gasped, then clutched his chest. He fell against her. She couldn't hold him up. He slipped to the ground. Kat screamed, "Call 911, Jocelyn."

Kat straddled his chest like she'd been taught in CPR class. The rhythm is…what is the song? Got it, "ah, ha, ha, ha, hmm, hmmm, alive." Her left arm was of no use. She pounded harder with the right, pushing all her weight into each compression. Would it work one-handed?

Pop seemed to be breathing but was out cold. Jocelyn wailed even louder after calling the ambulance. Why didn't she shut up? Crying never helped anything. Where was the blasted ambulance? *There—that siren's getting closer. Finally, they're almost here.* "Hang on, Pop. It's going to be okay." She kept the pounding rhythm going.

Jocelyn was his wife. Her place was in the ambulance with him. The EMTs told Kat she'd probably saved Pop's life. Jocelyn would only remember what happened *before* the sudden attack, not her rescue efforts.

Kat grabbed her phone off the kitchen table. Timmy was in tears, frozen in the spot from where he'd watched the ambulance leave. She took his hand and guided him into his booster seat in the back of the car.

"C'mon, honey. We need to go to the hospital."

Luckily, Timmy could belt himself in. She struggled to get her own seat belt fastened. She couldn't raise her left arm to get the belt under it. Finally, she gave up and clicked the strap in place over the limp, painful arm. She'd never driven one-armed before, but there was no choice. She had to know what was happening with Pop. If she wasn't at the hospital, she'd never know.

****

For the umpteenth time, Kat paced across the drab surgical waiting room with its worn Naugahyde-covered chairs and scarred end tables. No wonder people stared at her. She looked like she'd barely escaped from a pitched battle.

After they rushed Pop to the operating room, the emergency room nurse insisted on treating her scraped knees, legs, and elbows. They needed to "reduce" her dislocated shoulder and wanted to sedate her before they tried. She refused sedation. One of the nurses took Timmy out for a soda. He didn't need to hear his mom scream when the procedure ended in tears. She wasn't sure which hurt worse, Dirk jerking it out or the doctor putting the shoulder back in place. She would have to wear the immobilizing sling at least six weeks and gradually do stretching and strengthening exercises to get back to normal. How could she drive with that thing on? It was a lot more restricting than the one-armed drive to the hospital had been. No chance Jocelyn

6

would play chauffeur. Not for her.

How long does it take to do a triple bypass? No one told her. Jocelyn talked to the doctors. She never shared any information. Her father's wife sat alone on the other side of the room glaring at her.

Timmy happily ate a supper of root beer, peanuts, and cheese doodles from the waiting room vending machines, then curled up like a kitten in one of the chairs, totally unbothered by the lights, conversations, and general bustling. He slept.

The knot in her stomach kept Kat from eating. Pop had to be all right. She couldn't lose him too. She had hoped she'd never see Dirk again. If Pop hadn't rescued her, it would have resulted in far worse than scrapes and a sling. Her heart knew this wasn't the last time Dirk would hurt her. Would she survive the next one?

Kat bit her tongue when Jocelyn made it clear that she was his wife and she would be Pop's first and only visitor in the Coronary Intensive Care Unit. Okay, Jocelyn didn't want to lose another husband, but did she have to take such a hateful tone with everyone? The nurse told Kat not to take her mother's behavior personally. She quickly corrected the mistaken identification. That woman is *not* my mother. She's my father's wife. *It is personal. Nothing but.*

They'd been at the hospital all night. Timmy woke and needed breakfast. Kat called work. She wouldn't be in this morning. She wasn't sure when she'd be back with her shoulder immobilized. They weren't happy. She didn't care. She'd almost lost Pop. Jocelyn was being Jocelyn. Her worst nightmare was out of prison and had picked up his reign of terror right where he'd left off six years ago. This Monday morning was anything but routine.

****

The day Pop moved to the step-down unit, Kat picked Timmy up from school before afternoon visiting hours. They stopped at the hospital. Jocelyn was camped out in her husband's room. She occupied the recliner, the only chair in the room, reading while Jim dozed. She did not acknowledge their presence.

How Jocelyn felt didn't matter. Pop smiled broadly when they walked through the door. He introduced them to his cardiologist as, "This is my baby girl and her son—she's the one who did CPR on me until the ambulance got there." The doctor commended Kat for the quick thinking, repeating the EMT's opinion that she had saved her father's life.

****

Pop was released after five days in the hospital with a laundry list of do's and mostly don'ts to follow to speed his recovery. Jocelyn made sure everyone knew what they were.

Stop smoking completely—not even the Phillies victory cigar—if they ever started winning again that would be hard.

Get on a heart healthy diet. Absolutely no greasy Philly cheese steaks slathered in golden liquid imitation cheese. No hot dogs. No beer. No fried anything. Pop said it was the "if it tastes good, spit it out" diet.

No lifting more than ten pounds until his chest healed. So no going back to work any time soon.

Get more exercise. Walk every day. Do the cardiac rehab exercises.

Keep stress under control. Jocelyn glared directly at Kat when she read that one aloud from the list.

No wonder Pop was depressed. Who wouldn't be when their world had been completely flipped upside down? And Jocelyn, the Enforcer, made certain he followed the doctor's orders. To the letter. No exceptions.

The doctor put Pop, who had never needed routine medications, on a plethora of daily pills: for cholesterol, for depression, for anxiety, to sleep, to think more clearly. Kat believed the only way to truly help would be to stop taking *all* meds, but Pop couldn't sleep without something. If he didn't sleep, he wouldn't be able to function or go back to the garage. Then he *would* be depressed.

"If you hadn't been involved with that motorcycle-riding jerk, my husband would never have had a heart attack."

"And if I hadn't performed CPR on him until the ambulance arrived, you'd be a widow again!" The hateful comment spewed out of her mouth. The gloves were off. Arguing with Jocelyn sucked all the sweetness from Kat's soul.

The last three weeks had been brutal. Thankfully, Kat had returned to work by the time Pop came home. She couldn't lift trays, but she could take orders and wield a coffee pot. She'd gotten pretty good at one-handed driving. She wanted to make sure Timmy didn't miss kindergarten, and that took money. Part of each day she was at work and spared Jocelyn's barbed comments and unending hatefulness.

"Jim needs complete peace and quiet to fully recover. He doesn't need a five-year-old whirling dervish of activity constantly bothering him or the drama of waiting for your worthless scumbag lover to show up for round two. Next time, you'll kill your father as surely as if you put a gun to his head and pull the trigger yourself."

Pop and Timmy were together in the backyard doing cardiac rehab exercises in the sunshine. They hadn't witnessed the latest skirmish in the Russell Wife versus Daughter War. Kat couldn't take much more of the vitriol that rained down on her every time Pop was out of hearing. Someone needed to be the bigger person. It would be a cold day—everywhere—before Jocelyn had a change of heart. It had to be her.

Kat steeled herself with a deep breath. "Be fair, Jocelyn. Pop loves having Timmy around. He makes him laugh. Pop needs his grandson close. But you're right. He doesn't need any more drama...not from Dirk, and especially not from you and me."

"What do you mean? I'm doing what's best for my husband."

"Best would be for *us* to get along. I did some stupid things and you did some. Can't we call a truce?"

"Name one stupid thing I *ever* did. Nothing to hold a candle to your escapades. That's for darn sure."

"Please. Let's not fight. For Pop's sake."

"If you two moved out, we'd have peace and quiet and that lowlife wouldn't have any reason to come back here. Jim might be okay."

"I can't afford to move out. I don't know where I'd go, where we'd be safe living alone."

Jocelyn whipped out a checkbook with a bejeweled cover—her personal account—and wrote out a check she handed to Kat. *Great, now she's bribing us to leave.* She wanted to tell Jocelyn where she could stick her begrudging largesse, but she was going to need all the money she could scrape together. If Jocelyn got her way.

Kat nearly choked as she swallowed her pride, folded the check, and put it in her pocket. "I'll start working on a plan. Pop won't be happy if we leave, but his and Timmy's safety are my priorities. I'll figure it out."

"Do it. Something will come to you. You're always able to finagle things around to your advantage. You'll manage. And your father doesn't need to know about this transaction. It's just between us. He needs to believe moving out is all your idea. If he finds out anything different, I'll force you to leave anyway. Understand?"

The back door closed before Kat answered. She had no choice but to agree to Jocelyn's terms without discussion. Staying in Philadelphia wasn't safe. It wasn't a matter of *if* Dirk found them. It was *when*. Physical distance from that motorcycle-riding devil was the only solution, even though that wasn't possible without being away from Pop too.

After tossing and turning in bed for hours, Kat dreamt of visiting her grandparents in Wisconsin. She remembered the time years ago before she lost Mom and had to deal with Pop's jealous second wife. Before Dirk Crowe slithered his way into her life. She'd been so happy there. But it had been thirteen years since her last visit. Her grandparents were both gone. Who did she know in Lansdale now? It was a long way from Philly. A place Dirk Crowe didn't know had been part of her life. The perfect solution. She knew her mom sent those dreams to protect her and the grandson she'd never met. Kat put the wheels in motion for their cross-country move, convinced it was a solution sent from above.

Chapter Two

Timmy went on a play date and would spend the night with his best friend. Kat had a clear opportunity to present her plan to her father without any interruptions.

"Pop, it will be great. Do you remember Mrs. Ritterskamp? She was Gran's best friend. She said she attended your wedding. Her husband was a big, tall German. He's gone now and she's renting out a little upstairs apartment. It's perfect for Timmy and me. It has two bedrooms, a bathroom, and a sitting room. We'll have our meals with her. I'll get a job. You can come to visit. It's far enough away that we'll be out of Dirk's reach. When we're gone, he'll have no reason to bother you."

Kat rattled on, answering questions before Pop had a chance to form them. She tried to convince him that this was a well thought out plan. One destined for success. He stared at her as if she'd gone stark raving mad. Maybe she had. But there weren't any other options.

"She seems to have a good plan, Jim." Jocelyn added her approval with a smirk covering her face.

"You do not have a vote. Be quiet." Pop stared daggers at his wife. Kat had never seen Pop oppose Jocelyn on *anything*. His narrowed eyes and gruesome frown confirmed that he hated the whole plan. No matter whose idea he thought it was.

Kat hated causing her father such visible pain. She was about to cave, to tell him it wasn't definite. Maybe they didn't have to move so far away. She'd keep looking for a different solution. Then a motorcycle roared down the street, getting louder with each breath she took.

Danger! *Danger*! Her reactivated alarms sang out. She stopped talking and ran to the window. Kneeling on the sofa, she pulled the curtains slightly apart. The sound stopped. A motorcycle parked in front of the house. A red-helmeted rider. She ran and double locked the front door and held her breath.

One second, two, three. She cautiously parted the curtain on the door. The motorcyclist turned around and got on the bike again. It backfired, then roared off in the direction from which it had come. He didn't come to the door—*not this time*.

"Pop, he'll be back. We're not safe. Neither are you. Not as long as Dirk knows where to find me and Timmy. He's never heard of Lansdale. Mom was gone before I met him. We never talked about her or Wisconsin. Once we're gone, he'll move on. Maybe even to another city. He'd have nothing to hold him in Philly. It's the only way. You need peace and quiet to rest and recover."

He glared at his wife as if he recognized that those words were *hers* spewing out of his only daughter's mouth. "Peace and quiet is overrated. Lansdale, Wisconsin is a tiny, little town. It will be hard for you to find a job. It's not going to be the same place that it was when you were eleven. Things change. You don't need to leave me. I can handle the cretin. Next time the S.O.B. shows up, we'll call the cops. That's why I pay taxes. I can protect you."

"Pop, I'm twenty-three years old and live like I'm still a teenager. Don't get me wrong. I wouldn't have made it this far without you. But you can't be with us every minute of the day. Dirk can still get to me and to your grandson. I know you rescued me the night Timmy was born..." Kat couldn't continue.

If Pop hadn't intervened, if Jocelyn had succeeded in turning her away—she'd be *dead.* And probably Timmy too.

Pop looked like he'd been gut punched, not once, but over and over and over. And Kat was the one throwing the punches.

He stood, turned his back on his wife, and hugged his daughter. There were no words. Tears spilled down both their cheeks. He walked out into the backyard.

Kat's still-beating heart had been ripped out of her chest, and there was nothing she could do to stop the excruciating pain.

"See, that wasn't so bad. He'll be fine once you're gone. I'll make sure of that," Jocelyn said smugly.

Kat couldn't look at her. They had to leave. Dirk's parole, and Jocelyn's spitefulness, had changed everything that was good in her life to stinking, putrid garbage. *Everything.*

Chapter Three

The decision had been made. Pop had been told. Kat started packing before she had time to change her mind. She rehearsed the explanation for their trip. What would Timmy want to know?

There was so little to pack. The picture of her and Mom on her tenth birthday. The last family picture of the three of them a few days before the cancer diagnosis. The morning her son was born; Pop grinning from ear to ear holding Timmy carefully in one hand avoiding all his tubes. Not much "stuff" for twenty-three years. Of course, some of her childhood mementos had disappeared when she had been driven out of this house the first time. She'd never asked what Jocelyn did with those things. She couldn't bear to hear they'd gone out in the trash.

There was a knock at her bedroom door. Pop stuck his head in. "Have you got a minute?"

"Always for you."

He sat on the edge of the bed and motioned for her to sit beside him. "I know how scared you must be to even consider leaving home. I hate to admit it, but Crowe has proven more than once that he is dangerous and evil. If you stayed here to keep me happy and something happened to you or Timmy, I'd never forgive myself."

"Pop, I love you but..."

"You don't have to say anything. Since this seems to be the only viable solution at the moment, you have to do it the *right* way. Kat Russell can't be seen leaving Philadelphia or making the move to Wisconsin."

"But you just agreed this is the only option."

"Let me finish." He reached into the small bag he had with him and pulled out a pair of shears, hair dye, and a New Jersey driver's license for someone named Karly Rogers that was complete except for the photograph.

"I don't understand. What's all this? Who is Karly Rogers?"

"My daughter."

"You have another daughter? But Pop…wait…" She smiled. "I get it. Karly J. Rogers has the same initials as Katrina J. Russell. You want me to become Karly Rogers so she's the one who's going to move to Wisconsin. But what's the rest?"

"Honey, the hair has to go. You can't help but draw attention everywhere you go with that gorgeous, waist-length, blonde hair. Karly is a shorthaired brunette."

"Not my hair. Pop, you know, it's never been cut. I always kept it long, like Mom did. Do I have to go to such extremes?"

Pop sat back and took a deep breath. "Kat, why are you leaving me?"

"We've been all through that. You know why."

"Humor me and say it out loud."

"Because the man who nearly killed me and my unborn son is out of prison and has come looking for me."

"And you're afraid he'll finish the job." Pop

squeezed her hand.

"Yes. He's not going to stop until he kills me." Tears streamed down her face. "You're right that I'm worried, but I can't start a new life living a lie. How would I explain to Timmy that we are not only moving, but we're going to pretend to be someone else? He's confused enough about why lying isn't okay and tells little lies, like they don't count. This would be a whopper. He's only five. What are the odds that he could keep our secret? He could easily say the wrong thing to the wrong person, and all the deceit would be for nothing. Heck, I could mess up and answer to Kat instead of Karly."

"My grandson is smart. He'll understand, and he's the best little kid I know at keeping secrets. He never blurts out what your Christmas or birthday presents are even though he helped me buy them," Pop protested.

"It's not the same. You're talking about living a lie forever. I can't do it. Mom would never send me into danger, and I know she told me to go to Wisconsin."

"You are your mother's daughter. I'm certain in the same situation, her response would have been like yours. I admire your integrity. Truth be told, I'll worry about you—alternate identity or not. That evil beast is not sane and certainly not stable."

"Thanks for understanding."

"Will you at least cut your hair? It attracts way too much attention. It's something people remember seeing. It's a small sacrifice to pay for your safety. I don't think you want to risk going to a salon. You'd probably run into someone you know. Do you trust me to cut it?"

"Pop, I trust you with my life. Cut away."

When he had finished, Kat looked at the stylish

bobbed hairdo reflected in the bathroom mirror. "You do good work—especially for a mechanic!" She laughed and hugged her father's neck. "Where's what you cut off?"

"Right here. I put it all in this giant plastic bag. What are you going to do with it?"

"Donate it anonymously to the charity that make wigs for cancer patients. Remember, I wanted to cut my hair when Mom was getting treatment, but she wouldn't let me. If I get the package ready, will you mail it?"

"I'll do better than that. I'll drop it off at their collection center next week."

"Thanks. It will take some time to get used to this. The back of my neck is a little chilly. I probably weigh five pounds less."

"If aliases and disguises are out, I think you should leave your car here and take my truck."

"No, Pop. You'll need the truck when you go back to work."

"Then you can swap cars with Jocelyn."

"Really? You think she would? For me?"

"She will if I say so."

"No. I'm taking my car." *I won't give her more ammunition.*

"How did you ever get to be so stubborn?" Pop shook his head. "I've never been prouder of you than right now. Your mother had her mulish moments too, but you also got her inner strength. She was the strongest spirit I've ever known. I figured you'd insist on taking your birthday present. I wish we had time to repaint it. Drive over to the shop. Your uncle will do one last tune up. We need to make everything ready for you to hit the road."

"Thanks, Pop. Looks like you've thought of everything. I'll sit down with the atlas this afternoon and figure out my route."

"I can help you."

"I know, but I need to fully understand where I'm going. I need to do it myself."

After a quick trip to the shop with her remaining hair tucked in a Phillies baseball cap, she parked the car in the garage since Pop's truck was on the street.

Kat was upstairs sorting and packing clothes. No point in taking the things Timmy had outgrown. The back door slammed. Her son ran up the stairs hollering. He stopped at her bedroom door. "What's going on?"

"I'm packing our suitcases. We're going on a grand adventure. I didn't tell you earlier because it's a big secret. You can't tell anyone. Only Pop Pop and Jocie and Uncle John know," she explained.

"That's cool. We've never gone on an adventure before. Are we going to be spies?" Excitement shone in her son's eyes.

"No. Just a mom and little boy going somewhere new and exciting."

"Are Pop Pop and Jocie going too?"

"Not this time. This is a special adventure just for the two of us. When we get settled into our new place, Pop Pop and Jocie can come to visit."

"I'll miss them. Maybe we shouldn't go."

"Sometimes we have to miss people and go places far from them. It's part of growing up. So you and I get to grow up at the same time. I've never been on an adventure without Pop Pop before either."

"Okay," Timmy said hesitatingly. "Do I have the right clothes to take on an adventure?"

"I hope so. Let's go look." She led her son by the hand and went into his bedroom.

When Jocelyn returned from her day of shopping, she was pleased to see their suitcases in the front hallway. "I guess this means you're going to be leaving us soon." She smiled broadly.

Kat nodded. "No time like the present. We're all packed. Uncle John changed the oil and filters and tuned Thelma up this afternoon. We're planning an early start tomorrow morning."

"Jocie, next time you need your hair cut, we can save some money. I'll do it." Pop winked at Kat.

"No way I'd let you touch my hair."

"Who do you think was Kat's stylist?"

"Not you."

"It was Pop. Didn't he do a great job?" Kat pirouetted to show her new hairdo.

"It looks good on you, but he's still not touching my hair," Jocie grumbled.

There was carry out fried chicken and all the fixings for supper. While they ate, Kat brought her up to speed on the planned adventure. Jocelyn's smile never waned. Victory was within her reach. Soon, she would be alone with her husband. Kat and Timmy would be only memories.

After supper Pop pulled out the treasure trove of old videos and slides converted onto DVDs—Kat's Christmas present to him last year. "We better look at these one more time."

They started with Timmy coming home from the hospital almost six years ago. Hard to believe the energetic little boy on his grandfather's lap had ever been tiny enough to fit completely in those calloused hands. And Kat looked so young, a teenaged girl playing with her real live baby doll.

She hadn't remembered them being happy then, not like they looked in the pictures. *Guess surviving a near-death experience will make you see the brighter side of life.* Even Jocie had held Timmy in one of the rare family pictures of Kat, Pop, Jocie, and baby Timmy—after Jocie had thrown her out the *first* time. Funny what you remember. And what you don't.

Kat sent Timmy to bed at ten o'clock. He needed to get some sleep before they started out in the morning. He didn't want to miss anything, but when his mom threatened to cancel tomorrow's adventure, Timmy reluctantly said his good nights.

Jocelyn picked up her book and prepared to go upstairs. She warned Kat not to keep her husband up all night.

"Jocie, wouldn't you like to stay and see the older pictures?" Kat extended an olive branch one last time.

"Why? Am I in any of them? Jim, don't forget to take your night meds. Please don't stay up much longer. You need your rest. I'm going to the bedroom to finish this book."

"Don't worry about me. I'll have plenty of time to rest, tomorrow and every day after for a long while. Go to bed. We'll be fine," Jim assured his wife. She kissed his cheek and left without another word to Kat.

They were alone—for the first time in ten years—just Kat and Pop together, like they'd been during those few short months after they first lost *her.* Pop loaded the DVD player starting with pictures of him as a newlywed. Mom was so young, smiling shyly with shining eyes. Pop always told Kat she looked exactly like her mother. She finally saw the resemblance. No wonder Jocelyn didn't want her around. A ghost in the flesh. Was Kat really that beautiful?

There was the flowered sofa that used to take up the whole wall in front of the picture window. Mom loved it, even though Pop teased her about it being too frou-frou for *his* living room. Kat hadn't known until tonight that it was the second piece of furniture they'd bought together, after their bed. The living room walls used to be a pale yellow like the centers of the flowers on the upholstery. Now they were a bland cream color, and the sofa and chairs were covered in dark mahogany leather. Jocelyn had done a good job of removing every single thing Kat's mom had bought, painted, or made; any evidence that Jim Russell and Renata Schneckker were ever married—all of it—except their only child. Tomorrow the purge would be complete.

They turned off the auto advance slide show so they could linger over each frame. Pop had taken so many pictures of her, every significant event and lots of everyday ones, all immortalized on film.

Click. Kat in a lacy white baptism gown.

Click. Her third birthday party with all the neighborhood children.

Click. First day of nursery school holding her mother's hand tightly.

Click. At swimming lessons in her favorite yellow polka dotted swimsuit.

Click. A tan little blonde-headed girl running on the sand at the Jersey Shore.

Click. In an Easter hat and dress clutching a chocolate rabbit by the ears.

Click. Kat on Santa's lap.

Click. Kat and Mom in homemade, look-alike dresses for the Mother-Daughter Banquet.

Click. Kat's training wheels coming off her first two-wheeler.

Click. Her first skinned knees as she bravely fought back tears.

Click. Mom and Pop ready for a night on the town snapped by Kat when she was nine or ten. Jocelyn and her first husband are standing by the door waiting to go out with them. So Jocie *was* in at least one of the old pictures.

Click. Half a dozen grinning pumpkins lined up on the stoop.

Click. Christmas morning amid mountains of wadded up wrapping paper.

They laughed until they cried, remembering all they had been as a family—Mom and Pop and Kat. A lifetime ago.

Then the pictures stopped. Kat was thirteen. Mom was gone. The events in their lives weren't worth filming until Timmy came almost four years later. Kat still couldn't find the right words to explain to Pop, or to herself, what had happened nor why. It was simply a grief-filled, dark chasm in their family history.

She thought Pop didn't press her for answers because he didn't want to face the truth, even if she could tell him what it was, especially since his favorite photography subjects were leaving in the morning. Pop's hand in hers silently asked if she really had to go, even though they both knew the answer all too clearly. Warm, calloused, and comforting. She hated to say goodbye. When would she get to hold his hand again?

Kat volunteered to lock up and turn out the lights.

Pop held her tightly, then kissed her cheek. "Remember, honey, you are leaving Philadelphia tomorrow, but you and Timmy will always be here." He patted his chest, then went upstairs to bed.

She sat quietly in the middle of the sofa. She would be back. This couldn't be the last time she'd sit in this living room. But as long as Dirk Crowe had deadly unfinished business with her, and she had cashed Jocelyn's cursed check, leaving was the only solution. For now. The suitcases were packed. Timmy was eager for the adventure. There was no turning back.

Kat should have gotten a set of those DVDs for herself. Now it was too late. Who could have foreseen in December that Dirk Crowe would drive them from the only home they'd ever known in May?

Chapter Four

Kat glanced in the rearview mirror. The rising sun behind the vehicle wreathed Timmy's blond curls in a halo of flaming orange and fiery red. He slept. Good. The more of these escape miles that passed without his notice, the better. She focused her attention on the highway in front of her. Mile after endless mile yet to conquer.

Getting out of the city driving one-handed had been a challenge. But the automatic transmission made it easier. She lifted the seat belt away from the tender spot it had already rubbed on her neck. Not even that restraint could make her feel safe. Could they run far enough to find the peace her heart sought?

Timmy wholeheartedly believed he was on an exciting adventure. How long could she maintain his enthusiasm? Three hours wrestling with her pillow last night didn't help allay any fears. But she'd gladly exchanged elusive slumber for those last hours with Pop—alone. She would remember their time together long after the yawns and stiff muscles of today faded away.

Timmy had bounded into the room and onto her bed at five thirty. "Mom, we need to get out of bed, or we'll be late for our adventure!" Kat didn't dare let him know how dangerous this expedition was. Or how cautious they needed to be.

It was easier to leave early while Pop was still in a sleeping pill hangover. She knew he wished they would stay. Jocelyn left no doubt about *her* feelings—getting up hours before her normal rising time and forgetting her *bad* back long enough to help finish packing the car.

Kat punched the cruise control button on the steering wheel. "Okay, Thelma. Here we go. Your cruise control and GPS will make driving a little easier." Who knew her sixteenth birthday present from Pop would set off the chain of events that led to now? A little red car rolling west on the Pennsylvania Turnpike with Timmy perched on a booster seat in the back and the treasures of their entire lives thumping around in the trunk.

A motorcycle came up fast in the passing lane. She hit the cancel button on the cruise control, slowing as it sped past. The bike didn't hesitate. The black-helmeted driver never glanced in her direction. She forced her breath out, slowly and deliberately. A sour taste filled her mouth. It wasn't Dirk. Not yet. How long until it would be? Were all their precautions enough? Could they outrun evil? Could anyone?

"Mom, I'm getting hungry." The cat nap was over.

What did that sign say? Blue Mountain *Tunnel* in thirty miles? How had she forgotten the tunnels? As a child, she'd hated even riding through them on their annual road trip to Wisconsin.

Two miles down the turnpike, she pulled off at the oasis. Time for breakfast and research. She scoured the atlas Pop had insisted she bring, in case of bad cell service. No options there. Maybe the maps on her phone were more up to date. Same answer. They were in the middle of Pennsylvania on the only road that actually went due west from Philadelphia. There wasn't just *a* tunnel. There were four—the Blue Mountain Tunnel followed by the Kittatinny, Tuscarora, and Allegheny. All in the short space of an hour and a half of driving.

Kat's mouth grew dry just thinking about it. She gulped her juice and coffee. No relief. There was no way to continue going west on the turnpike except through the tunnels unless they turned around and went back to Philly—where Dirk was surely waiting—then they'd have to take a completely different route farther north before turning west. It had been hard enough to leave Pop this morning. She didn't think she could summon the strength to do it twice in the same day. She had to run *from* danger, not back into it. Tunnels weren't nearly as scary as what they had left behind.

Twenty minutes later, the entrance to the Blue Mountain tunnel loomed ahead. She pulled off on the shoulder to prepare them both. She couldn't deal with a panicky passenger while she tried to keep from hyperventilating.

Kat told her son they would play a game to see if he could keep his eyes shut all the way through the tunnel. The prize would be a dessert of his choice at supper tonight. Timmy smiled declaring, "I love dessert!"

She eased back into the lane of traffic approaching the gaping maw. *Breathe. It will be okay as long as you breathe. Go!* Her passenger tightly closed his eyes. Hers were wide open. She clutched the steering wheel to steady her shaking hand and managed to take one deep breath and hold it. *There's the sunshine. We made it through. Breathe.*

They repeated the drill three more times. Timmy was delighted that he'd won four desserts. Her right shoulder ached from hunching over the steering wheel in focused concentration searching for the glimmer of sunlight that signaled their successful passage through the tube that seemed to keep narrowing in on her. The immobilizer on her left shoulder seemed embedded in her skin. Her head throbbed. She smelled sour. The back of her shirt was soaking wet. But she wasn't tired any longer. *Must be the adrenaline.*

The sign read *Rest Area One Mile.* Good. Kat needed ibuprofen and a dry shirt. Timmy needed to go to the bathroom. They might as well eat the bologna sandwiches she'd packed. Get everything out of the way at once. Maybe after a break she'd be stable enough to crawl back in the car and continue their journey. No maybe. She had to be.

"Mom, I'm not a baby. I can go to the bathroom by myself. I promise I'll wash my hands." Timmy tried to get free from his mother's iron grip. Heat flooded her face as people stared at them. *So much for not being noticed.*

"C'mon, I want you to go with me." She dragged him a little farther before he planted his feet and refused to budge.

"Give me one good reason why I should."

"Because I'm the mom and I say you're going to." She hated resorting to that, but he had learned long ago not to argue when she played the mom card in her sternest tone of voice. *How long will he continue to be cowed by that?*

"Fine, but don't hold my hand." He shook free

from her grasp and walked at her side into the women's restroom.

By the time they'd gotten the cooler out of the trunk and found a shady picnic table, Timmy's embarrassment at the restroom indignity had faded away. He ran around between bites of sandwich alternating between being an airplane and a quick draw cowboy. The ibuprofen conquered her headache and relieved the stiffness in her shoulders. The clean shirt smelled fresh, almost hopeful. They were ready for the next obstacle on this trek. She couldn't be lucky enough for this to be the only one on their adventure. Probably not even the only one today.

"E I E I O." Timmy applauded when they finished the song for the third time. It was a big farm full of pigs, cows, chickens, horses, geese, sheep, donkeys, and ducks. Thank goodness he couldn't think of any other farm animals. Then he launched into "Row, Row, Row Your Boat," another favorite from his school music programs. She was glad he could entertain himself on their first ever cross-country trip. He noticed her looking at him in the rearview mirror, and made faces at her, then giggled in a way that never failed to make her smile.

Thelma's gas mileage was great on the highway, even at seven years old. She didn't have many miles on her. She'd rarely been outside the city. Pop kept her tuned and running well. Who would work on her now? It certainly wouldn't be free. Pop automatically dealt with so many things for her. Every day. Now she would be the only person to take care of things, for both of them. What's the saying? You don't know what you've got until you don't have it? Truer words were never spoken. Kat certainly had it made. Now she was entering a brave new world. Alone. No, worse than that, fleeing evil, and responsible for her son's safety.

They passed the Mansfield, Ohio exit, and she immediately regretted not stopping. Timmy complained that his bottom was tired. Hers was almost numb, except for the spot where the seat belt had bruised her right hip. They'd left home ten hours ago. She shifted in her seat. The ibuprofen had worn off. Then a billboard beckoned, "Visit Marion, Ohio, the Home of President Warren G. Harding. Next Exit." There would be motels near a tourist attraction. Wouldn't there?

Kat took the Marion exit. There was a Mom-and-Pop circa 1950s motel and restaurant, the Pine Woods Motel, on the left. The vacancy light flashed. She drove around its circular drive. Most cars parked in front of the rooms had out-of-state plates, so it probably wasn't a No-Tell Motel.

The restaurant parking lot was full of local cars. Must be the best place to eat for miles; that could be a good sign or a bad one. The food didn't have to be great, just something to eat without having to get back behind the wheel to find it. The Pine Woods Motel looked like it would meet their immediate needs. They had a clean room in their price range. She paid cash. Dinner was served until nine.

Timmy told the waitress he was too tired to eat supper, but just awake enough to eat one of the desserts he'd won in the tunnel game. Kat decided a desserts-only supper was appropriate for two intrepid adventurers and ordered them both their own triple-decker ice cream sundae complete with a chewy, chocolate brownie, a mountain of whipping cream, and a cherry on top. Her son may have won the game, but Kat had *driven* through four tunnels today. That alone deserved a creamy celebration.

First, a bath for Timmy, then they called Pop to update him on their first day of travel. It rang once. Pop started talking without slowing down to say hello. Timmy told him about the tunnels and the desserts for supper. "Mom said not to get used to it. It's only because we're on an adventure." He handed the phone to his mother.

"Honey, I'm sorry about the tunnels."

"Pop, I know it's my fault. I didn't ask you the best way to go."

"You're going the best way, the shortest one, anyway, but you have to do tunnels. Sounds like it was fine. I worried all day about you driving after so little sleep last night. I miss you both already. Remember, there's always a bed for you here, no matter what."

"Thanks. It's time for me to see if I can live without you being right there ready to catch me when I falter. I think I'm ready. After all, I made it through four tunnels today."

"I know, my Kat is all grown up. Just remember, you're never too big for me to love. Honey, be sure the car is secure, and keep the double lock on in the motel room. A woman traveling without a man needs to be extra careful."

"I'm a city girl. I know how to be careful. Locking up was the first thing I did."

"A city girl who's moving to the boondocks. I hope it's the right place for you—for now."

"I think Lansdale is the best place for us. I can almost see Mom smiling."

"I love you. Hug that grandson of mine. I'm hoping you land on your feet, baby girl. Keep me posted. Good night, Kat."

"Love you too. Thanks for understanding."

Timmy was snoring. She jumped in the shower. Warm water was supposed to be relaxing, right? Her son hadn't moved while she was in the bathroom. Not even the jet-engine roar of the hair dryer had disturbed him.

She crawled under the covers. How was it possible to be both totally exhausted and completely wide awake—simultaneously?

Car doors slammed in the parking lot. Laughing people paraded past their room casting ominous shadows on the wall. Pop was right. Traveling could be dangerous. Was anyone watching them at supper? Did they know there was a woman with a small child alone in Room 6A?

She wished he'd kept the fatherly advice to himself. Maybe she wasn't quite as ready to solo in life as her bragging made it sound. But she had made it through the first day's obstacles—leaving the only home she'd ever known, driving one-handed, four tunnels, dragging her son to the women's restroom against his will, and crossing a state and a half. *Think positively. It will get easier. Maybe.*

****

What time was it? Later than she'd planned to sleep. "Timmy, we need to get up if we're going to make Wisconsin today. I'm hungry. What about you?"

"Yep. Ice cream just melts and leaves lots of room in your tummy."

Pop's warning echoed in her mind as they walked

into the café. When the server asked, "Only two today?" Kat looked cautiously around the room to see who might have overheard. Timmy started innocently talking about Wisconsin. She shushed him and told him to finish his breakfast. The cashier asked where they were headed today. She responded, "On our way."

Timmy struck up a conversation with a trucker eating at the counter while she was paying the check. Kat grabbed his arm and hurried him out of the café in mid-sentence.

"Mom, what's wrong with you? That man was just being nice to me," Timmy asked grumpily as they walked across the parking lot back to their room.

"We don't talk to strangers."

"But everyone here is a stranger."

"Exactly. Don't talk to anyone. And don't tell people we're going to Wisconsin. Okay?"

"Sure."

They were barely up to speed on the highway when an eighteen-wheeler blew his horn as they passed. Why would he do that? The answer was apparent in the rearview mirror. Her passenger was waving at the driver.

"Mom, it's my friend from breakfast. See, I told you he was nice."

"Please don't wave at people. When they honk, I lose my concentration. It makes me think there's some kind of problem."

"Sure. Guess I'm not supposed to have *any* fun today." He pouted for about fifteen minutes. She wanted him to enjoy this rapidly deteriorating adventure, but pouting was better than attracting attention from passing truckers who could clearly see there was no adult male in the car.

Timmy said, "Mom, I'll help you concentrate. I'll tell you about everything we're passing so you don't miss it or have to take your eyes off the road, okay?"

"Great idea." At least he'd found some way to entertain himself that didn't involve singing about farm animals again.

"The old barn we just passed needs paint, and it's falling down. It looks worse than old Mr. Caruther's house by the church, but the pigs seem to like it. Oh, yuck. Be glad you can't see that, some kinda animal got runned over. No head and its guts are all black and ugly. I bet it stinks. Oh, there's another one. Must be the baby. Sure is yucky."

"Honey, isn't there anything pretty to see?" *Let's squelch the roadkill narrative.*

"Sure, Mom. There's black and white cows, lots of them and baby cows."

"Calves."

"Yeah. And there's a big black horse trying to race with us. He looks like the horse I'm going to have when I'm big. I'll teach him to eat out of my hand like the pony at the petting zoo does. I'll name him Blackie." Timmy continued his travel monologue for over an hour. Thankfully there was very little roadkill, or he took her advice and concentrated on reporting only the pretty things.

Kat pointed out when they crossed the state line between Ohio and Indiana. "You just entered another state. Three so far on this trip, and the Shore is in another state, New Jersey. Only forty-six more and you'll have been in all fifty states."

Timmy sang "Twinkle, Twinkle, Little Star" and

"Mary Had a Little Lamb", then moved on to "This Old Man", before returning to the farm and rowing boats.

After finishing the sandwiches from the cooler at their lunch time rest stop, Timmy's enthusiasm began to wane. When they crawled back in the car, the whining began. "How much longer 'til we're there?"

It was hard to sound upbeat between her aching shoulder and nonstop yawning after a second sleep-deprived night in a row. "We're almost to Chicago in the state of Illinois. I promise, we'll sleep in Wisconsin tonight. You'll have been in six states by the time you go to bed."

He told her Ohio and Indiana seemed pretty much the same and he never did see any of the state lines she kept talking about. Illinois was pretty boring. He finally perked up when they saw the tall buildings in Chicago on the horizon.

"Which are taller, Mom, buildings in Philadelphia or in Chicago?"

"They both have tall buildings, but Chicago has the Willis Tower. It's taller than anything in Philadelphia."

"Darn it. I was hoping our town would win."

The combination of hard rain and heavy traffic made travel around the city very slow. "Honey, please be quiet. Mom has to concentrate. This is hard driving." He stared out the window, quietly humming to himself.

Traffic began to thin out on the other side of the city. Kat pulled off the toll road at the first over-the-road travel plaza. Timmy got up from the table several times to watch the cars and big trucks run beneath his feet and come out on the other side, enthralled with the way the restaurant spanned the width of the multi-lane highway beneath them.

On the way back to the car, Kat splurged on a set of pictures from a photo booth. Timmy had never been in one and was amazed when three minutes after they posed it spit out the strip of pictures. It was a little extravagant, given their resources, but she wanted a memento to help turn the feel of this trip into a true adventure, instead of the urgent flight to safety she knew that it was.

Mile after mile crept by. *Wake up, girl. You're drifting over the center line.* She fought the hypnotic effect of the white stripe fading off at the horizon. She coaxed Timmy into singing again and joined in, hoping the noise would keep her awake. Even being on that old farm again would be better than silence. The lower the sun drifted in the sky, the harder it was to focus on the road.

They passed through another little burg where a motel called to her touting their clean rooms and reasonable rates. But they couldn't stop. She'd promised that they would be in Lansdale tonight. Last night's intermittent light sleep had worn off hours ago. Every part of her body ached and was going numb at the same time.

They clapped and cheered when they saw the large, brown, "Welcome to Wisconsin" sign shaped like the state. But they *still* hadn't arrived at their destination. Two hours later, they were finally in Lansdale. Timmy created a song whose only lyrics were the word "happy" with clapping as punctuation and sang it in honor of their arrival.

The GPS led them down North Jefferson Street to a two-story white house with bright blue shutters. They were expected. All the lights were on. Kat pulled in the driveway as Mrs. Ritterskamp had instructed. Finally, they were there.

A short, plump woman with a riot of snow-white curls capping her head came out on the porch to greet them. Mrs. Ritterskamp hadn't changed in thirteen years. She looked exactly as she had at Kat's grandparents' funeral.

When Kat saw the ad in the online edition of the local paper and called to check on the apartment, she couldn't believe that Gran's best friend would be her landlady. Mrs. Ritterskamp's encouragement helped her decide they could make this move successfully.

Mrs. Ritterskamp's crystal-blue eyes twinkled when she smiled, and she hugged them as if they were long-lost family. "Would you like some supper?"

"Thanks, we ate at a plaza on the toll road."

Timmy piped up, "It was really neat. The cars went right under our table."

She put her hand on her son's shoulder. "Timmy loved it. I'm sorry to be rude, but I'm beat, and I think he is too. Tonight all we need are showers and beds."

"I'm sure you're tired. Such a long trip driving alone, and it looks like you've been injured. Everything is ready and waiting." Mrs. Ritterskamp led them upstairs to the apartment.

"The rooms are lovely and larger than I expected." Kat put Timmy's suitcase in the smaller bedroom.

"Thank you. No one has stayed in them since my mother-in-law passed away fifteen years ago. We kept saying we were going to take in boarders, but we never got around to advertising. After the last six months, I'm ready for some company. I guess we were saving them for Hannah's granddaughter and her son. I'm happy to have you here and hope you'll enjoy your new home."

Mrs. Ritterskamp kissed Kat's cheek and patted Timmy's head on the way out of the room. Timmy was thrilled to have his first grownup bed, a full double, and there was a night light in the hall so he could find the bathroom if he woke up at night.

After bathing him and tucking her son into bed, Kat went downstairs to give Mrs. Ritterskamp the rent from her travel money stash of one-hundred-dollar bills before turning in herself.

"Thank you. This could have waited until morning." Mrs. Ritterskamp slid the money into an envelope in a napkin holder in the middle of the kitchen table that appeared to be full of billing statements instead of napkins. "I wanted to tell you about an opportunity for an experienced waitress. Isn't that what you told me you do?"

"Yes, and I need to find work as soon as possible."

"Wonderful. Muriel Whistler is looking for someone to start right away. One of her waitresses left last week."

"Whistler's? The place on the square with the long counter, red-topped twirly stools, and two rows of booths?"

"That's the one."

"Great. Our bank account is close to needing life support."

"I don't want to butt in. However, I thought if we had breakfast there tomorrow morning, I could introduce you to Muriel. Then you wouldn't just be a stranger off the street looking for work."

"That would be wonderful. I wouldn't have to leave Timmy in unfamiliar surroundings on our first day here, and I'd get an early start on the job hunt. You're so kind to think of this. I don't know what to say."

"I find that 'thank you' is usually enough." Mrs. Ritterskamp smiled and hugged her.

Timmy slept peacefully in another strange bed. Maybe this one would be *his* bed for a while. Such an adaptable little guy.

She unloaded his backpack, checking for food remnants among the toys. In the very bottom she unearthed a fat, manila envelope labeled "Kat's Rainy Day Fund" in Pop's familiar scrawl.

In her room, Kat perched on the edge of the bed and punched "1" on her cell phone's speed dial. Pop answered on the first ring.

"I guess you're finally there. Getting all settled in?"

"We are. Got here about an hour ago. I found something in the bottom of Timmy's backpack. Did you hide it there because you knew I wouldn't take it otherwise?"

"Well, would you have?"

"No, but that's not the point."

"That is *exactly* the point. You had good reasons to insist on this whole moving-away-from-home-with-my-only-grandson episode. But I am *still* your father. Please, let me help you. Since you're going to be so far away, money is the only way left to me. If you don't need it, you can give it back the next time you see me. Deal?"

"Deal. But you know Jocie doesn't like you spending money on us."

"My wife has nothing to say about what I give my

daughter."

If you only knew. "I love you, Pop. Sorry for all the upheaval we created for you and Jocie."

"I wouldn't have missed a single moment of Timmy's life. Thanks for sharing it with us." His voice wavered. "I wish I hadn't missed any of yours. But that's water under the bridge. Thanks for letting me know you're there and safe. I'll sleep better."

"And I have a lead on a job. Mrs. Ritterskamp is going to introduce me to the owner at Whistler's Diner in the morning. They need an experienced waitress. Everything seems to be falling into place. I think I can be on my own. I can do this."

"Okay. I understand. I'll back off and give you some space. If I don't hear from you for a while, I'll operate on the no news is good news theory, but remember to call *me* first—if you need anything at all."

"I promise. I love you. Good night."

"I hope you land on your reliable cat feet again, baby girl. Hug Timmy for me. Good night."

I guess I'll always be his baby girl. Well, we're here, but I think our adventure has only begun...

She snuggled under the covers in the comfortable bed. No tunnels. No strangers. No more miles until she got there. She was safe. Loved. Asleep.

Chapter Five

"Mom, I found you."

She stirred awake. "Was I lost?"

"No, you were right across the hall from me, just like you're supposed to be. The same place you were at our other house."

Kat patted the side of the bed for him to sit down. "Isn't that wonderful? This morning we're going out to breakfast with Mrs. Ritterskamp so I can check about a job."

"Breakfast in a restaurant three days in a row! Are we still on our adventure?"

"We are. If we do it right, this adventure could last a long time."

"But not too long. Pop Pop and Jocie will miss us. And I'll miss them."

"Let's just take it a day at a time and see what happens, okay?"

"It's a deal. You better get out of bed. You can't go out to breakfast in your nightgown."

"And you can't go in your pajamas." She tousled his hair. He scooted across the hall to his room.

Kat got dressed but left the shoulder sling on the chair in her room. It had been four weeks. She'd done the strengthening and stretching exercises religiously, even while traveling. The shoulder needed a test run. Who would want to hire an injured server?

Let's hope this adventure includes getting a job. Today.

****

A wave of comfort and happy memories gently washed over her. The diner looked exactly the same. She remembered Grandpa Schneckker lifting her onto one of the red vinyl-covered stools at the counter. She was officially all grown-up when she didn't need his boost to get on a seat during one of their secret afternoon excursions to Whistler's for root beer floats.

Kat could almost taste the caramel richness of root beer and feel the fizz tickling her nose as she'd twirl to the right atop her perch at the counter. A little bite of the creamy, cold, vanilla ice cream teasing her tongue, just a tiny one to make it last as long as possible, and then a twirl to the left. Grandpa usually had a cup of coffee, but sometimes she could coax him into a taste of her delicious treat. He always made her promise to eat all her supper so Gran wouldn't find out they'd been eating between meals.

The red-topped stools and cool to the touch granite counters beckoned, but this morning, she followed where Mrs. Ritterskamp led and slipped into a red vinyl-covered booth against the wall.

The place sounded the same. A low hum of people greeting the day punctuated by a shrill laugh or hardy guffaw. It even smelled the same, a not unpleasant mixture of coffee, cinnamon rolls, bacon frying, chocolate, and a whiff of what she was certain was Grandpa's brand of after shave.

The diner teemed with businessmen breakfasting before opening for the day, hospital workers after or about to begin their shifts, and tables of grizzled older

43

men, that had once included Grandpa, drinking coffee and solving all the world's problems. If only someone would listen to them.

Sitting there with Gran's best friend completed the feeling of safety and security that comforted her. For a moment, she was a child again, in the place where she had laughed, always felt loved, and never experienced a single second of fear. Could it be her sanctuary now?

Timmy gobbled down his breakfast as if he hadn't eaten in days. Susie, their waitress, teased that if he was still hungry, she would have Walt cook up some more chocolate chip pancakes for him. He wiped the whipping cream mustache off his mouth, then rubbed his tummy, and giggled.

Kat finished the last swallow of coffee in her mug. "A friendly server, fast service, great coffee, and good food. I think I'd like working here."

"I'm glad to hear you say so. Muriel just came in. I'll bring her over to meet you." Mrs. Ritterskamp went to the front register, and an energetic, lean woman followed her back to their table.

"Good morning, young lady. A little Emma bird just told me that you're the answer to my prayers—an experienced waitress." The woman chuckled and extended her hand. "Muriel Whistler."

Kat grasped the extended hand. "Katrina Russell, pleased to meet you. I hope I can help. I don't know about being divinely sent, but I am experienced and looking for a job."

"Let's go to my office where it's a little quieter and get better acquainted."

Kat kissed the top of Timmy's head. "Will you stay with Mrs. Ritterskamp until I'm finished?"

"Sure, maybe we could go over and look at the neat fountain across the street," he suggested hopefully.

"An excellent idea. I think there might be some goldfish in it. Katrina, we'll be across the street when you're through." Mrs. Ritterskamp picked up the check and took her charge by the hand.

"Thank you. I'll get the tip." Kat left several bills on the table, then followed Mrs. Whistler to a room at the back of the diner.

The neat, small office seemed to reflect the calm, orderly woman on the other side of the desk. "Mrs. Whistler, I've been working for over five years in a busy, family-run diner in Philadelphia."

"Please, it's Muriel. You're kinda far from home, aren't you?" Muriel looked at Kat over the top of the glasses perched halfway down her aquiline nose.

"Yes and no. I grew up in Philadelphia, but every summer until I was ten was spent here. My grandparents were Lee and Hannah Schneckker," Kat explained.

"That's why you look sort of familiar. Are you the little girl Doc brought in for the root beer floats he thought Hannah didn't know about?" Muriel laughed. "It's a small world. Your timing couldn't be better. Vicky left me last week. I've been dreading breaking in an inexperienced waitress. Why is it everyone thinks they can do this job? They don't realize how much harder it is than it looks. Emma told me she would be your personal reference. Her endorsement and your experience mean you're hired. When can you start?"

Muriel pulled a packet of paperwork from her desk drawer and slid it across the desktop. "The starting rate is on the top page, as well as information about other benefits, such as they are."

Kat glanced through the papers. The hourly rate was better than it had been in Philly. No fully paid insurance, no surprise there, but it was offered at a discount and through payroll deduction. She'd definitely need the employee plus one rate.

"This looks great. If I can find daycare for my son today, I could start as soon as tomorrow. What's the uniform?"

"White tops and black bottoms. I don't care if you wear skirts or slacks, but clean and in good repair. If you need uniforms, I'll give you a voucher to go to the Budget Boutique across the square. They'll bill me, and I'll deduct it from your pay, spread over your first four paychecks. Mondays are payday, plus you keep all your own tips. You can bring the completed paperwork with you in the morning."

"I will need the uniform voucher. What time do you want me here?"

"Five a.m. to set up. The doors open at five thirty with the coffee pots full and available for the invading hordes."

"I'm used to an early schedule. I'll be here. If something happens and I can't get Timmy settled today, I'll call you."

"Come in through the back door. You can park in one of the spaces in the alley. Welcome aboard, Katrina Russell. Let me introduce you to Susie and Doris. They'll be here in the morning. I usually get in around seven thirty or so. My husband, Walt, is the cook, so he's the early bird."

"Sounds wonderful. Please call me Kat."

Muriel introduced her to Walt and her coworkers,

then walked her to the front door. She could see Mrs. Ritterskamp and Timmy through the window. How could she thank her landlady? A job on the first day. She shook Muriel's hand, turned quickly, and ran nose-to-chest into a man who had materialized out of thin air between her and the door.

"I beg your pardon," he said as he moved aside.

"Please, excuse me," Kat mumbled. "Sorry!" A blush flooded her face with heat as she escaped out the front door.

"Vicky's replacement?" Chase Merrick asked Muriel.

"Yep. Experienced. Emma Ritterskamp's new boarder. She's an Easterner too, not Boston, Philadelphia."

"I'm sure she'll fit right in here in no time, just like Libby did. Just a coffee and sausage biscuit to-go. I'm sure Dr. Jones is anxious for me to relieve him. Thanks, Muriel."

He leaned on the counter to wait. A tall, sun-browned man in overalls walked over to him. "The fishing's been great this spring. I haven't had a bit of problem with my foot, and I've been out there most every day. You'll have to play hooky one afternoon to join me. Bring the boy. Happy to see you any time."

"Thanks, Hank. I will. He'd love it." Chase smiled. Hank shook his hand, then joined his friends in a back booth.

The new waitress was walking to Emma's car holding the hand of a boy who looked like he might be Trevor's age. *An Easterner with a young son. Wonder what her husband does? Mom will probably have all the details from Emma by the time that I get home tonight.*

Muriel brought the to-go order to the register. "Say, Doc, I need my blood pressure pills renewed pretty soon. Would you call it in?"

"I will, but get on my office schedule. Seems like it's about time for your annual checkup, okay?" he gently chided her.

"Will do. See you in the morning." Muriel smiled and rang up the sale.

Some people said Chase Merrick had been in a rut for the past six years. Every morning, if his schedule allowed, he had breakfast at Whistler's while catching up on emails and journal reading, and sometimes dispensing medical advice over cups of strong, black coffee. If it *was* a rut, he was happy to stay in it.

He reveled in the comfortable, satisfying rhythm of his life as a small-town physician. He'd been grateful Libby willingly left her Boston roots behind to move to his hometown in rural Wisconsin. It was a great place to raise kids with loving neighbors who always had your back, in good times and, especially, in sad ones.

Mom never would have understood if we'd turned down the offer to come home. She loves being a hands-on grandmother. She's been my rock.

Chapter Six

Kat couldn't stop smiling. She jaywalked across the street to where Mrs. Ritterskamp and her son were admiring the fountain in front of the courthouse. She teased that she'd tell them all about the job interview once they got home.

Mrs. Ritterskamp smiled as they walked into the kitchen and said, "Never play poker, Katrina. Judging from the grin on your face, I believe I'm looking at Whistler's newest employee."

"You are right! Thank you so much for breakfast, for introducing me to Mrs. Whis…Muriel, and especially for being my personal reference. She hired me on the spot and wants me to start tomorrow. I need to get my uniforms today and find a place for Timmy to stay while I'm at work. At least until school starts in the fall."

"My dear, doesn't your shift start awfully early in the morning?"

"I have to be there at five a.m., just like in Philly. I used to take Timmy to daycare in his pajamas. They had a little cot for him. Once he got up again, they dressed him and took him to school next door. I picked him up when his school day ended. In the summer, they had all kinds of outings and educational programs. They even had a late pickup option that I had to use more than once." Kat continued down her mental checklist of things to remember to ask a daycare provider. Would a small town have anything so convenient?

"I'll be here when he wakes up," Mrs. Ritterskamp quietly stated.

"You'll take him to daycare or school for me? That would be *so* helpful." She checked transportation off the list.

"No. I'll *be* his daycare. Once school starts, he can catch the bus right in front of the house, and if you're still at work when school is over, I can be here to meet the bus. There are scads of fun things we could do together this summer."

Mrs. Ritterskamp, his daycare provider. That would be amazing. Kat stammered, "How much do you charge for daycare?"

Even though her waitress salary was better than in Philly, she'd have to allocate a lot of it for rent and insurance. She'd never paid Pop anything for room and board. Her only expenses had been for her son's care. The Rainy Day Fund would wash away in a flood of daycare expenses.

Pop tried to help with her escape plan, but she had to prove she could handle it on her own. Talk about lack of planning. This was an even bigger obstacle than the tunnels. They'd have to go back to Philly. Danger or not. They couldn't afford to stay. Tears welled up in her eyes.

"Nothing. No extra charge. You're already paying room and board. He'll just be home more of the day than you will." Mrs. Ritterskamp smiled broadly.

"I'm sorry. What did you say? It sounded like you said you would look after Timmy for free. That can't be right," Kat said distractedly, fighting tears.

"There is nothing wrong with your hearing. It *is* what I said."

"I may have to work some evenings too. I can't ask you to do this," Kat protested, while frantically trying to think of any viable alternative.

"You didn't ask me to do it. I volunteered. Why should Timmy be uprooted every day to go stay with strangers when he can stay home? What do you think, Timmy?" Mrs. Ritterskamp directed her question to the energetic little boy at Kat's side.

"Mom, I think it's a good idea. You won't have to come to pick me up somewhere else when you're tired from working all day. Besides, Mrs. Ritterskamp gives great hugs," Timmy said earnestly.

"I'm outnumbered," Kat sighed. "You are too kind. Somehow the obstacles we've encountered are being magically removed."

"I don't believe for a minute that it's mortal magic. God has a plan, even when we haven't formed one yet or the ones we have don't quite work out as expected. We just have to be smart enough to recognize the solution when He puts it in front of us. I'm looking forward to Timmy's company," Mrs. Ritterskamp proclaimed enthusiastically.

Divine intervention would certainly explain how this ill-conceived adventure was falling into place. *If* she believed in divine intervention.

"Thank you. I don't know how I'll ever be able to repay you. I'm beginning to understand why you were so special to Gran." She hugged her landlady.

"I see a lot of Hannah in you. I'm glad I can help you since she isn't here to do it herself."

Kat turned to her son. "We have lots to celebrate. What do you think about a picnic in the park and some fishing?"

"I can't."

"It's not like you to pass up a day in the park."

"I'd like to go, Mom, but I don't know how to fish."

"Lucky for you, your mom does! My grandpa taught me how to fish when I was just about your age." Her son stared at her wide-eyed. "We'll pick up the supplies after we stop to get my uniforms. Unless you don't want to go because you're afraid of worms!"

"I ain't afraid of nothing!"

****

It had been far too long since they'd enjoyed mother and son time alone in the pursuit of pure fun. Timmy's expression was one of total awe when his mom could not only pick up the slimy worms they had for bait, but she knew how to put them on the hook so they wouldn't wiggle off. None of the fish they caught were big enough to eat, but the sound of Timmy's laughter was balm to her soul. They were together...having fun...and safe.

****

The mouthwatering aroma of supper emanating from the stove greeted them at the kitchen door. "Did you have fun? You're just in time for supper. Get washed and we'll eat." Mrs. Ritterskamp finished setting the table.

"It was great. We caught lots and lots of fish, but we threw them back. We're saving them until they grow a little," Timmy reported enthusiastically.

After some soap and water to remove the fish

smell, Kat and Timmy sat down on either side of Mrs. Ritterskamp. She reached out to them with her head bowed and eyes closed. Timmy grabbed a fresh-from-the-oven biscuit off the platter in front of him and took a bite.

The heat of embarrassment flooded Kat's face. "Honey, put down the biscuit. Hold hands with us. Close your eyes and bow your head."

"Gee," Timmy started to protest. One look from his mother and he did as she instructed.

After she said the blessing, Mrs. Ritterskamp served the tasty meal—savory pot roast, mashed potatoes, tender carrots, and juicy onions, all covered with creamy mushroom gravy, and the already sampled warm biscuits with honey butter.

"I'm sorry. Next time he'll know to wait to dig in until after the blessing."

"I expect playing in all the fresh air makes a guy extra hungry. I take it as a compliment to my cooking."

"Thanks for understanding."

Timmy reached for another biscuit.

Kat shook her head. "Vegetables first."

"It's nice to have someone to feed again. It's not really worth the effort to make a full meal for just one person. My husband, Godfrey, always had a good appetite. He worked outside most of the day and always wanted a hearty supper. No soup and sandwiches, and definitely no rabbit food for supper."

"Rabbit food?" Timmy cocked his head.

"He meant salads. He didn't understand how lettuce could possibly be filling enough for a meal." Mrs. Ritterskamp laughed.

"I remember you and your husband coming over to

Gran's to play board games in the evening. I always thought Grandpa was a big man, but he was dwarfed by your husband. I thought he was a giant straight out of a fairy tale."

"He was six foot six, probably did look huge from a little girl's perspective."

"What kind of work did he do?"

"He owned a dairy with his brother Karl. We came here so they could work the business together. Now that they're both gone, our nephew and his sons own it. Your grandpa was our veterinarian. In fact, I met him before I met Hannah, right after we moved here over fifty years ago. It's been a good place to be." She seemed lost in the past for a moment. "I hope it will be for you."

"So far, I couldn't ask for anything more. A cozy place to live, Gran's best friend to watch Timmy, and a job to start tomorrow, all in the first full day here."

"Don't forget teaching me to fish, Mom," Timmy interjected.

"Oh, yes, and Timmy learning to fish. We're off to a terrific start. I think Mom and Gran would both be glad we're here."

After her son snuggled into bed, Kat called Pop to give him an update. He wasn't waiting for her call tonight. She never meant to hurt his feelings by asking him to give her space. She still needed him. She left a message about landing the job and Mrs. Ritterskamp's offer to watch Timmy averting a budgeting near disaster. They were both finding their way in this new long-distance, father-daughter relationship.

****

After dinner, Chase said to his mother, "I literally

ran into Emma Ritterskamp's new boarder today. Muriel hired her to replace Vicky at the diner. Why would Emma have someone from Philadelphia renting from her?"

"Oh, you're talking about Katrina Russell, right? An attractive blonde with a little boy Trevor's age," Claire Merrick replied.

"She may have been attractive. I didn't get a good look at her, but she did have a little boy with her."

"There's a logical reason for her to be here. Her mother is from Lansdale. You never knew her because she moved away before you were born. But you knew her grandfather. He was Dr. Schneckker."

"Our veterinarian? I remember him."

"I was sure you would. Katrina used to spend summers here with her grandparents. You had already left for college when they passed away. She's only twenty-three."

"I probably met her at the clinic. There used to be a little blonde girl with what I thought was a funny accent who liked to pretend she was running the office. I'm certain she was in there the last couple of times I took Duke to the clinic before I left for college."

"I'm sure she was Katrina. Hannah Schneckker always said how lost they were when she went back to Philadelphia every fall. She loved working with her grandfather when she was a little girl," Claire remembered.

"Well, she definitely isn't a little girl any longer. Maybe Trevor will get to meet her son. He always likes having new friends to pal around with."

"There will probably be an opportunity for them to play together. Emma is going to be the boy's daycare provider."

"Small world."

Chapter Seven

The unmistakable roar of a motorcycle echoed through the diner. Kat stopped where she stood. Her lungs wouldn't refill. She gripped the counter to steady her trembling legs. Out the front window she saw a red-helmeted rider atop a motorcycle pull out of a space in front of the diner and drive away.

Impossible. Not here. He couldn't know she's gone. Not yet. *Other people with red helmets ride motorcycles. Get a grip, girl! People are staring. Stop scowling.* She wiped away the tear that slipped down her cheek, plastered on what she hoped was a pleasant smile, and resumed pouring coffee. She needed to make a good impression. She had to keep *this* job. There weren't many employment options in a town of four thousand.

The breakfast crowd cleared around ten thirty. After the last table was bussed, Kat's coworkers approached to get better acquainted. Susie Powell was their waitress yesterday, a tall woman who looked to be in her mid-thirties, self-described as a "married single mom" since her husband's job on a tugboat on the Mississippi had a thirty days on, then thirty days off schedule. From the patter she kept up with the customers, she seemed to enjoy the work.

Petite Doris Keith told Kat she had been known to live up to the feistiness her auburn hair color predicted.

She was single, confessed to being twenty-seven, and had an ever-present smile. You might say she was perky, but Kat sensed that was *not* a description Doris would like.

"From your demonstration this morning, you sure know your way around a diner," Doris complimented Kat. "I see why Muriel hired you on the spot. I was a little worried about getting someone from out of town. I don't know anyone else from Philadelphia, but you fit right in."

"Thanks, I've been working in a diner for the past five years. If I'm the first person you've met from Philly, I hope I made a good impression."

"Oh, you did," Doris quickly responded.

"It's nice to have someone on our shift who keeps going until the job is done. Most mornings will be like today. They start a little slow, we run like crazy from six to ten thirty, have a short break, and then the lunch crowd until the mid-afternoon lull. Then it's either clocking out or working the supper crowd. You just have to keep smiling and never sit down, or you'll realize how much your feet hurt." Susie laughed. "If you're looking for love, one plus about the job is that all the single guys in town eat here."

"Good for her, if she's single, but probably not for us. A Whistler's romance is how we lost the last girl," Doris volunteered. "Vicky married a traveling salesman from Green Bay. It was love at first order. He stopped in every couple of weeks for a year before he popped the question. She didn't hesitate to say 'yes.' "

"I am single, but definitely not looking for a relationship. I'm here strictly for a paycheck to care for my five-year-old son."

"Growing boys cost a lot to feed," Susie said. "Wait until he's fifteen like mine! My kid's always hungry and eats constantly. He's skinny as a rail and shooting up so quickly that his pants become high-waters almost before the first time they're washed!"

"Well, if you change your mind about romance, at least you'll know what kind of table manners the local Romeos have. If any of them look interesting to you, talk to me first. I've probably dated them, *if* they're worth thinking about twice." Doris rolled her eyes. "Bottom line is we're glad you're here. Nice not to be working shorthanded."

The lull was over. At eleven, exactly as Susie predicted, the lunch crowd started coming through the doors, almost as if they had been queuing up on the sidewalk waiting for the dinner bell to ring.

When a tall, dark-headed man in a utility company uniform came in, Doris glanced at her reflection in the front panel of the metal milk machine, tucked a stray strand of auburn back in her hairnet, and said, "Speaking of worth dating, I have some business to take care of right now." She led the handsome customer to a table at her station.

Susie chuckled. "I'm not sure Doris will be footloose and single much longer. Jason's been in for lunch every day for the past two weeks. Always at her station. They've been out together too. Good thing we were able to replace Vicky so quickly."

The day whirred by. Kat crawled in the car at the end of her shift, then her feet reminded her she hadn't sat down all day. Being busy was good. The less time she had to dwell on the past, the better.

****

"Mom, you're home!" Timmy raced to the door to meet her. He hugged his mom. "Guess what. Nana knows how to make my favorite pancakes—chocolate chip!"

"Nana?" Kat questioned.

Mrs. Ritterskamp came out of the kitchen drying her hands on an apron. "I hope you don't mind. Mrs. Ritterskamp seems like a lot for a little mouth to repeat all day long."

"Timmy doesn't call anyone else Nana. I think it's wonderful. It can be his special name for you." She sat down and pulled her son onto her lap. "What kind of fun did you have today?"

"We went to the store. Good boys, like me, get free cookies. Nana needed my help to hang the sheets on the clothesline 'cause one person can't do it alone. I learned a new song, but it's in French so I probably need more practice before I sing it for you." Timmy stopped. "Nana, what else did we do today?"

"I can't believe you don't remember. You beat me playing the ladder board game three times!"

"Oh, yeah!" Timmy whispered, "Nana's not very good at games, but I like to play with her."

"I wouldn't get too used to beating Nana. She'll get the hang of it after she plays a while, then she'll start beating you. I had a good first day too. I met some new, interesting people, and I have lots of food for your piggy bank."

Timmy held out his shirt to catch all the tip change his mom brought home to feed his pig. He was saving for a bicycle or a pony or a football, depending on when you asked him. He went upstairs to add today's haul to his stash.

Kat walked into the kitchen. "What can I do to help with supper? It smells delicious."

"Please set the dining room table. We're just about ready. The plates are in the cabinet on the left side of the sink, glasses above the plates, and silverware's in the drawer by the stove." Mrs. Ritterskamp started putting food in serving dishes.

Timmy sat down and immediately reached out to hold hands for the blessing. Mrs. Ritterskamp quietly said the prayer, then helped him get a leg off the platter of fried chicken in front of her.

"Mom, I forgot the most important thing. Do you know what happens tomorrow?" Timmy asked almost breathlessly.

"I don't. Are you and Nana doing something special?"

"*Yes!*"

"Hey, little man, inside voice, please," Kat cautioned.

"Sorry, Mom. This is so exciting. I'm gonna have my very own swing set, right in Nana's backyard."

"Really?" She looked over to Mrs. Ritterskamp for confirmation.

"A family at church was moving away. The swing set was in their garage sale last Saturday, so I bought it. The men's prayer group is coming to install it tomorrow. It was a great bargain."

"You're amazing. Thank you, Mrs. Ritterskamp. How wonderful to have a play set right in the yard."

"You're welcome. Please, Katrina, call me Emma. We needn't be so formal. You can't call your son's Nana, Mrs. Ritterskamp."

"Thank you, Emma. Timmy, what do you have to

say to your sweet Nana?"

"Quack. Quack. Quack," Timmy sang out.

"What does that mean?" Kat asked.

"It means I'm a lucky duck. Thank you, Nana." He giggled.

"Indeed you are. Promise me you'll only play out there when an adult can watch you. I don't want you to fall and hurt yourself."

"I promise, Mom." Timmy got up from his chair and hugged Emma's neck.

Dessert was juicy, blackberry cobbler. "This is simply marvelous," Kat said smacking her lips. "Still warm, like Gran used to serve it."

"I'm not surprised it reminds you of her. It's her recipe."

"Well, you did Gran proud. It tastes like she made it herself. I don't have any of her recipes. I'd love to have a copy."

"We can look through my recipe box after we do dishes. I have several of hers. I'd be happy to share any that you want," Emma offered.

"We're getting spoiled rotten, and we've only been here two days."

Timmy wanted to play with his trucks while Emma and Kat did dishes. His mom told him to go upstairs so Nana could have some peace and quiet, but Emma insisted they both keep her company in the living room, so the trucks came downstairs.

After Timmy was in bed, Emma and Kat sat side-by-side on the sofa leafing through the recipe files.

"I hope you're all right with Timmy calling me Nana," Emma began.

"He doesn't call anyone else Nana. My mom was

gone long before he was born. My father's second wife didn't want any old-sounding grandmother name, especially since we're not *her* blood relatives. She insisted on being called by her first name, even with Timmy. His father isn't from Philadelphia. I've never met his parents."

"I'm glad I can be his first Nana."

"He was still talking about the swing set as he drifted off to sleep. I know you'll keep a close eye on him. At five, he believes he can do anything. Sometimes I have to remind him that he's breakable."

"I'm glad he's excited. Maybe he'll miss you less if he's playing hard all day. He was a little anxious first thing this morning. I offered to take him to Whistler's for lunch so he could see you. He told me he wasn't a baby. After he got busy playing, he seemed to relax. He's a sweet child. I enjoy being with him."

"I'm so lucky to have found you again. I feel like we're part of your family. I was under a lot of stress about this move, but you smoothed everything over for me. It sounds like you're doing the same thing for Timmy."

"It was getting way too quiet in this old house. I'm glad to have you here."

"After we've been here a while, you may be wishing for a little peace back." Kat laughed.

"Six months was enough silence for a lifetime. You're both welcome—noise and all." Emma stood. "I'm afraid it's time for me to call it a day. You have an early morning too. Have pleasant dreams, Katrina."

"Good night, Mrs...Emma."

****

"Well, hello. We meet again," Kat's first customer

of the morning greeted her as he sat down at the counter.

"I don't believe I know you. This is only my second day here."

"You could say we *met* briefly on Monday morning." The man smiled.

Kat didn't recognize the perfect white teeth or the deep-blue eyes ringed by dark, lush eyelashes any woman would envy. At first. Then her ears grew warm, and she knew a bright red blush flooded her face. "*Met* is being kind. I apologize again. I was so excited about getting this job that I wasn't watching where I was going. Let me take this opportunity to meet you properly."

She took one step back, turned completely around, then stepped to the counter again and said, in her most professional tone, "Good morning. I'm Kat, and I'll be your server. What would you like for breakfast?"

"Chase Merrick. Very nice to meet you." He shook hands with her. "My usual—two eggs lightly scrambled, crisp bacon, rye toast, and black coffee. Thank you."

She walked to the window at the back of the diner to place his order. Mr. Merrick seemed awfully good natured considering she practically knocked him down on their first encounter.

When she delivered his breakfast, Mr. Merrick looked up from his phone long enough to say "thank you," then went back to responding to emails between bites. He ate quickly.

"Will there be anything else?" Kat asked when she brought his check.

"Thanks, not this morning. I know Muriel is glad

you're here. Hope Lansdale agrees with you. My wife loved it here, once she got used to being away from Boston." He picked up the check.

"I guess you can tell I'm from out of state because I don't have a Wisconsin accent."

"Accent? Don't you know, Wisconsinites don't have accents." He laughed, left a five-dollar bill under his mug, grabbed his white lab coat, paid Muriel, and was out the door.

What a great tip. Was he always so generous? Kat smiled and pocketed the bill. He was wrong about one thing. Kat's Philly trained ears definitely picked up a Wisconsin accent.

****

Timmy didn't let his mom sit down when she walked in the kitchen after work. He pulled her out the back door into the yard. "Tada!" he said with a great flourish. "Isn't it awesome? You should've seen them putting it up. There were six guys here and a great big truck and tools and everything."

The *swing set* was not at all what she expected. This wasn't a basic, tubular-metal-legged, backyard swing set. This was a cedar play fort complete with three swings, a spiral slide threaded through a tunnel, a tall tower you could access by a rope ladder or stair steps, and a trapeze bar swing—all secured in concrete footings.

"Oh, my! Awesome is right." Kat walked all around the layout.

Emma came out the back door. "Doesn't it look splendid? The men's prayer group came early, about mid-morning, and had it up in no time."

"This must have cost a fortune, Emma."

"Well, I did have to feed my labor today, but the whole thing was still a steal. If Timmy enjoys himself, it will be well worth the price. Speaking of feeding, supper's about ready if *someone* wants to set the table," Emma hinted.

"I'm on it, Nana." Timmy raced in the back door.

"I'm impressed…with the swing set *and* your helper. You run a first-rate daycare, Mrs. Ritterskamp."

Timmy needed help reaching the plates and glasses from the tall cabinets but had the napkins and silverware on the table by the time Kat and Emma walked into the kitchen.

Emma and Timmy worked together the same way that she used to help Gran. Emma had made this move the right thing to do. *Thanks, Gran, your friend is an amazing gift to us.*

Chapter Eight

Kat watched as the man in dark glasses made his way to the counter and took a seat on the third stool from the left. His German shepherd guide dog made itself comfortable on the floor. She squeezed in between his stool and the wall of the counter, out of the way, but nearby.

"Good morning, sir. Would you like some coffee?" she asked cheerfully.

"Where's Vicky?" The man frowned. "Oh, I remember, she ran off and abandoned me. Everybody knows me. Charlie Bishop's the name. This little sweetheart is Sheba. She's my eyes. Who are you?"

"My name's Kat."

Sheba growled. "Shush, don't let Sheba hear you say C-A-T. She hates 'em; starts growling at the mere mention of those pesky critters. Had a bad encounter with an especially cranky Siamese when she was a pup."

"Sorry, I didn't know. My full name is Katrina, if you'd rather use that."

"Seems kinda formal. We'll be seeing each other regularly. Might even be friends." Charlie thought for a moment. "If it is okay with you, I'll call you Kitty. What do you think?"

"I like it. Nice to meet you, Mr. Bishop and Sheba. What would you like?"

"The name's Charlie. Got any specials this morning?"

"Today's are a short stack of blueberry pancakes with bacon; a ham and cheese omelet with home fries and toast; and sausage, egg, and cheese on a homemade biscuit. What'll it be?"

"Vicky used to read me the whole menu until I decided what tickled my taste buds today," Charlie said with a mischievous grin.

Kat was skeptical but began reading the breakfast items from the menu out loud.

"Prices, too. Have to see if I can afford what I want."

She started again with the prices, stopping briefly between items to see if any of them struck Charlie's fancy.

Chase Merrick listened to the server patiently read each item. When she got to the sixth one, he interrupted, "Charlie Bishop, you should be ashamed of yourself. Tying up all of this young lady's time when there are other people waiting to order. I'm pretty sure you have the entire menu memorized by now. It hasn't changed in five years."

"But she has such a sweet voice. I could listen to her all day." Charlie smirked. "I'll have the short stack special. And, for the record, I *do* know the menu by heart. Just making sure Muriel doesn't raise prices on me."

Kat mouthed a "thank you" to Mr. Merrick when she poured him a cup of coffee.

Charlie finished his breakfast and signaled for the check. "Young lady, I hope you know I was just funning you. I only need to know the daily specials next time, but you do have the voice of an angel from on high—when you talk it's like you're hugging my ears. Would you mind letting me *see* your smile?" He lifted his hands toward her face.

Intrigued, Kat leaned over the counter toward him. "Please, go ahead."

Charlie gently touched her face from ear to ear and eyebrows to chin. "It's a beauty, just like I knew it would be. No makeup either. A looker like her doesn't need any help from the cosmetic counter. Modest too, judging by that blush."

"How do you know I'm blushing?"

"Can feel the heat. We'll be in again. We always sit in this spot. Good to have you here." When the dog sensed her master moving, the shepherd stirred and stood at Charlie's side.

"It was nice to meet you and Sheba, Charlie. Enjoy your day." Kat gave him the check and told him the total.

Charlie put money on the counter saying, "I'll leave this with you to take to Muriel. Keep the change." Sheba and Charlie got all the way to the door before she caught up with them.

"Mr. Charlie, you left me too much money."

"I told you to keep the change."

"I think you might have pulled out the wrong bill." She leaned over and whispered in his ear what it was.

"It's the right bill. Sheba likes you. So do I."

Kat opened the door for them, paid Muriel, and returned to her station after adding the change to the growing sheaf of ones in her "tip pocket."

Chase Merrick had watched the whole episode. When Kat delivered his check, he said, "Charlie was right." Then got up and paid his bill.

Charlie had the softest hands. Before today no one had ever "seen" Kat with their fingers. She had a funny story to tell Timmy and Emma tonight. What did Mr. Merrick mean about Charlie being right? He left another five-dollar tip. Timmy's piggy bank would eat well tonight.

This was a good job. The customers were mostly friendly, and she never heard a complaint about the food Walt sent out of the kitchen. It was tasty and delivered quickly. She soon learned the names and usual orders of her *regulars* like Charlie and Sheba; Mr. Peterson, the pharmacist; Mr. Merrick; and, last of all, the eccentric Miss Althea Schumacher.

She had recently retired, at age eighty, after a sixty-year career as the librarian at the Stintson Public library. Their first encounter did not start off well.

"Young woman, just how long do you expect me to patiently wait for service?" questioned the petite, silver-haired woman who had sat down at the counter only moments ago.

"No wait at all. What would you like?" Kat responded cheerfully.

"I have eaten the exact same breakfast sitting on this very stool for over thirty years, and you have to ask what I would like? Are you addled or simply too lazy to try and remember?"

Kat stammered, "I'm sorry. Today is the first time I've waited on you."

"Well, I never…excuses, excuses. Young people don't want to work anymore."

Susie came to the rescue, taking Kat aside to reveal what Miss Schumacher's *usual* breakfast order was—

one poached egg with done whites and runny yolks; four half slices of dry white toast; extra, extra crisp, not burnt, bacon; and a cup of Earl Grey tea with honey. Bring an extra pot of hot water.

Kat quickly put the cup of tea with honey and extra pot of hot water in front of Miss Schumacher and went to the back to place her order. She thanked Susie for her assistance. "Was Vicky a blonde?"

"Nope. Inky black hair and twice your age. We think Miss Althea orders the same thing every day because she doesn't see well enough to read the menu anymore. Not sure she hears much either." Susie smiled. "You'll be fine as long as you stick to her usual."

Kat delivered Miss Schumacher's breakfast, exactly the meal Susie had described. The only response was a derisive snort.

****

After dinner, Timmy played on the living room floor while Kat and Emma visited. "Mom, when can I see Pop Pop? I miss him so much," Timmy asked while he examined the truck in his hands. "He gave me this. The hood even opens just like the ones he and Uncle John work on."

"I know you miss Pop Pop, honey, so do I. But we just got here. I don't have any vacation time, so I wouldn't get paid. Why don't you write a note to Pop Pop and Jocie, maybe send them a picture. I know they'd like to hear from you," Kat suggested hoping to placate her son.

While he went to get paper and crayons, Emma asked, "Were you living with your father before you moved here? Timmy has talked all day about Pop Pop and Jocie. Who is Jocie? A pet?"

Kat laughed. "No, Jocie is my father's wife. They've been married since shortly after I lost my mom when I was thirteen. Timmy and I were living with them in my childhood home."

"So Jocie's your stepmother."

"She prefers to think of herself *only* as my father's wife, and I'm fine with that."

"What does your father do?"

"He's a mechanic, in business with his brother, John. They can fix anything with a motor. Sometimes Pop picked Timmy up at day care and took him to spend the day at Russell Motors. I know he misses getting to go to the garage."

"Timmy sure thinks the world of your father."

"I'm proud of Pop. I hate to be so far from him, but protecting Timmy comes first." Kat shook her head sadly. "I may have overreacted coming all the way out here. I didn't think how it would affect Timmy to be uprooted from his regular routines. But we're here now, and we need to make it work. Someday, I'll tell you about all the whys when we don't have little ears listening."

Timmy went to the dining room table with crayons, pencils, and paper. He was just learning his letters, so Kat slowly spelled out each word for him to complete his note. Fortunately, it was short. He concentrated on drawing a picture of Pop Pop working on a bright blue car with the hood open. Timmy was standing beside him with a wrench in his hand. You could tell he'd seen underneath a car's hood from all the detail on the engine that was complete with spark plugs, fan belt, and a radiator. She added a note to the bottom of the letter: *I miss you too. Lots of love, Kat.*

Emma found an envelope, but no stamps. "Don't worry. We'll go to the post office first thing in the morning to get stamps. I'll put it on the counter right by the door so we don't forget." The envelope was addressed to James and Jocelyn Russell. *I guess it's more common these days, for young women to keep their maiden names. But don't children usually take the father's?*

****

Chase was on duty in the Emergency Department Saturday morning. He just had time enough for a quick breakfast alone.

"Regular coffee, black, two eggs lightly scrambled, crisp bacon, rye toast—did I get it right?" a cheery voice asked as a mug of steaming hot black coffee appeared in front of him.

"Exactly. You catch on quickly. The girls must have told you, I'm a pretty predictable guy, at least about what I want for breakfast." He smiled and went back to checking his phone messages.

When Kat delivered his check, Mr. Merrick whispered, "Please give me the check for the Hollises, the couple at the end of the counter. Today's their fiftieth wedding anniversary."

"How sweet. What should I tell them when they ask for their check?"

"Tell them it's been paid and to enjoy their anniversary."

"I'm sure they'll want to thank you."

"Don't tell them it's from me. Tell them it was paid by a fan of enduring love." After leaving a large tip on both checks, Mr. Merrick paid the bills at the register.

Kat heard a motorcycle rev up, just like she had every morning since she had started at Whistler's. She hurried to the front window in time to see Mr. Merrick put on a red helmet, then pull his bike away from the curb. What a waste of energy worrying all week. *It was him all the time. Dirk must still be in Philadelphia. He's nothing like Dirk.* She let out the breath she'd been holding and relaxed.

****

Thank goodness she had a garage to park in, out of the gusty wind and pouring rain. After leaving the diner, she had barely closed her car door when a popup thunderstorm started. It was almost ten minutes before the windshield cleared enough to safely pull out of the parking space.

All the way home, she found herself thinking about Mr. Merrick. Pop would say he was a presence, someone who instantly commands attention and respect, just by walking in the room. When she told the Hollises, "Happy Anniversary from a fan of enduring love," they quietly said, "Thank you," and walked out of the diner hand in hand. His appreciation of their obvious mutual affection touched Kat's heart.

He's so thoughtful and generous. After Dirk's foul moods, it was nice to have kindness, instead of snarling, greet you at breakfast time. Mrs. Merrick was a very lucky woman.

Kat turned off the car. She rested her head on the steering wheel a moment before summoning the energy to go in the house. Her legs and feet ached. Those two fingers on her left hand throbbed with remembered pain. They ached unceasingly when she was overtired or when the weather was rainy and damp. Tonight, she was getting the mega-pain daily double. Her shoulder definitely needed some stretching exercises tonight. Had she jumped the gun removing the sling?

Emma always left the light on over the stove to show Kat the way into the still unfamiliar kitchen. There was a note from her and a picture from Timmy on the table. The picture showed Kat in her uniform with a heaping tray of food and drinks, all easily balanced on one hand, her other hand resting on her hip. She laughed out loud, glad that she made her job look so effortless to her son.

It had only been a week, but things were going so well. Was it too soon to believe they were free of Dirk? *If* their escape continued to be successful, it would be worth the homesickness she was feeling.

A plate of fresh baked, white chocolate, macadamia nut cookies—Kat's favorite—waited on the table. Before going to bed, she poured herself a glass of milk and sat down with a cookie, something she hadn't done since the last visit to her grandparents, years ago.

Dear Kat,

I hope you enjoy the snack and didn't have to work too late. I know it's been a long week, moving, and starting right to work. Timmy's been a perfect angel. He's happy to entertain himself or to help me with projects. What a blessing!

If you're not too tired in the morning, I'd love to have you both join me for church. Sunday School is at nine thirty, church at ten thirty. We'll talk about it at breakfast. Have pleasant dreams.

Blessings, Emma

She checked the time. It was after eleven. She'd covered for a call-in on the late shift. The last customer hadn't left until well after normal closing time. Next week's paycheck would be more than welcome, and the tips had been generous, but she was thankful the family-run diner was closed every Sunday.

Emma had been a life saver. She hated to disappoint her, but Kat really needed a day off. She wasn't interested in sitting in the middle of strangers being preached at, scolded, and made to feel more guilty about her life choices than she already did. Hopefully, Emma would understand.

After rinsing off her dishes, she peeked in on Timmy, his blond curls spread across the pillow. She kissed her son's forehead. He stirred long enough to kiss her cheek.

She didn't remember anything after her head hit the pillow.

****

If storms passed through during the night, Kat hadn't heard them. She'd slept soundly, knowing there wouldn't be any alarm to disturb her. The sun shining through a gap in the curtains woke her.

She ran a brush through her hair, pulled on a tee shirt and jeans, then after finding Timmy's room empty, went downstairs. It was quiet. The welcome aroma of brewed coffee wafted to her nose.

"Timmy? Emma? Anyone home? No wonder. It's after ten o'clock. I've slept half the day away." There was a note on the kitchen table.

Dear Kat, You were still soundly asleep when I checked on you after we finished breakfast. I'm taking Timmy with me. I'm teaching Children's Church so he'll be able to meet some other children there.

A plate to reheat for your breakfast is in the fridge.

Please take out the pot of chicken and dumplings and put them on the stove on low about noon for our dinner. Hope you are well rested. Blessings, Emma.

She zapped the waiting breakfast, poured a cup of coffee that tasted as good as it smelled, and sat down to read the Sunday *Madison State Journal* she'd found on the kitchen table, thankful that Emma understood what she needed without any explanation.

She glanced through the paper, then poured herself a second cup of coffee and stepped out the back door. The coffee cup warmed her hands. The cool air nipped her nose. Emma's backyard was lined with blooming lilac bushes growing parallel to the privacy fence. She breathed deeply, enjoying their light scent.

"This is a perfect, safe place for Timmy. It's so beautiful and peaceful, just like Emma," Kat said aloud to herself. "It's still a tad chilly out here. Time to get dinner on the stove."

Today was her son's first Sunday School experience. Going with her mother had been an important part of Kat's early life. Mom told her that a loving, caring God watched over His creations. Even when the cancer wracked her body, that faith never wavered.

Kat stood at the stove stirring the chicken and dumplings. The raising garage door groaned. Moments later, the kitchen door flew open.

"Mom! Mom!" Timmy called out at top volume, streaking to her side.

"Please use your inside voice." She led him to a kitchen chair, hugged him, and pulled him onto her lap. "Did you have fun?"

"Mom, I have a new best friend, Trevor. He's

'zactly the same age as me. We had the best time. Look what I made you. It's my handprint, but don't touch it. It has to dry. Happy Mother's Day from me to you! Do you like it?" He barely slowed to take a breath.

She hugged him again while examining the neon pink clay handprint. "It's beautiful. I'd forgotten about Mother's Day. Did you thank Nana for taking you with her?"

Timmy ran to Emma, who was at the stove, and hugged her waist. "Thank you, Nana. You were right. Mom loves her present. Thanks for taking me. It was way fun."

Kat called him back over to her and pulled him onto her lap again. "Who loves Timmy more than anyone?" It was a game they'd played since he first started to talk.

"Mom loves me! Who loves Mom?" Timmy's little voice sang out.

"Timmy loves me!" she responded.

"Jesus loves Mom too! He loves me and Nana and everybody! Did you know that? I learned it in Sunday School," Timmy added cheerfully.

Kat laughed a little uncomfortably. "Yes. I knew. I'm glad Jesus loves everybody." Her son kissed her, then ran to his room to change clothes before dinner.

The chicken and dumplings were wonderfully satisfying, reminding Kat of Sunday dinner with her grandparents. No wonder they called it comfort food.

While they did dishes after dinner, Kat and Emma watched from the kitchen window as Timmy played in the backyard. He was giving the swing set a workout. Emma's instincts had been perfect.

Kat was lost in thought when Emma said, "I know

it's asking forgiveness after the fact, but I hope you're okay about Timmy going with me."

"No apologies are necessary. I needed the sleep, and he seems to have had a great time." She pointed to the handprint. "This is the first Mother's Day gift I've ever gotten."

"I'm surprised your husband never bought you one. Maybe this will be the beginning of a new trend."

"His father wasn't with us for a Mother's Day. I'm sure you could tell Timmy had never been to Sunday School before today. Religion hasn't had a place in our family, at least not since my mom died."

"No time like now to change that trend too, if you want to. You're both welcome to come with me any Sunday. I think Timmy and Trevor instantly bonded. Trevor's grandmother, Claire, is a very dear friend of mine. They're good people. Thanks for helping with the dishes. Let's go outside and enjoy the sunshine."

Emma picked up her work basket. She was knitting a warm, red, wool sweater for Timmy's September birthday, just the thing for next year's cold, snowy winter.

From the patio, they could watch him swing and slide. Kat helped him on the trapeze bar. Soon he was fearlessly swinging as if he was the main attraction under The Big Top.

Chapter Nine

Doris and Susie had warned her that Monday mornings were especially busy. Kat was ready for action. It was her first Wisconsin payday too, an opportunity to replenish the funds eaten up from traveling.

She was making another round refilling coffee cups when Mr. Merrick stopped her. "Excuse me, Mrs. Russell?"

She hesitated a moment. Had she told him her full name? "Regular, right?" Kat started to pour him more coffee.

Mr. Merrick moved the mug out of her reach. "No, thanks, I don't need any more coffee. I think I met your son, Timmy, yesterday at church."

"Oh, that explains how you knew my last name. He went with my landlady, Emma Ritterskamp." She set down the coffee pots.

"It was definitely your son. He looks so much like you. My son, Trevor, told me Timmy Russell was his new best friend."

"Funny, that's what Timmy told me about Trevor. It's nice knowing you're the father of my son's new best friend. Sorry, but I have a lot of other customers needing a little more caffeine." She picked up the coffee pots.

"I didn't mean to keep you. I need to be going too."

He put on a white lab coat and paid his bill.

Kat wasn't surprised to find his regular tip under Mr. Merrick's mug. The girls weren't kidding when they said he was a great tipper. A motorcycle revved up. She frowned. Even though she knew it was Mr. Merrick, her heart skipped a beat.

"For the record, he'd definitely be classified as dating-worthy. So, what's up with you and the Doc?" Doris asked laughing.

"Did he need a to-go cup or something more?" Susie chimed in.

"The Doc? Mr. Merrick is Dr. Merrick? Guess I should've figured it out from the lab coat," Kat said self-consciously. "You both have overactive imaginations. Our sons met at Sunday School and decided they were best friends. He wanted me to know he was Trevor's dad. It isn't any big deal."

How would Timmy fit in with a doctor's son and his friends? Her paychecks were fully spoken for. They barely had enough money to make ends meet. She couldn't disappoint Timmy when he was so elated about finding a best friend. She would have to figure out a way for him to keep up with Trevor. Another challenge on this adventure.

****

"Mrs...sorry, Emma, if I keep eating like this, I'll get fat. You'd think someone who works around food all day would get tired of it. But not me! The lasagna was wonderful. I don't know when I've eaten better apple dumplings. Thank you so much." Kat stood and started clearing the table.

"It wouldn't hurt you to have a little more meat on your bones. You're such a slender slip of a girl." Emma beamed at the compliments.

"Kind of you to say, but I need to pace myself or I'll have Grandma Russell's ample hips in no time. Hey, Timmy, one of my regular customers is your friend's dad. Trevor told him that you were his best friend." Timmy looked up from where he was playing on the living room floor and grinned.

Emma suggested, "Maybe Trevor would like to come over to play one afternoon. If it's okay with you and his dad, I'd be happy to have them both here."

Timmy jumped up to plead, "Please, Mom, that would be so fun. Please, will you ask his dad?"

"Thanks for offering, Emma. I'll ask Dr. Merrick the next time I see him." Kat grabbed a dish towel to take up her regular duty of drying and putting away dishes.

****

Moments after the doctor sat down, Kat hurried toward the front counter.

"Boy, am I glad to see you, Dr. Merrick."

"I like the sound of that." He smiled.

"Susie's in the back passed out. We laid her down on the sofa in Muriel's office. I hate to impose, but she needs a doctor." She signaled for Dr. Merrick to follow her.

"Susie's one of my patients. Did she drop the tray I heard crash to the floor when I came in?" He went in the office and closed the door. In a few minutes, he came out and instructed Kat, "Please send John Peterson, the pharmacist, back here as soon as he comes in. You know who he is, right?"

"I do. I'll find him." She returned to the front of the diner.

About five minutes later, Mr. Peterson came in. Kat sent him directly to Muriel's office. He met briefly with Dr. Merrick, then left quickly. Kat and Doris covered their stations and Susie's, but they were anxious about what was happening in the office. Mr. Peterson returned fifteen minutes later and handed a package to Dr. Merrick who was waiting in the office doorway.

"Thanks, John. This is exactly what we needed. When Susie comes over to get the whole prescription filled, please use The Fund." The doctor closed the office door again.

Kat refilled Charlie's coffee. "Doc said someone wasn't having a good day when he heard the clatter. Did you say it was Susie who dropped a tray?"

"Yes, she passed out. Dr. Merrick and Mr. Peterson are helping her now."

Thirty minutes later, Dr. Merrick and a pale, but upright, Susie came out of Muriel's office. Kat put a cup of black coffee in front of him.

"If you have time, I'll put in your usual order. Should Susie be working?"

"Yes to breakfast, and yes, if she feels like it," Dr. Merrick answered, never taking his eyes off his patient.

Kat and Doris kept a close watch on their coworker, who insisted she wasn't sick, just foolish. When they were all at the kitchen window, Susie confessed, "Doc put me on a new heart medication two weeks ago. He gave me a sample to try before I had the prescription filled. It ran out three days ago. When I went to get the medicine, the co-pay was going to be more than Todd's baseball cleats. The shoes won. Doc scolded me pretty good. He told the pharmacist to fill my prescription out of his fund until my insurance improves its coverage. He's a prince."

"What's his fund?" Kat asked.

"Doc works with drug reps to get medication samples and discounts to help people out. I have insurance, but it won't pay much on brand new medications like this one. My co-pay was almost the total prescription cost, in the hundreds," Susie explained.

"You're right. He's a prince," Kat agreed.

"You're lucky Doc and Mr. Peterson were here this morning," Doris added.

"Yep, I'm glad they're both creatures of habit," Susie acknowledged.

Kat dropped off Dr. Merrick's check. "Thank you for taking care of Susie. Don't know what we'd have done if you hadn't come in when you did."

"Lately, I've been put in the right place at the right time. I told her to let me know if she has any more problems, but I'll give you my card, in case you need me again." He handed her his business card with his cell phone and home numbers on it.

"Thanks."

Dr. Merrick was gone before she remembered to ask about the play date. Hopefully, tomorrow would be back to normal. Maybe then she'd remember.

During the morning lull, Kat checked her phone. Timmy wanted to know if he could go to the matinee at Movieland with Trevor and his grandmother. Keeping up with the Merricks was starting already. Timmy rarely went to movies in the theater since waiting for the video was a better fit for their budget. She called home to double check with Emma about her friend taking the boys to the movies. After Emma confirmed Claire Merrick's reliability and driving skills, Kat agreed to the outing and asked Emma if she could lend Timmy some money. She'd settle up when she got home.

Emma's so good with him, but he needs playmates his own age. Today's tips would have to repay Emma instead of feeding Timmy's pig. How could she tell her son movies had to be a once in a while special treat, not a regular thing, without making him feel inferior to his new friend? Another challenge.

****

When Kat came in from work, Timmy and a blond-headed boy who could have been his twin were stretched out on the living room floor. An elegant looking woman was seated beside Emma on the sofa.

"Mom." Timmy jumped up and hugged her. "This is my best friend, Trevor."

Trevor stood and extended his hand. "I'm pleased to meet you, Mrs. Russell."

"It's nice to meet you, Trevor." Kat turned to the woman on the sofa. "You must be Trevor's grandmother. I'm Kat Russell."

The woman stood and shook hands. "Guilty as charged. I'm Claire Merrick."

"Thank you for taking Timmy to the movies. Emma, how much do I owe you?"

"Claire wouldn't take my money," Emma responded.

"Please. It was my pleasure," Claire insisted.

Kat hesitated a moment. "Thank you. Timmy, did you thank Mrs. Merrick?"

"Awww, Mom. I know how to be polite. Of course,

I did," Timmy assured her, and Claire confirmed with a head nod.

"Come sit with us." Emma patted a spot on the sofa between them. "I hope you don't think we're terrible gossips, but we've been talking about your mother."

Kat sat down. Claire examined her profile. "You are Renata Schneckker's clone."

"You knew her?" Kat asked excitedly.

"I'm a little older than Renata. She dated my brother-in-law, Noah, off and on. I saw her often at family events, that is until Jim Russell came to town for Glen Myers's wedding. In two short weeks, he swept her off her feet, they got married, and she moved to the big city," Claire reminisced.

"I remember Pop saying he'd never have met Mom if he hadn't been his Army buddy's best man. Mom was the maid of honor, so they were paired up the whole weekend. He always claimed he carried her away before she knew what hit her. Mom would blush and say very little about the short courtship. I'd say two weeks definitely qualifies as a whirlwind. Wait until I tell Pop I've met someone who witnessed the whole thing."

Claire continued, "Some romances are meant to be. Renata didn't need a lot of time to decide. Jim was quite handsome with a full head of wavy hair and gorgeous eyes. Being from Philadelphia made him seem even more exotic and exciting."

"I've always wondered what Grandpa and Gran thought about Mom and Pop getting married so suddenly. Did they approve?"

Emma laughed. "Hannah couldn't say much in protest since Lee had swept her off her feet when she was a year younger than Renata was then. She said she wouldn't be a hypocrite; she'd just let the relationship take its course. Lee said he knew from his handshake that Jim Russell was a good man, and more importantly, he could see that Jim loved Renata as much as she did him. There wasn't anything else to be said."

"I guess I have something to look forward to, coming from at least two generations of dramatic romantic actions," Kat said.

Claire said, "Of course, Noah was devastated when she told Jim 'yes,' but they remained friends. He was one of the groomsmen at their wedding."

"I think I know who Noah was. When I was a little girl, I memorized Mom's wedding pictures—the snapshots Grandpa had taken. Was he the one on the end, tall and good looking?"

"That's Noah. He still lives here in town, married a girl he met in college."

"I know Glen and Edith Myers too. They were the best man and matron of honor for Pop and Mom."

Claire hesitated a moment. "I heard you lost your mom to breast cancer. I'm so sorry."

Kat took a deep breath. "Mom's been gone ten years, although sometimes it seems like it happened last week. It was only three years after Grandpa and Gran Schneckker passed away."

"I knew your grandparents from church and your grandfather took care of all our pets. Did you know we live in their old house? Chase and Libby bought it when they moved to town. You'll have to come over and see how it looks now," Claire invited.

"Thanks. I've always loved that grand house. I

used to dream about living there when I got married. I'll make a point to stop by soon."

Claire stood. "Trevor, we need to get going. Your dad will be home for supper shortly. Please help Timmy carry the toys back upstairs."

"Okay, Gran," Trevor said cheerfully. In no time, the playthings were stowed away.

Another person who thought she looked like her mom. How much did Mom love Pop to leave everyone and everything she'd ever known, and follow him to Philadelphia? It must have seemed like going to the ends of the earth. Would Kat ever find a love so strong? So far she hadn't proved herself to be a good judge of husband-worthy men.

Timmy chattered all through supper about the movie he saw, even singing some of its songs for them. Then he suddenly asked, "Mom, do you like Trevor?"

"I do. He's very polite. I like him almost as much as you," Kat teased.

"Be serious, Mom. I'm your flesh and blood. You have to like me the most."

"You're right, but you two look enough alike to be brothers. You even have the same laugh."

"We do? But you like me best, right?"

"Yes, I do. I'm a lucky mom to have such a smart, cute, adorable, little boy."

"Awww, Mom. I'm not so little anymore. I'm almost six."

Kat mussed his hair when he walked past her. "You're right. When you're six, we'll have to get you a grown-up haircut, then all those gorgeous curls will be gone."

"Like a buzz cut?" he asked hopefully. "That

would be really neat."

"No buzz cuts. Just trimming enough off to make you look a little older."

Timmy mumbled about a buzz cut as he helped clear the table.

After Timmy was down for the night, Kat joined Emma for another cup of coffee, decaf. "So Dr. Merrick's mother lives with them? I've always wondered if it would be hard to share a house with my mother-in-law."

"Yes, she does now, but Chase's wife never lived with her. Claire didn't move in with him until after Libby died," Emma explained.

"Dr. Merrick is a widower?"

"Yes, he's a single parent too. Something you two have in common. Dr. Merrick returned to Lansdale after his residency. He and Libby had just been married a year, and they were expecting Trevor. They met when Libby was a nurse and Chase was a resident at Massachusetts Medical Center. Such a striking pair. We teased that they looked like the models for the popular doll couple."

"What happened?"

"They were renovating a room to be the nursery. Chase was doing all the painting; he didn't want Libby going up and down the ladder. While he was at the hospital, she started putting the wallpaper trim across the top of the walls. They think that she missed a step coming down the ladder. Chase found her on the floor in premature labor. An emergency C-section saved Trevor who was a seven-month baby. Libby never recovered. It was tragic. The whole community mourned with Chase. Thankfully, Claire was here to help him as he tried to put his life back together—a young widower with an infant son."

"It sounds like Trevor and Timmy have a lot in common. He was a seven-month baby also," Kat said trembling as she remembered the circumstances of her son's birth.

"Maybe that's why they were drawn to one another in Sunday School," Emma speculated.

"Dr. Merrick has been through so much, yet he's kind and generous. No wonder Trevor is so sweet natured."

"Chase was zombie-like for over a year. After all this time, Claire still worries about him ever being willing to risk love again. They're in my prayers every night, just like you and Timmy are. We all need a little divine protection."

"Indeed," Kat said, then hugged Emma, and went upstairs.

****

Kat poured a mug of black coffee for Dr. Merrick. "I put in your usual order after you got stopped as you came in the door. Hope you haven't changed. It seemed like it was taking longer than it normally does to check on all your patients between the door and the counter."

"Thanks, I appreciate it. I'm running behind today. My mom said she met you yesterday."

"She did. It was kind of her to take Timmy to the movies. He loves being with Trevor. In fact, Emma suggested an afternoon play date one day soon. Would it be okay with you?"

Susie slid Dr. Merrick's breakfast in front of him. "Don't run away yet, Susie. No more ill effects? You got your prescription filled?"

"None, Doc, everything seems to be hunky dory. Got it filled the same day. Thanks for the discount." Then speaking to Kat, Susie said, "Doc's breakfast is on me this morning. Mr. Peterson's too, when he comes in."

"Thanks, Susie, it's not necessary, but appreciated. Glad things are returning to normal." Turning back to Kat, he said, "Where were we? Right, a play date. Let me double check Trevor's schedule. Seems like he always has lots on his calendar. My five-year-old has a better social life than I do." He laughed as he wolfed down his breakfast. "Sorry to eat and run, but the hospital is overflowing. Hope the Emergency Department was quiet last night. I'll let you know about the play date in the morning. Looks like you're getting busy." He grabbed his lab coat and left.

"Good morning, Kitty," Charlie said as he headed to *his* stool.

"Hi, Charlie. How's Sheba?" Kat told him today's specials and took his order.

****

"Timmy, I saw Dr. Merrick this morning. You'll be glad to know I invited Trevor for a play date. He'll tell me a day that will work when I see him tomorrow morning."

"Thanks, Mom. I think Trevor's almost as much fun as me."

"Almost...we need to work a little on your humility."

"My what?" He looked confused.

"Never mind. I'm glad you're confident. That's important."

Chapter Ten

"Good morning, Miss Shumacher. Isn't it a beautiful morning? Are you having your usual today?" Kat cheerfully asked and delivered the cup of tea.

"What else would I have?" Miss Shumacher harrumphed. "What makes you so all fired cheery today?"

"Just happy to be here. I'll go put in your order." Kat walked back to the kitchen.

"I think that girl is touched in the head," Miss Shumacher said out loud to no one in particular.

Dr. Merrick watched the whole exchange, then said, "I think she's rather charming. You should try looking on the bright side of life, Miss Althea. Might even help some of your aches and pains feel a little better."

Miss Shumacher mumbled to herself, but loud enough for her physician to hear, "Doctors, you think you're so smart. You don't know *anything* about how I feel."

****

Shortly after lunch, Doris approached Kat. "Say, do you have any plans for Saturday night?"

"I'm not sure. Why?"

"Jason's childhood pal, Dennis, is coming to town this weekend, and I'm looking for someone I wouldn't mind spending the evening with to double date with us," Doris explained.

"I'm flattered," Kat began. "But I think I'll have to pass this time. I hate to impose on Emma to babysit, and I don't really know anyone else I'd trust Timmy with for the evening. Remember, I told you I'm not interested in a relationship right now."

"This isn't for relationship building. Just doing a favor for me. Maybe Susie could babysit." Doris sounded desperate.

"I'm sorry. I can't," Kat repeated. "I'm not comfortable with blind dates, even if they're not intended to lead to anything."

"Great. Now I'll be stuck Friday and Saturday night with two guys goofing around like they're fifteen again. Nothing like having to be the adult in the room." Doris wheeled around clearly unhappy with Kat's response.

Welcome to my world. I have to be the adult every day.

****

Friday afternoon, Trevor Merrick was still playing with Timmy when Kat got home. As soon as she walked through the kitchen door, Timmy asked, "Mom, can Trevor stay for supper? Nana made ham and scalloped potatoes. It's Trevor's favorite. We have plenty."

"I'm sure Trevor is expected at home," Kat said tiredly.

He continued pleading, "Please."

"Fine. Hi, Trevor."

"Hi, Mrs. Russell. I can call home and ask Gran if it's okay for me to stay," Trevor said politely.

"Sure. I'll be happy to tell her it's all right with

us."

After a brief conversation, Trevor handed the phone to Kat. "Hi, this is Kat. We'd love to have Trevor stay for supper."

Claire said, "It would be fine. What time should his dad pick him up?"

"Seven, if that works with Dr. Merrick's schedule."

Supper was full of knock-knock jokes and laughter. The boys gobbled up everything on their plates knowing ice cream sundaes were waiting for dessert. Emma dipped the ice cream, bravely allowing them to put on their own toppings. The only rule was they had to eat every bite of their creations.

A little before seven, the doorbell rang. Kat answered the door. Dr. Merrick stood on the porch in a black tee shirt and black jeans. She invited him in. "Sorry for staring. It's just I haven't seen you in clothes before."

"I beg your pardon," Dr. Merrick said with a grin.

"I'm sorry, I mean, at the diner you have on your work clothes and lab coat. Today, you just look like a regular dad, not doctor dad," she stammered.

"I hope it's the clothes and not my dad bod making you say that."

She felt a blush start on her neck but said nothing. *If that's a dad bod, then men everywhere will want one.*

Chase stepped into the living room and gave Emma a hug. "Thank you for the play date and supper invite. Trevor has talked about Timmy Russell all week."

After inspecting the spread of trucks, cars, building blocks, and dinosaurs on the living room floor, Chase said, "Trevor, you and Timmy need to start putting things away. It's time to go home."

"Dad, can we play just fifteen minutes more, please?" Trevor asked hopefully.

"Always the negotiator," Chase said to Emma and Kat. "Okay, but only fifteen minutes, then you have to clear the floor. Timmy shouldn't have to put away this mess all by himself."

Emma went to get Chase a cup of coffee. He stared at Kat sitting across from him on the sofa. "I'm sorry for staring, Mrs. Russell. I've never seen you in clothes either."

She laughed. "Please, call me Kat."

"Okay, but what is Kat short for?"

"Oh, it's Katrina. Pop gave me the nickname."

"Why?"

"I was a bit of a daredevil, but I always managed to get out of dangerous situations alive, so, like a cat, I must have nine lives. Pop said no matter what happened I always seemed to land on my feet and keep on going."

"Kat would be an appropriate nickname, but if you don't mind, I'd like to call you Katrina. I like the old-world sound to it. It seems to suit you. Please call me Chase. How are you adjusting to being in the great Midwest again?"

"Lansdale has been a welcome surprise. So few things live up to your childhood memories, but it does. I've met several people who knew my mom and grandparents, and even some who remember me visiting here as a little girl. It's made the whole move less difficult. Of course, Emma has been wonderful. She's a natural Nana and spoils both of us rotten. We couldn't be luckier than being under her care," she said enthusiastically.

"I'd say that we are the lucky ones," Chase said

looking directly into her eyes in a way that made Kat a little uncomfortable. "Lansdale has a welcome new addition to town, and Trevor has a new best friend. Life is good." Now she *knew* she was blushing.

Chase finished his coffee, stood, and pointed to his watch. "It's time, buddy. Let's see how fast you two can clear this toy battlefield."

Reluctantly, the boys got it all collected and put away.

At the door, Chase hugged Emma and patted Kat on the shoulder. "Next play date needs to be at our house, and you can have supper with us. Emma, I hope you'll come too. Mom loves visiting with you. Thank you again for Trevor's meal. And it was a pleasure to see you outside Whistler's, Katrina Russell."

Trevor joined his father saying, "Thank you for inviting me over." Then the gentle father and his polite little boy were gone.

****

The Saturday morning crowd at Whistler's fell into two categories: the early arriving, coffee drinking, tables full of the same old men who were there on weekdays holding court, and the later arriving families needing booster seats and highchairs so they could tank up on waffles and eggs before heading out for a day of family fun.

Kat felt a little guilty about working instead of taking Timmy out for brunch. But if last week was any indication, the Saturday tips were too good to pass up. And Timmy keeping pace with Trevor's social life was going to take some extra funds.

About ten thirty, someone came and hugged Kat's waist. A child's voice said, "Good morning. Mrs.

Russell, will you be our waitress?"

It was Trevor with Chase and Claire. "Good morning, Merricks. I'd be delighted to wait on you. I think we have a booth right here in the front. Will it work?"

They were immediately ready to order since they knew the menu by heart—this was a regular outing for the Merricks any Saturday that Chase wasn't on duty at the hospital.

Chase watched Katrina as she worked. He'd thought about her on the way home last night. His mom said she came from good people. Her mother had been a caring, sweet person. Her grandparents, the Schneckkers, had been pillars in the community. She showed the joy in her heart, through her patience with customers like Charlie, and shared a caring spirit, even with the always crabby like Miss Althea. Her physical attractiveness was just icing on the cake. There was no question he had a strong attraction to this woman.

Her shy smile was the first thing Chase thought of this morning. No woman had affected him like this since he first met Libby Michaels. Something about Katrina had hit him hard. After so long, it was scary and more than a little surprising. Hard to believe only two weeks ago, she was living in Philadelphia.

Right after delivering the Merricks' food, Kat got too busy to visit, barely having a chance to leave the check. After things slowed down, she saw they'd finished eating and were gone. Chase left the money for the check and the tip on the table. On the back of the check, he had written: *Have a great day. Hope to see you in church tomorrow.*

Sunday again so soon? Timmy would want to go to

church. She could hear him saying, "But, Mom, we have to go so I can see my best friend," as if they hadn't seen one another since last week.

Kat hadn't been inside a church since her mother's funeral—the day she believed God abandoned her. Would things be different now?

She knew Emma would be thrilled to take them with her. Emma had done so much for her above and beyond a normal landlady's role. Kat certainly could spare a few hours of her day off to do something near and dear to Emma's heart. And she had a written invitation from Dr. Merrick. That piqued her curiosity.

****

Chase Merrick came out of the Children's Sunday School classroom as Emma and Katrina were headed in. He bowed to them. "We meet again."

"Don't worry, they'll be fine," he said nodding to their sons. "Would you like to come with me to the Young Adults Class?" Chase extended his hand to Katrina.

"Emma, where will you be?" Kat asked in a concerned voice.

"Not in the *Young* Adult Class." Emma laughed and winked at her. "I'm in the senior group. You're in capable hands. I'll save you a seat for church."

Although she was trembling on the inside, she took Chase's offered hand.

There were about fifteen people between twenty and forty years old in their class. Katrina attracted a lot of attention when she walked into the classroom hand in hand with the handsome widower. Some of the single women looked at her with very un-Christian expressions. In particular, one brunette with close-cropped hair and no wedding ring glared at her from the moment she walked through the classroom door at the doctor's side.

Chase introduced Katrina. Everyone made introductions and told a little about themselves. Several people recognized her from Whistler's. The glaring woman was Joan Schneider who didn't volunteer any information except her name. Kat was pleased to see Doris in the back row with her current beau, Jason Demming. The guy next to him was the friend, Dennis.

Everyone was very pleasant. Only Joan didn't fit the mold. Maybe she wasn't happy about seeing Chase with someone else. Did they have a history?

Kat had very little to contribute to the lively class discussion since she'd never before been in an adult Sunday School class. She was a little surprised that there was some debate among them; everyone did not come to the same conclusion about the takeaways of the lesson.

After class, she followed Chase into the sanctuary where Emma and Claire were seated in a pew about halfway toward the front. The two women had their heads together talking softly and, occasionally, laughing. Chase and Katrina walked into their row at the opposite end from them. She sat next to Claire with Chase on her left. Emma leaned forward and waved at her, smiling broadly as if she was pleased about something.

Chase's rich baritone sang out loudly and confidently, although he never looked down at the words. The hymnal was only open for her benefit.

As they were leaving the sanctuary, a patient stopped Chase. Kat continued out of the building and saw Emma and Claire had the boys with them, standing at the top of the steps, grinning like co-conspirators.

"Katrina, dear, Claire and I decided to pool our resources for dinner today. Claire has a roast in the crock pot big enough for all six of us. We'll provide the dessert, the cherry spice cake I made last night. We'll take the boys over to the Merrick house now. Would you and Chase stop at home to get the cake? You may want to get some play clothes for Timmy since those two are planning a backyard adventure after dinner. Thank you, dear." Emma patted her hand and winked as she headed to her car trailed by Claire, Timmy, and Trevor.

After dispensing a little free medical advice, Chase came out of the church. "Where is everybody?" he asked coming down the steps to where Katrina stood all alone at the edge of the parking lot.

"We're victims of a sneaky plot. Our families have decided we're all having dinner at your house. We've been dispatched to pick up the dessert from Emma's kitchen. And I've been told we're staying for some playtime after dinner."

"That suits me. This way, madam, your chariot awaits." Chase held his arm out, leading her to a red SUV in the middle of the nearly empty parking lot.

She hesitated after he opened the door. "I'm not sure my dress is made for stepping up into this car."

"Mom complains about how high the step is too. That's probably part of the reason she wanted Emma to drive her home. Put your hand on my shoulder and step up." Chase put his hands around her slender waist. Heat rushed to her ears when his strong arms lifted her into the seat.

"Nothing to it!" Chase closed the passenger door and got in on the driver's side.

At Emma's, Kat quickly changed into slacks and a sweater to make getting in and out of the car easier. They picked up the cake and play clothes for Timmy.

"You're certainly a quick change artist," Chase commented when they were back in the car in less than fifteen minutes.

"It's because I love to sleep until the last possible minute. I learned in high school how to get dressed quickly so I could have a few more minutes of shut-eye."

They pulled into the driveway of the stately, three story, brick mansion on the corner. Katrina smiled. "The old porch did need rebuilding, but I'm not sure I can get used to the shutters being green."

"The porch pillars were rotting. We poured concrete for the floor, so it shouldn't have to be replaced again. How did you know the shutters used to be white? Never mind. I remember, Mom told me your grandparents lived here."

"Yes, the Schneckkers. I spent some of the happiest days of my life in this house," she said, momentarily lost in thought.

"Dr. Schneckker took care of every dog I ever had. They weren't still living here when I moved back to town. We bought the house from the Taylors next door."

"They're still alive? I remember Mr. and Mrs. Taylor very well. I'll have to stop and see them. When my grandparents died, they bought the house from Mom. She would've loved to move back here, but Pop is a full-blooded city boy who had no interest in living in the boondocks, his pet name for Lansdale. He had a thriving business with his brother in Philly and wasn't ready to pull up stakes and move halfway across the country. Mom said the Taylors knew how special this house was to her and would care for it like she would have. Mr. Taylor said he bought it so he could have a little control over who he got for next door neighbors." *Chase was easy to talk to. Too easy.*

"The house was empty when we moved in, almost seven years ago. When did you lose your grandparents?"

"They've been gone for twelve years. After sixty years of marriage, they died within three days of one another. Losing them both at nearly the same time was hard on Mom, but I think she was glad they were together, even in death. It might've been harder to see one without the other. The last time I was here was for their funerals. You must have passed Mr. Taylor's 'who I want for a neighbor' test! What a strange serendipity to have your family living here." *Why did she keep spilling out all her personal history to an almost perfect stranger?*

"Maybe it's more than serendipity, Katrina." Chase hesitated. "I hope you can make more happy memories here… We'd better get in the house before they send out a scout party."

After dinner, Katrina pushed her chair back from the table. "What a delicious meal. I'm sure Gran and Gramps are looking down and smiling at seeing me here. Growing up, I thought Lansdale, Wisconsin was the most magical place on earth. My friends all vacationed at the Jersey Shore or in the Poconos every summer. I was the only kid in my class who got to go to

Wisconsin. It was so much farther away than most of my friends had ever been, almost like a foreign country. I really missed those trips after my grandparents were gone. I wonder if my secret hiding place is still there."

"Where was the hiding place?" Claire asked.

"Behind two loose bricks in the back of the fireplace. I remember putting some treasures in there so I would have them every year when I visited. I didn't think to get them when we came for the funerals. Too many other things were going on. Do you mind if I look?"

"Be my guest," Chase said.

Kat knelt in front of the fireplace and reached in the back of the chimney on the right-hand side above her head. "Well, the bricks are still loose." She pulled down two bricks, then a small dusty red metal box tied with a faded ribbon that might have been blue at one time. "My treasure box. It's still here." She carefully put the bricks back in place.

"What's in it, Mom?" Timmy eagerly asked. He and Trevor were standing over her. She sat on the floor with eyes closed and the red box in her lap.

"I don't remember everything. It was a long time ago. Let's see." She untied the ribbon and carefully opened the box, then laughed. "Well, you can see what were treasures to my eleven-year-old self. There are two bird's feathers—one brownish and one black. An especially pretty rock, at least I thought so." She pulled out a tiny, plastic, purple figure. "Oh, my special fairy. She could grant wishes and keep me safe from harm. If you believe in her, she's quite powerful."

In the very bottom the box was a piece of notebook paper that had been folded into a small, fat, square. In a childlike scrawl on the outside it said, "*Don't open 'til growed up*." Katrina chuckled. "I'm not sure I can open this yet."

"Come on, Mom. Read it to us," Timmy begged.

She carefully unfolded the page. Tears filled her eyes. "Mom, we want to know what it says," Timmy pleaded. Kat took a deep breath and began reading quietly aloud:

"When I am growed up, I will be a very beautiful lady married to a brave and handsome king who is not 'fraid of spiders or snakes or dragons or any creepy things. We will live in a huge castle with our ten kids. We will have ice cream every day and candy whenever we want. We will play outside with our ponies all day long. We will be happy all the time because it is the law in our land. Love and kisses, KJR."

"What is the J for?" Chase asked.

"Joy. Mom said she gave me that middle name so she would always have a little Joy in her life." Kat wiped away the tear on her cheek. "She was an unfailing optimist." She smiled and hugged Timmy and Trevor. "Would you boys like the feathers?"

"Yes, please," Timmy and Trevor shouted in unison.

She carefully packed the letter, her rock, and fairy back in the box, tied the faded ribbon around it, and hugged it to her chest. "Thank you for another reminder of the wonderful memories I made in this house."

Afraid that Katrina was going to cry harder, Chase quickly volunteered, "Since you lovely ladies made the scrumptious feast, we will be on KP duty. Mom, why don't you and Emma go out on the patio with your coffee, and the boys can play in the new sandbox."

Trevor and Timmy didn't have to be asked twice. They headed to the sandbox—a tractor tire filled halfway up with new brown sand—clutching toys and their new feathers.

Katrina washed and Chase dried. For a long time there was no conversation, then Chase noticed a single tear sliding down her cheek before she had a chance to wipe it away.

"Hey, I thought you said this was a place full of happy memories. No crying, unless those are happy tears."

"This is so nice. I'm crying a little for happiness and a little for sadness. I'd begun to forget how much I enjoyed being here—in this house. After Mom died, there was no discussion about coming back since there wasn't anyone to visit."

"You lost her ten years ago?"

"Yes. She was diagnosed with Stage Four breast cancer. She spent her last four weeks in the hospital, hooked up to tubes, in and out of consciousness. I was thirteen. I couldn't believe God would take her away from me. Before today, the last time I was inside any church was for her funeral. I was angry with God. I guess in some ways I still am. I'm sorry. I didn't mean to blurt all that out." She turned away from him.

Chase patted her back and stood beside her breathing in the floral scent of her shampoo. "Katrina, I think it is normal to be angry at God when you lose someone you love. It's even a recognized stage of grief. I was angrier than I've ever been when I lost Libby, then almost Trevor too. At first, I thought, and sometimes I still do, that I was responsible for her death."

"Emma told me what happened."

"It wasn't right. I was a trained emergency medicine physician and couldn't save my own wife. I was angry at the whole world, even at Libby, for leaving me alone with a tiny infant struggling for his life. All because she'd been too impatient to wait for me to get home to finish the redecorating. Mostly I was angry at God. It took me over a year to go back to church. I don't know what I would've done without Mom being here to take care of Trevor, and of me. She was my lifesaver, my rock. Wasn't your father able to help you through your loss?"

"Pop was there, but he remarried just two months after Mom died. I thought it would be a good thing. Jocelyn was Mom's widowed best friend. I liked her. Pop was so afraid of being alone. He made her the center of his life, and my world changed dramatically." *Why am dumping out my soul to him?* She picked up the dishcloth as another tear slid down her cheek. "We've talked enough about sad things. What about finishing the dishes and joining the crew out in the yard to enjoy the lovely afternoon?" They finished the chore in silence.

Katrina stood in a corner of the patio away from everyone else, lost in thought, watching the boys building a city in the sandbox. They drove their trucks and tractors all over the newly created domain. The feathers were posted like giant flags atop the tallest buildings.

"Penny for your thoughts," Chase said as he walked toward her. "You appear to be far away and deep in thought."

"I'm not far away in space. I'm right in this

backyard, but long ago in time. It's funny, the sandbox is in almost the exact same spot it was then. It was an exhilarating feeling staying here—running all around the neighborhood, all over town. It was so safe and secure.

"I didn't have that kind of freedom in Philadelphia. I believe that's why Mom thought it was important for me to visit her parents. Until they died, I spent two months every summer here; basking in my grandparents' love; being adored and spoiled rotten. It was wonderful. I thrived here."

"I'm glad being here makes you happy. I love hearing you laugh—it is a uniquely joyous sound. You need to do it more," Chase said as he took her hand in his. "I'm sure you think I'm being presumptive, but Katrina, I want to know you better. Even though I only met you a short time ago, I want to see more of you, and not just in the company of our sons.

"I haven't been interested in anyone since I lost Libby, but you kind of snuck up on me. For reasons I can't explain, I am attracted to you in a way I thought was dead and gone forever. I look forward to seeing your smiling face each morning. I'd like to see it outside of the diner."

"Why me? How can you possibly know so soon that you want to see more of me?"

"I don't know, but haven't you ever met someone whom you reacted to differently than anyone else? Almost immediately?"

"I don't think I ever have. When I was ten, I might have believed in love hitting you like a cartoon lightning bolt. I didn't expect that you—an educated man past thirty who'd been married before and a father—would subscribe to that kind of thing."

"All I can say is when I am with you, even sitting across the counter from you, it feels natural—as corny as that sounds."

"Please don't misunderstand, Chase. I like you and your family. In the short time I've known you, I've discovered you have lots of wonderful qualities: patience, kindness, thoughtfulness. You're a terrific dad and good son."

"Katrina, stop. Those sound more like you're evaluating my qualifications for a scouting merit badge than as a future romantic interest."

"You'll have to forgive me. The last ten years of my life have been pretty short on happy-ever-after moments. I don't believe I can live in the fairy tale of my dreams."

"Why not? You more than deserve it. You'll see. One day you may even ask for my help to slay your dragons."

"I'll keep that in mind. At this moment, things are moving too quickly for me. We've only been here two weeks. I'm not starting a relationship right now—with you or anybody. There are issues…"

"I know you've hardly had time to get settled here, but sometimes serendipity can be a sign of good things to come that shouldn't be ignored. Katrina, if I can help resolve your issues, I am more than willing to try." Chase sounded so confident, so reassuring.

"I appreciate your offer, but I'm on my own for the first time in my life. Timmy has to be my focus. I can't think about anything else. It wouldn't be right for me to encourage you. I still have to resolve major problems from my last relationship."

"We all have things in our past that, given the chance to turn back time, we would do differently."

Tears welled up in her eyes. "Chase, it's dangerous to be too close to me. Timmy's dad didn't die. He left us and recently made an unwelcome, unexpected reappearance in our lives. He is a threat to the people who are important to me. Could we stop talking about our possible relationship? Please?"

"Of course. I didn't mean to press, but if you're in danger, you want me at your side, not at a distance." Chase wiped away the tears flowing down her cheeks. "And I need to find the right words. Mine seem to make you cry. That's the last thing I want to do. Just remember, we all have to battle demons and get over the lingering guilt born of our actions. But whatever our trials, they are easier to face if we're not alone."

Timmy and Trevor came racing across the yard hand in hand. "Mom, I need a sandbox. Did you see everything we made today? Please, can I have one?"

"Where would you put it? You have a marvelous swing set in your backyard."

"You're right. Trevor, we can play in the sandbox at your house," Timmy began.

"And the swing set at your house," Trevor finished his thought.

"Now, you need to help Trevor put everything away because it's time we were getting home."

"Awww, Mom, do we have to leave so early?" Timmy complained.

" 'Fraid so, big guy. Let's see how fast you can get everything put away!"

The boys gathered up and rinsed off the toys and their feet with the hose. Claire sent home leftovers for supper so Emma would not need to cook. Emma left the Merricks some cherry spice cake for their dessert.

After buckling Timmy in the car seat, Kat closed the door and turned right into Chase's arms. He hugged her. "Have sweet dreams tonight. Thank you for coming for dinner. I'll see you at breakfast in the morning."

"Thank you for listening and understanding. Sweet dreams to you." She returned his embrace and crawled in the passenger's seat.

When they were almost home, Emma said, "You and Chase are hitting it off as well as I thought you would."

"Hmm…what did you say Emma?"

"Chase seems to like you very much. Do you feel the same?" Emma asked anxiously.

"Too much," Katrina said before thinking. Realizing she'd answered aloud, she added, "I think we should try to get along given how much the boys adore one another."

"Oh, so you like him because he's the father of your son's best friend?" Emma chuckled.

"Right. I don't think we need to talk about it now." She motioned to Timmy in the back seat.

"Okay, dear, I won't tease you anymore." Emma smiled knowingly.

Only two weeks. Kat needed to refocus. They were still in danger. Dirk didn't walk away so easily. The other shoe would drop. It was only a matter of time. She didn't regret dismissing Chase's attentions today. He must stay at a distance. For now.

Chapter Eleven

"Nice to see you yesterday. You could've knocked me over with a feather when you strolled into Sunday School class on Doc's arm. That's quite a coup for a girl who isn't looking for a relationship," Doris said snidely.

"What do you mean?" Kat asked.

"You walked in with Lansdale's most eligible catch. No one has ever gotten him to bite. There's a long list of women who have been trying to get his attention for years. You did it in only two weeks. It's amazing. What's your secret?"

Kat stiffened a little. "Dr. Merrick and I are NOT dating. Our sons are best friends. We'd met in the boys' Sunday School classroom, and he offered to show me the way to the young adult class. He was being nice."

"Whatever," Doris said flippantly. "He may not have asked you out yet, but from where I sat, it looked like he brought you to class with him. I'm not the only one who made that observation."

"Feel free to correct your friends' misinterpretations. I expected a Sunday School class to have a more charitable viewpoint." Kat frowned remembering Chase's declaration yesterday afternoon.

"I think the lady doth protest too much. For what it's worth, the double date wouldn't have worked out; Dennis said you're not his type."

"Good morning, Doc." A lean, balding man greeted Chase as he took the stool next to him.

"Bobby Murphy, it's good to see you out and about." Chase shook his hand. "I was just about to order breakfast. Hard to make up my mind what I'm most hungry for...do you ever have that problem?" He signaled for Kat to come over.

"Sometimes, I just order toast and coffee when I can't decide," Bobby said timidly.

"I'm awfully hungry today. I think we both need a big breakfast. What about..." Chase gave Kat his usual order. "Would you join me, Bobby?"

"Well..." the man hesitated.

"My treat today. Miss, we'll have two orders like that, please." Chase quickly dismissed Kat before Bobby had a chance to object.

They chatted all through breakfast, which Bobby ate with the relish of a truly hungry man. He stepped down off the stool after his third cup of coffee. "Thanks, Doc. Enjoyed the company even more than the meal, and the meal was very tasty. Something about company while you eat makes everything taste better."

"Couldn't agree more." Chase shook Bobby's extended hand. "Hope to see you again soon. Enjoy the rest of the day. Looks like it's going to be glorious."

When Mr. Murphy left, Kat brought Chase the check. "I've never seen him have anything but toast and coffee. How did you know he couldn't afford a full breakfast?"

"I just had a feeling that today I needed to treat Bobby to a meal." Chase picked up the check. Before he turned to leave, he added, "Remember, I'm here if you need me, and Bobby can attest that I'm a good listener." He smiled broadly.

"Thanks. I know you are. When I'm ready to share, you'll be the first to know."

Was she being silly? This was the beginning of their third week in Wisconsin and nothing bad had happened. No Dirk. Could she begin looking forward instead of watching for her unwelcome past to slither back into her life?

****

"Mom, you're not listening to me," Timmy said across the dinner table.

"Sorry, Timmy, I have a lot on my mind. What did you want?"

"I need you to answer a very important question."

"I'd be happy to, what is it?"

"Trevor used to have a mom, but she went to heaven when he was born. He said everyone has to have a mom and a dad. Did my dad go to heaven when I was born?"

Startled, Kat made herself take a deep breath hoping her voice wouldn't betray her fear. "No, your father is alive, but he's never lived with us."

"Why doesn't he live with us? Where is he?"

"It's kind of complicated. He got into trouble and had to go away right after you were born."

"What kind of trouble? Where did he go? Is he ever coming back?"

"So many questions." They were bound to start. She might as well answer them honestly. "He was friends with bad men who sold drugs and hurt people. The police caught him, and he was sent to prison."

"Like a criminal?"

How does he know that word? "Yes, I'm afraid

so."

"My teacher, Miss Mueller, told us you're never supposed to take drugs, not ever. They can make you sick and you do bad things because drugs can make you crazy."

"Miss Mueller is right." Before he could ask more questions, she said, "Why don't you help me with the dishes so Nana can have the night off, okay?"

"Good idea, Mom. Thanks for dinner, Nana." He began clearing the plates off the table. They finished the dishes without any more dad questions.

Trevor's friendship was creating more challenges than keeping her son in spending money. It had taken a long time for him to start asking questions about his father. If it hadn't been Trevor, some other kid would've asked about his dad.

****

"Have you seen Susie?" Doris sounded concerned. It was nearly six thirty, and they were getting busy.

"No," Kat said as she picked up an order at the window.

"If she's not here in the next fifteen minutes, I'm calling her house. I know she got her new meds. I hope she's okay." Doris picked up full coffee pots to go on refill rounds.

Kat and Doris watched the door and tried to make sure no customer waited, despite being shorthanded. Muriel was expected by seven thirty, and she didn't like it when one of them was late.

At six forty-five, when Doris was ready to call her house, Susie raced in the back door putting on her apron and hair net in flight. "I'm so sorry. Rich got home last night—I wasn't expecting him until Monday.

114

We got a little carried away getting reacquainted." Susie blushed deep crimson.

"Getting used to being married again?" Doris teased.

"Yeah, thanks for covering for me." Susie grabbed a coffee pot.

"We were starting to get worried. Glad you're late for a happy reason," Kat said.

Susie caught up on her tables, and everything was running smoothly by the time Muriel walked in. She immediately told her boss what had happened and why. Muriel laughed and said, "I was young once too. Thanks for confessing. Like to know I have such honest employees."

Irene Schmidt, one of the evening waitresses, called shortly after the lunch rush. Her mom had taken a turn for the worse. She wasn't sure when she'd be able to come back to work.

Muriel asked for volunteers to cover until closing. Doris' social life would suffer—her relationship with Jason was definitely on a high boil. Rich was back after being gone a month, so Susie would rather be at home. Before she volunteered, Kat called Emma to talk it over. She was the logical choice to work the extra shifts but didn't want to take advantage of her landlady's good nature.

Emma encouraged her to work the shift. She assured her that she and Timmy would be fine, so Kat agreed to cover. She hated being away from her son such long days, but their bank account could really use the boost. Less thinking, more working.

"Kitty, have you been bad?" Charlie Bishop asked as he came up to his usual spot at the counter. "Is

Muriel punishing you by making you work late?"

"No. I volunteered since Irene's out unexpectedly. I didn't know you came in for dinner too. Want to hear tonight's specials?"

"Nope, I came because on Tuesday night it's always chicken livers, at least it has been for ten years. That's right, isn't it?"

"Yep. You want the mashed potatoes, gravy, and green beans?"

"Sure. Walt knows to put a little extra gravy on my livers too. They go together."

Kat put the order in. When Charlie finished eating, he signaled for his check. "Sure is nice to start and end my day with you, Kitty. Have sweet dreams. Know I will."

What a charmer. She'd be worried if he was forty years younger. He always brightened her day.

****

Friday morning, Chase said, "If you have to work tomorrow, I'd like to take Timmy with us. We're going fishing down on the river. He could stay overnight, and you could pick him up Sunday morning at church."

"Timmy would love it. He has a cane pole that we bought the first day we were here."

"I asked you before I told Trevor he could invite him, in case it wasn't okay. I think those two would live together if we'd let them." Chase chuckled. "We'll see you for breakfast before fishing. I'll pick Timmy up at eight thirty in the morning."

Kat called home on her break. Trevor had already called with the invite, and Timmy was anxious to get permission for the fishing trip.

Chase certainly knew the way to Timmy's heart.

His dad must have taken him fishing.

****

Rain.

Timmy's going to be so disappointed. What will Chase do with them now?

Early in the afternoon, the boys came in the diner for lunch. Timmy was wearing something Kat had never seen.

"My goodness. Looks like you must have gotten wet. Where did those clothes come from?" she questioned.

"They're Trevor's. We're the same size. We got muddy. Mom, it was so fun. Dr. Chase put up a tent on the riverbank so we could fish from inside."

"Then how did you get muddy?"

"When the fish stopped biting, the boys went wading and started a mud ball fight. I was the target," Chase explained.

"Dad can't get us both if we gang up on him," Trevor volunteered grinning.

"Mom, I taught Dr. Chase and Trevor how to bait their hooks so the worms can't escape—like you showed me."

"Nice technique, Katrina. Timmy's a good teacher." Chase mussed Timmy's hair. "Now, we're starving. What'll you have, boys?"

All three quickly devoured their jumbo cheeseburger baskets and root beer floats.

"Mom, we're playing board games tonight AND we're gonna have a pizza delivered right to the house," Timmy said excitedly.

They got up to leave, and Timmy hugged her before joining Trevor. Kat stopped Chase. "Thank you.

Timmy has missed getting to do guy things since we moved. I really appreciate you including him in your father-son outing."

"He's a great kid. He and Trevor get along well and like the same things. It was my pleasure. Hope you have a quiet evening. See you in the morning."

About eight thirty, Mary Buford, the other evening waitress, told Kat to go ahead and go home. Since it was so quiet, she'd close up on her own.

"Thanks for the help. I can do a shift alone, but not nearly as well as I could ten years ago. Enjoy the long weekend."

"Thanks. I'd forgotten we were closed Monday for Memorial Day. I won't know how to act with that much time off. See you Tuesday."

****

Kat visited with Emma for a while to unwind before getting in the shower and to bed. "The boys seemed like they were having a blast even in the rain. Chase is so thoughtful about including Timmy."

"Yes, maybe he has a special reason to be thoughtful."

"What would that be?"

"Maybe he's trying to impress Timmy's mom," Emma gently teased.

"No...I think he really cares about Timmy. Why do you think he wants my good opinion?"

"You can see how much Chase cares for you just by watching his face when he's with you."

"We haven't been here long enough for him to really know me. I have a lot of baggage. You heard me tell Timmy over dinner that his father was sent to prison. He was unexpectedly released, and I moved here to escape him. There are things about me that a man like Chase wouldn't understand, much less approve of—we've led very different lives." Kat tried not to sound irritated.

"I can see you don't want to talk about it. I didn't mean to upset you. It was merely an observation. I'll butt out." Emma picked up her knitting and checked her pattern for the next stitch.

Kat had hit the wall—emotionally and physically. Multiple double shifts in a row. Worrying about her son. And now, Chase being more than a little interested in her. She couldn't put him and his family in danger too. Tears rolled down her cheeks and onto her lap. She was too tired to sob.

"Katrina, my dear, there is nothing so bad that it should cause tears. You're just exhausted. Get in the shower and let it wash away your worries. I'll wake you for church in the morning. Everything will look better then." Emma helped her to her feet.

Kat bent down and kissed the top of Emma's head. "I'm sorry. I hope you're right." Slowly, she made her way upstairs.

The shower warmed her and forced her to relax.

Chapter Twelve

Life in Philly seemed to be from a long-ago dream—scratch that—a lifetime-ago nightmare and she was slowly awakening.

The cell phone buzzed with an alert. There were a dozen missed calls, all from an unknown Philadelphia number, no messages, only attempts. Had Dirk gotten this number? Who else wouldn't leave a message?

Kat blocked the number in case it was him. Then she punched "1" for Pop. It went straight to voice mail. He'd probably taken his sleeping pill and was in bed. Jocelyn usually turned off the ringer when he went upstairs each night. *Guess no one was supposed to have nighttime emergencies.*

"Pop, I think Dirk is looking for me. I just blocked a suspicious number that keeps calling. If he bothers you, don't hesitate to call the cops. You know how dangerous he is. Please, be careful. I love you. Bye."

Only three weeks of peace before Dirk figured out they were gone. She left Philadelphia to protect Pop from Dirk. It had to work. There was nowhere else to run.

Kat tossed and turned, drifting in and out of a sleep that was rife with nightmares of life with Dirk. At two a.m., her phone vibrating on the bedside table woke her and saved her from his fists.

The caller ID said Nancy Raymond, her coworker

from Philadelphia. "Nancy, are you okay? Why are you calling in the middle of the night?"

"Who do you think you are, blocking MY calls? Where in the **** are you?" Dirk snarled.

His hard voice dripping with anger. She should have hanged up without speaking, but she couldn't push the END button.

"It is none of your business," she said, trying to keep the terror in her heart from infecting her voice.

"I have to see you now. I've spent two days and nights watching and waiting down the street from your house. I *know* you're not at your dad's. Where in the **** are you?"

"If you keep cursing at me, I'm hanging up."

"I'll talk to you any ***** way I please. Are you forgetting what happens when I'm not happy, you stupid *****?" Dirk barked.

That was enough. She pressed the END button, shook her head sadly, and gripped the phone tightly. How could she have believed he had loved her? How could her sweet little son have come from that vile animal?

She took a deep breath. Where was he? Would he hurt Pop? How did he get Nancy's phone? Did he take it from her friend or had she been betrayed...again? Her phone vibrated. She hit the answer button, but didn't speak.

"I knew you'd answer Nancy's phone, compassionate, little Kat; always the reliable friend."

"Why would she give you her phone? Or my number? Did you hurt her?"

"She's fine. Let's say she understood that it's a matter of life and death. She cooperated fully. This is serious, Kat. I'm stressed out. You know how much I love you. I've never stopped. Really, babe, you gotta believe me," Dirk sweetly pleaded.

"What's the emergency?" She bit off the words.

"I can't talk about it on the phone. I've gotta see you in person. I'll meet you anywhere you say. We don't have to be alone. You name the place."

"Not possible."

"Not possible or you refuse to help me?" he growled angrily. The sweetness had instantly disappeared.

"Not possible."

"Where are you and where is my son?" Dirk's speech was rapid and getting louder.

She laughed harshly. "Your son? You mean the brat, or is it the bastard today? Why are you concerned about MY child—the one you tried to keep from being born? I won't let you near him."

"Kat, you're being childish. Have a heart."

"I don't have one. You ripped it out of me. Get out of my life and leave Pop alone, or the police will pick you up." She pressed *End* with trembling hands.

Holding her breath, she waited. He didn't call back. She turned out the light and lay staring at the ceiling. This wasn't over. Her heart knew the terror had returned. And she had foolishly believed the nightmare had ended. It had only begun.

Kat was barely asleep when the alarm blared. Her arms were wrapped tightly across her chest as she tried to protect herself. Dirk had raged in her nightmares each time she finally drifted off. Her fingers throbbed and her head ached. She couldn't go to church looking like a zombie and feeling like she'd been running for her life all night.

There was a soft knock at the door. Emma. "Katrina, are you awake and ready for coffee?" The door slowly opened, and the aroma of coffee wafted in. "My dear, you look as if you haven't slept a wink. Are you sick?"

Kat wiped her face with the sleeve of her robe. "Emma, I can't go today. I know I must look a fright. I've been battling demons all night."

"I'm sorry I upset you so much." Emma sat down on the edge of the bed.

"Sweet Emma, it isn't you. My worst nightmare is back. I'll figure out what I'm going to do, but I'm too tired to think right now. Would you mind bringing Timmy home with you? I can't face everyone at church looking like this."

"Of course. Try and get some sleep. You'll be in my prayers this morning." Emma rose to leave, then said, "I'm a good listener. I'm here any time you need to share your burdens. Sometimes it helps to remind yourself you're not alone." She kissed the top of Kat's head and closed the door on her way out.

After several hours of wrestling with her pillow without a wink of sleep, Kat finally conceded. She made her way slowly downstairs for more coffee. How could she have coped without Emma's love?

"Emma, if you know any prayers to keep motorcyclists from Pennsylvania out of Lansdale—now would be the time for them," she said aloud as she paced the kitchen.

Emma's landline rang. She answered it. Timmy called to ask if he could stay over with Trevor one more night.

Kat asked to talk with Claire, who confirmed the invitation, and said he could borrow some clothes from Trevor for tomorrow. Claire said they all thought it would be a good idea to give her more time to rest.

Emma got on the phone. She was eating at noon with the Merricks. Kat said she'd have a sandwich if she got hungry, and that she appreciated their thoughtfulness.

Dirk had an instinct for knowing who cared about Kat. Their kindness made them all targets for his hate.

She walked outside and sat on the middle swing. For a long time, she didn't move. Then she pushed off and pumped her legs, flying higher and higher. She stopped pumping and came to rest, then burst into tears that threatened not to stop. "What am I going to do? I need to talk to Pop. Now."

She pulled out her phone. She had to know. Had Pop seen Dirk? Was he safe? She punched "1". Thank goodness he answered the phone. She couldn't deal with Jocelyn today. It was so good to hear his comforting voice.

She tried to control her wavering voice. "Hey, Pop, just checking in."

"Kat, are you okay? You sound strange."

"I'm okay. Timmy is too. I miss you. How are you?"

"Go to the doctor Tuesday afternoon. Guess he'll tell me how I am." Pop laughed. "How's the job?"

She told him about her quirky customers and Emma's continuing kindness. As they talked, a blanket of calm enveloped her. Calling Pop was the absolute right thing to do.

Then to the real reason for the call. "Pop, last night

Dirk called, so I blocked his number. I don't know if you heard the message. Then he called from Nancy's phone. Not sure why she let him have it. He was furious that he couldn't find me. Said he had to see me. Has he bothered you?"

"No, I didn't hear your message, and I haven't seen hide nor hair of the slime bucket. Jocie hasn't said anything about him either. If he dares to show his face here, we'll call the cops. We won't wait until he causes more trouble. Did he know where you were?"

She hesitated. "No. I think that's part of what made him so angry. Please let me know if you see him—after you call the cops." Her voice faded.

"You're worried about me. That's why you called, isn't it?" Pop asked quietly.

"You know me too well. Yes. It was a shock to hear his voice. After three weeks, I wanted to believe we'd successfully escaped."

"You're going to be all right. No one else knows where you are. John didn't even tell Judy. You probably ought to block Nancy's number, just to be safe. Honestly, I was surprised you two stayed friends after she told Crowe you didn't have the abortion."

"None of it was her fault, but giving Dirk my number... You're probably right, as usual. Pop, I love you and miss you. Let me know what the doctor says."

"I promise I'll talk to you later in the week after the appointment. Love you, baby girl. Hugs to my grandson."

Why was she crying again? Pop was fine. Timmy was safe at the Merricks'. Dirk didn't know where they were. Only that they were gone. No one would tell him. Only Pop and Jocelyn and Uncle John knew their secret. They couldn't be safer.

She hated knowing Nancy had been involved again. It saddened her to block the number, but it was necessary. Dirk was right. Kat had always been a reliable friend. Even when other people deeply disappointed her. Another piece of her life was over. Now she had to show a laser-like focus on recovering from this setback and make their adventure a great one. Like it was meant to be. It *had* to be.

****

A hand grasped her shoulder. "*No!*" Kat tried to protect her head with her arm.

"It's me. Emma. I won't hurt you," a gentle voice said.

She slowly opened her eyes. "*No!*" She stared at the face inches from her own. She refocused. "Emma?"

"You were dreaming." The voice was so soft. She must still be asleep.

"I'm in Lansdale?"

"Yes, of course, you are."

She must have nodded off on the sofa. She sat up. Emma sat next to her. Kat looked around wildly.

"Where's Timmy?"

"He's at the Merricks'. He's staying with Trevor again tonight. He talked to you earlier today, remember?"

Kat shuddered. A tear slid down her cheek. "He could be here any time."

"Timmy's just staying one more night... Oh, who are you talking about?"

"Dirk Crowe," Kat sobbed and put her head in her hands.

Emma quietly waited for further explanation.

Kat took three deep breaths letting each one out slowly. "Emma, I hardly know how to begin. Until early this morning, I thought we were safe here. Then my son's violent, unstable father called and wanted to see me."

"The father would be Dirk Crowe?"

She nodded. "When he got out of prison, we had to leave Philadelphia so Timmy would never meet him, and Pop would be safe. Where will we go if he finds us here?" Her words stumbled over one another.

"Go? You and Timmy are staying here," Emma declared. "You need to face this monster with people who love you."

"Wisconsin's such a long way from Philly. It might be too far for him. But if he *does* come to Lansdale, then everyone I care about is in danger. He's capable of extreme rage. He's beaten me before, and now, he's even angrier because I left with Timmy. If he hurts any of you, I'll never forgive myself."

"Katrina, we should let Chief Davis know about Dirk Crowe so we're ready if he does come here," Emma counseled.

"I could be wrong. He's on parole. Surely he wouldn't risk going back to prison to see me. I'm overreacting. He might be trying to scare me. Couldn't we wait and see?"

"I don't think waiting is wise. If he's only trying to frighten you, he has already succeeded—and me too. It costs nothing but a little time to be prepared."

"I keep hoping…"

"We're going to do more than hope and wait helplessly. We're praying." Emma wrapped her hands around Katrina's. "Dear Lord, please protect us from the evil in Dirk Crowe, and shelter us all in your abiding love. Amen."

"Amen."

****

No alarm. Sleeping all night. Yea! The positive side of being totally exhausted. Gran always said, "Some good can come from bad." Kat's reflection was ashy and haggard, but at least her eyes no longer showed that she'd cried herself out yesterday.

Around eleven o'clock, Timmy came in the front door with Trevor, Claire, and Chase close behind him. "Hi, Mom. The Merricks brought a picnic for us to have in the backyard. I told 'em it would be okay. It is, isn't it?"

Kat didn't immediately answer. Emma came out of the kitchen saying, "I think it would be lovely. I just baked a lemon meringue pie that will be perfect for dessert. Come in."

Chase carried the picnic basket into the kitchen where Claire and Emma began to unpack it. He walked over to Katrina. "I know we should've called and asked first. But honestly, I was afraid you'd say no. I wanted to see how you were feeling today."

"I've caught up on my sleep. I'm fine," she said tersely.

Her tone surprised Chase. "Maybe this was a mistake. If it is, it's all on me. I'm sorry. I guess I don't know how to give you the space you need. Forgive me?" Chase asked sheepishly.

"Of course. Sorry. I'm a little touchy. Let's go out and join the picnic."

The boys were defending their fort from unseen invaders. Katrina was lost in thought. A hand brushed against her back. Spinning around, she barked, "What do you want?"

"Whoa. You weren't kidding about being touchy. I've been trying to get your attention for several minutes. You didn't seem to hear me. Otherwise, I never would've put my hands on you." Chase backed away from her.

"Sorry, I have a lot on my mind. I'm afraid I'm not very good company today."

"I hope it's not because of me."

"No. Well, yes. It's complicated. I just need some breathing room."

"Sure. Only thought I could help." Chase went into the kitchen to carry drinks out to the picnic table.

The boys didn't seem to notice that their parents were both very subdued through the lunch. Several times, Katrina caught Emma looking her direction with concern on her face. She simply couldn't worry about Pop and Timmy *and* the Merricks. She needed to keep Chase at a distance. Even if it hurt his feelings. Later he'd thank her for protecting him and his family.

They had cleared away the paper plates and divided up the leftovers when it began to sprinkle. Soon, it became a full-fledged downpour. The Merricks stayed about an hour longer until there was a brief lull in the storm. Before they left, they got in a few raucous games of hippos eating marbles as quickly as they could.

Even after two days and nights together, Timmy wanted Trevor to stay overnight with him. Trevor asked, but Chase said, "I think Timmy needs to spend some time with his mom. She's working a lot and doesn't get to see him as much as she wants to. We need to go home and give them some alone time together. You can play later in the week, and I'm sure Timmy will be coming to your birthday party on Saturday."

"Thank you for understanding," Katrina said quietly to Chase.

After the Merricks left, Emma went to read in her room leaving mother and son next to one another on the sofa.

"Mom, do you really miss me like Dr. Chase said?"

"Yes. I do. I'm sorry I have to work so much. I hope Irene will be back soon." Kat hugged her son. "Want to read together? We can take turns with the new book you got. I'll read a page, then you can read a page."

"Great idea, Mom." He ran upstairs to get the story, and they spent the next hour snuggled together reading. Timmy was able to sound out words he'd never seen before with surprising accuracy.

Protecting their life in Lansdale was her top priority. Maybe Pop was right. Dirk couldn't find them. But all of her instincts screamed that somehow he knew exactly where they were and their newfound security was about to be shattered irreparably into millions of jagged pieces.

Chapter Thirteen

Breathe. In. Out. Again. Two o'clock. Breathe. Kat's chest ached with each gasp. Something had shifted in the universe. Overwhelming evil was coming. Searching for her. For them.

The distance.

The secrecy.

Parole restrictions.

None of it would stop him. Dirk Crowe wouldn't be happy until she ceased being. Completely. He *was* coming. No one had to tell her. Her bones ached with the knowledge. Her heart trembled in fear.

Kat sat in bed staring out the window, as if she could see him on the motorcycle, riding straight for Lansdale. She turned off the buzzing alarm. She dragged herself to her feet, hoping the shower would revive her and wash away the signs of the sleepless night. She couldn't face people at Whistler's with the red-eyed, ashen countenance that stared out from the bathroom mirror.

****

A big post-holiday crowd this morning would keep her too busy to dwell on the evil who could be there, in the flesh, very soon. She would figure out some way to survive. She needed to channel her inner feline one more time to land safely on her feet. She had a least one of her nine lives left. She would need it.

Chase saw Katrina and was immediately concerned. Her face was a smiling mask, but there was no joy in it, no twinkle in her eyes. Was she still upset with him?

When she began reciting today's specials, Charlie interrupted, gently patting her hand. "Kitty, where are the angels this morning?"

"What do you mean?" she asked softly.

"No joy in your voice. Only dark fear."

She took a deep breath. "I'm sorry. My mind is somewhere else. You don't need to be worried about my troubles."

Before she finished taking Charlie's order, Chase saw her brush a single tear off her cheek. Charlie must have sensed it. He gently said, "I'm sending my prayers to scare the evil away so the angels can come home. It will be okay."

"Thanks. I can use all the help I can get." She hurried to the back to put in Charlie's order.

Kat gave Chase his check. "Is there anything I can help with? Anything at all?"

"Chase, I appreciate your concern. I don't need a doctor. You can't fix my problems."

"If a friend can do anything, please remember I'm here. For now, I'll add my prayers to Charlie's."

"Thanks. That helps more than you know."

Maybe his mom could learn something from Emma about what was tormenting Katrina.

****

Kat checked her phone before going to bed. Pop had left a message saying the cardiologist was very pleased that he'd lost weight and was sticking with his exercises. He planned to return to work on Wednesday morning. Good news at last. It was definitely too late to call him at home. Instead she called the garage and left a "welcome back to work" message on the machine there. It was comforting to hear Pop's voice on the recording. Maybe tonight she would sleep.

Kat tossed the covers off, then shivering, pulled them back on again. She punched the pillow to fluff it up, then tried to flatten it out. Nothing worked for very long. The roar of a motorcycle woke her more than once. Each time she got out of bed, raced to the window, and peered into the darkness. No Dirk. Not even a headlight. The sound echoed only in her mind. This must be what it was like to slowly go totally, certifiably crazy.

****

Chase watched Katrina as he finished breakfast. She was even paler than yesterday. Swollen eyes revealed she hadn't slept well. Again. His mom hadn't learned anything. Emma said Katrina's news wasn't hers to tell. Besides, Emma didn't think she knew the whole story—yet. Chase didn't know what to do. He hadn't felt this helpless since the day he walked into the nursery and found Libby on the floor. He shuddered. Not a feeling he wanted to relive. Ever.

****

The string of long shifts ended when Irene returned to work on Wednesday evening. Kat was certain her danger radar was right. Nothing else could invoke the sense of dread and terror she carried deep in her heart. Every day it grew heavier.

Since she was off the night shift, Kat could take Timmy to Trevor's birthday party on Saturday. Now the challenge was to agree on a present that wouldn't bust their fragile budget. She took Timmy shopping on Thursday afternoon after work. He'd agonized all week about what would be the perfect birthday gift for his best friend. Finally, he settled on an ant farm. She was thankful he chose something they could afford. She hated to have to keep telling him "no" on so many of his desires.

****

Emma went over Saturday morning to help Claire with party preparations. Kat and Timmy arrived right at the two o'clock invitation start time. They had to park three blocks away due to the cars already in front of the Merrick house. Kat made a mental note— Midwesterners show up for things earlier than the stated start time, an important piece of information. In Philly, no one came to a party until at least thirty minutes past the time on the invitation.

The Merrick backyard was transformed into a mini fair for the celebration. A clown walked among the children making balloon animals; three buff colored Shetland ponies provided rides around a small, makeshift corral; and there were games of chance to win little prizes by picking up numbered ducks or shooting water into a clown's mouth. There were at least two dozen children in attendance, boys and girls, and their parents. The adults sat or stood in small groups visiting as they watched their progeny racing from one fun event to another.

Chase waved to them from the other side of the yard where he manned a large gas grill with a grate full of hot dogs, hamburgers, and bratwurst. Claire made frequent trips between the kitchen and patio to keep the snacks replenished. Emma kept the punch bowl filled with bright green fruit punch with ginger ale fizz. Timmy spotted Trevor and ran across the yard to join in the fun. Kat went inside to see if they needed any help in the kitchen.

From the crowd there, other moms had the same idea. Kat recognized three women from the young adult Sunday School class. She noticed several of them did not have on wedding rings. Maybe they were divorced or other single moms.

Kat began mixing the next batch of punch for Emma. The conversation in the kitchen continued at a low murmur. Finally, Joan Schneider, the willowy brunette from Sunday School class, turned to Kat and asked from out of the blue, "Is it true this house belonged to your grandparents?"

A little surprised at Joan's tone, more than at the question, she responded, "Yes, it is. They were the Schneckkers. Did you know them?"

"No, I didn't. I haven't lived here that long. Them living here should make it all very convenient for you," Joan said in the same hateful tone.

"I must have missed part of your conversation. Convenient for what?"

"For you, my dear. You know, for when you finally manage to lasso the highly eligible Dr. Merrick and persuade him to marry you. It will be easy to move in here. You'll already know your way around. I heard you've had your sights set on the good doctor since the first day you hit town," Joan continued, her voice dripping with venom and sarcasm.

Kat's ears burned as she blushed bright red. How could she respond to this vitriol from a woman she'd only recently met?

Claire was not at a loss for words. Her tone was clipped and forceful as she stepped between Kat and Joan saying, "Mrs. Schneider, *if* it is any of your business, Dr. Merrick is the one trying to attract this delightful young woman, not the other way around. I think it's time for you to go outside to check on your children. Your help is no longer needed nor welcome in here."

Joan glared at Claire and Kat, shrugged her shoulders, and said, "Too bad for him," then went out the door trailed by the two other women without wedding rings.

"I'm so sorry, my dear. Divorce brings out the worst in lots of people. Joan Schneider was never the soul of kindness, but since her divorce, she's been positively hateful. I'm sorry for her pain, but her behavior is unlikely to bring her husband home. She probably sees you as a threat. I'd heard shortly after her divorce that she was more than a little interested in Chase. Thankfully, he didn't take her bait."

Kat couldn't believe what she'd heard—not from Joan—but from Claire. "Chase told you he was attracted to me?"

Claire pulled Kat into the pantry for a little more privacy. "He didn't volunteer it. He wasn't breaking a confidence. I guessed, and he couldn't deny it. A mother can sense these things. Wait until your Timmy falls in love. You'll know before he does.

"I'm so thankful you decided to come to Lansdale. Chase has only been going through the motions of life since Libby's death. There has been no one he'd even consider dating, much less think about falling in love with. Your presence here is truly a blessing." Claire hugged Kat.

"Thank you for coming to my defense. This is all happening too quickly. I hope you understand. I need more time. Only one short month ago I was living in Philadelphia. Chase is so certain about me. I'm a little confused right now."

"When he makes up his mind, my Chase can be a force to be reckoned with. It must be overwhelming. He's a lot like his dad in that regard. He's a good judge of people. Take your time. Remember, there are two sweet boys who will be affected by this possible relationship," Claire said reassuringly.

Kat took the punch refill out to the backyard. As she passed Emma, their eyes met. Emma smiled and said, "Don't look so worried. It's all going to work out. Just have faith. You can stay outside. I'll help Claire. I'm sure someone is probably looking for you." Emma nodded her head in Chase's direction.

Chase was laughing and talking with a group of dads. He waved and smiled beckoning her to his side. After the encounter in the kitchen, Kat was a little reluctant to meet more people, but she headed to the group at the grill.

"Gentlemen, this is Katrina Russell, the mother of the blond boy on the pony. Don't get any ideas, all you single guys. I have first dibs!" Chase squeezed her around the waist.

She was unaccustomed to being the center of attention but made no move to leave Chase's side. The conversation around the grill was much more pleasant than the one in the kitchen had been. Soon, everything was ready to eat.

Chase called out, "Soup's on. Let's form a circle."

When the not-perfectly-round circle was made, he continued, "Dear Lord, thank you for Trevor's sixth birthday celebration and all the friends and family in attendance. Please bless this food to our nourishment that we may serve you better. Amen."

Everyone piled their plates with meat from the grill and all the wonderful salads and sides from the buffet table. They found seats at the picnic tables scattered around the yard. Kat helped Timmy with his plate before filling her own.

"Mom, isn't this the best birthday party ever? Can I have a pony at my birthday party in September? And a clown? I hope Trevor likes his present from me. These are the best hot dogs I've ever had. Don't you think they're great, Mom?" Timmy kept chattering. He didn't quit talking until his mouth was full.

Kat had no idea what it cost for this kind of extravaganza. They definitely wouldn't be able to keep up with the Merricks in the parties category.

"September is still a long way off. Let's not worry about it yet." Kat ruffled Timmy's hair. "You have lots of wants—vacations, ponies at birthday parties, bicycles—we'll have to decide what we want the most and work toward it, okay?"

"Sure, Mom. I love you. I'm having so much fun." Then Timmy raced over to where Trevor was beginning to open his birthday presents.

Kat was concerned when she saw all the expensive gifts Trevor received—lots of electronics, gift cards—things well beyond anything she could afford for a six-year-old boy's birthday gift.

Trevor opened Timmy's gift. His expression was one of pure joy. He hugged his best friend. "Thank you,

Timmy. We can hunt for ants tomorrow after Sunday School. This is so cool. Thank you."

Timmy beamed at the special recognition. "Mom, I'm so glad we got the ant farm. Trevor really, really likes it. Thanks for moving to Wisconsin. You're the best mom ever."

Was it true? Was coming to Wisconsin the right thing to do? Could her radar be wrong? Was Emma right? Would it all work out?

The party ended after hours of food and fun. Kat and Timmy were the last to leave since they stayed to help clean up. They walked the three long blocks to their car with Timmy chattering away about how much fun he'd had and how he looked forward to populating the ant farm after church tomorrow. Kat began to relax.

She put the key in the ignition. What was the paper stuck under her windshield wiper? Looked like someone advertising their lawn mowing service. The same flyer was on other cars parked on the street. Since she had no lawn to mow, she pulled it off and folded it in half to throw it away.

Wait. Something was scrawled in pencil on the back. "*Hi, Kat. You don't have to miss me anymore! I'm here. See you soon.*" It didn't need a signature.

"No!" She tore the page in two. Then she stopped. *This is evidence. Proof he's here. The police will want it.* She wadded up the two pieces and shoved them in her pocket.

"Are you okay, Mom?" Timmy reached over the front seat to touch her shoulder.

She took a deep breath. "I'm fine. We need to get going." She looked up and down the street. Then checked again.

The waiting was over. Her danger radar had been deadly accurate. Was he watching them now? Had he seen Timmy? How long had he been in town? Did he know where they lived?

Kat sent Timmy upstairs to start his bath as soon as they walked in the door. Then she went in the kitchen to find Emma. "He's here." She pulled the wadded-up note from her pocket and handed it over, certain that her friend could read the fear in her teary eyes and trembling voice.

"It's time to make the call." Emma went straight to the phone and dialed the number for the Lansdale Police Department.

They spoke with Chief Davis who assured Kat that a parole violator crossing state lines could be picked up, even if there was no other violation. He promised to alert both the Pennsylvania and Wisconsin State Police. Chief Davis would check in with them as soon as he had any new information. Kat was instructed to call if she saw Dirk.

After she hung up, Emma hugged her tightly. "God will watch over us, Katrina. Get Timmy to bed, and you should go too. It will be time for church before we know it."

She wanted to call Pop, but he was just getting back to work. He didn't need to be worrying about them. Maybe Chief Davis would pick Dirk up tonight. It would be over almost before it started. Could she be so lucky?

Chapter Fourteen

In Sunday School, Joan Schneider and her two friends did not speak to Kat but were quite talkative with Chase. He didn't seem to realize they were snubbing her. Clearly, Claire had not told her son about the episode in the kitchen yesterday afternoon. All Kat had to do was sit next to Chase in class and Joan's green-eyed monster made itself known.

The Merricks came to Emma's for dinner after church. Being together on Sunday was beginning to be a regular thing. That was a concern for more reasons than not being ready to commit to a relationship.

Chase volunteered to dry dishes, if she would wash. She couldn't escape being alone with him.

"I know you've had a full week between work and yesterday's festivities. I really appreciate you making time for this, for me, on your only day off." Chase took a plate out of her hand.

"You know the boys never pass up an opportunity to be together, and Claire and Emma always enjoy an opportunity to visit."

"So that's the reason you spend time with me? Other people make you do it? Not exactly what I hoped to hear by now." Chase frowned.

"By now? We need to slow down. It's too soon. You still don't know me. I haven't led the same kind of life that you have."

"Katrina, the past is past."

"Please, let me finish. I know we're both single parents of sons who adore one another, but there are some significant differences in how we got to this place."

"Of course there are. It doesn't mean we can't have a very happy, shared future together."

"That might be true—someday—but not now. Not yet. I need some space. I want you to be safe. I haven't got the right words to explain it."

"Maybe I can help."

"I know you think you can, but this isn't anything you can magically fix."

"Well, the perfect opportunity to give you space is coming soon. Trevor and I are going to Boston for a week leaving on Tuesday."

"Oh, no. Does Timmy know? He'll be lost without Trevor."

"I'm hoping *you'll* be a little lost without me too." The sadness in Chase's voice tugged at her heart. "I'm going to a medical conference on pediatric trauma surgeries, and Trevor is going to spend time with Libby's parents out on the Cape. They haven't seen him in three years. We planned this visit last fall. I don't really want to leave you for so long, especially since you seem to be upset, but I need to make sure Trevor feels connected to his grandparents."

"Don't feel bad about leaving. You need the training, and Libby's parents need to see their grandson. Hopefully by the time you return, my issues will be resolved."

Their moment was interrupted by the boys racing over to see if they would play whiffle ball with them.

Chase patiently showed the boys how to grip the bat and swing with the perfect amount of force. He helped Timmy perfect his pitching stance so the ball was harder to hit.

Initially, Kat took the outfield and Chase pitched. When they were up to bat, Timmy pitched and Trevor played outfield. They played until Claire said it was time to go home before it got dark.

Chase and Kat never had an opportunity to continue their private discussion. It was just as well. Their absence was timed perfectly—at least for her. Dirk would be captured before he realized how important Chase was to her.

It was well past Timmy's bedtime when Kat finally tucked him in after washing off the grime of a day playing outside. "Mom, I wish I had a dad. Trevor is such a lucky duck to have a dad to play ball with him and teach him special secret dad stuff."

"Hey, what am I? Don't I count? I teach you all kinds of stuff. Didn't I teach you how to fish? I was out there playing ball today too, you know," Kat argued with a smile.

"I know, Mom. But you can't teach me secret man stuff. That's way different. I need a dad to teach me those things. You're a girl. You don't know everything boys need to know."

"Think about all the secret mom stuff I'm teaching you that Trevor can't learn because he doesn't have a mom. Doesn't mom stuff count for anything?"

"It counts plenty, but, Mom, every boy really needs a dad."

"I agree, honey. But you won't get a dad until I marry someone who wants to love us both. Someone who wants to be a husband to me and a dad to you. That's how it works. We're a package deal."

"Cause my dad isn't coming back to live with us ever? Even if he found out how much I need him?"

Kat was heartbroken. "The problem is that I don't love your father and he doesn't love me. That's no way to be married. We can't be a family without caring deeply for one another."

"Couldn't you try to love him…for me?"

"It's complicated, and I'm afraid too much has happened for me to ever love him, even for you, as much as I would like to make you happy."

"I figured it was something like that. I just need a dad, somehow, some way. Will you work on it, Mom? Please."

"Sure. I'll make it a priority, my little man. Remember, you are learning some secret man stuff from Dr. Chase, like how to pitch the ball today."

"Wait, Mom, I almost forgot to say my prayers." Prayers had become a nightly event since the first time Timmy stayed overnight at Trevor's. He jumped out of bed and knelt with his eyes closed and his head bowed. Every night she marveled at how comfortable he was talking to God, as if He was a good friend her son had known his whole life.

"Dear God, Thank you for this day. Please bless Mom, Nana, Dr. Chase, Gran, Trevor, Pop Pop, and Jocie. And please bless me. I'll keep trying to be a good boy. Oh, and, God, please help Mom fall in love with someone who loves me too, so I can have a real dad like Trevor's. Amen." He jumped back into bed.

She kissed her son good night and added her own prayer to his, "Please keep all of the people I love safe from harm. Amen."

****

At the end of her shift, the roar of a motorcycle assaulted Kat's ears. Chase was at the hospital. She ran to the window. A red-helmeted rider was circling the square. Pennsylvania plates. Driving too fast. She ran to the back of the diner and called Chief Davis.

"Dirk Crowe is circling the square. He didn't see me. I don't know what to do." Her wavering voice betrayed the terror in her heart.

"Stay there. I'll have someone take you home," Chief Davis said.

"I don't want to leave my car here. Can someone follow me home? I keep it in Emma's garage, so it won't be obvious where I am. If you hurry, he may still be downtown."

"We can. Sit tight. After we check the square, I'll have someone in a patrol car come to the alley in just a few minutes."

The officer who responded to the call recommended she get her Wisconsin license plates as soon as she could. The little red car with out of state plates was an easy link to her.

The policeman waited for the garage door to go down before leaving. Kat physically shook as she came in the kitchen door. It was going to be okay. Emma was fixing supper, and Timmy was playing on the living room floor. Just like any normal evening.

Emma saw the patrol car pull away from the front of the house and looked questioningly at Kat. Nodding at Timmy, "Later" was all she said.

After Timmy was in bed, Kat told Emma about seeing Dirk.

"You told the chief like you were supposed to. The officer is right, though. You'd better get new license plates, the sooner the better. Maybe you could step out a few minutes during the day. Explain to Muriel what's going on. I know she'll help in any way she can."

"You're probably right. I just hate to drag more people into the middle of this."

"Tell Muriel you need Wisconsin license plates. You don't have to say why. It's a perfectly normal thing for people to do when they move somewhere new and they're going to stay. You are staying, aren't you?"

"Yes, we're staying. There's nowhere to run. I think we're safer here than alone on the road." Kat surprised herself with the strong positive response.

****

Chase didn't have time for a sit-down breakfast. It was just as well. They would be gone tomorrow. She could only juggle so many problems at one time. She didn't want to break down and spill all her secrets overwhelming him before he left.

Charlie and Sheba made their way to the counter. Kat got his order and made the rounds to refill coffee cups. When his order and Miss Althea's were ready, she put them on a tray.

"Walt's pretty fast today," Kat said as she walked to the front. She told the new customer at the counter, "I'll be right with you, sir."

The stranger caught her eye. He smiled broadly and winked. The tray dropped to the floor. Hot coffee, eggs, and bacon flew everywhere amid shattered china. She immediately bent down to gather up the debris and recover her composure.

She had the mess corralled in a dishpan and

struggled to stand. Where was he? She knew *he* had been sitting at the counter right between Charlie and Miss Althea.

"What clumsiness," Miss Althea began raring. "They should take the cost of all those dishes out of your paycheck."

Kat stared at the stool she knew he'd been sitting on. "Mr. Charlie, wasn't there someone else at the counter, sitting right next to you?"

"Yep. Insisted he knew someone who worked here and he was waiting for her. Sheba didn't like him one bit. You know she's a good judge of character." Sheba continued her low growl.

"How long must I wait for breakfast?" Miss Althea was getting louder.

"I'll get it now. One more question. Miss Althea, what did the man look like? What color was his shirt?" Kat asked trying to get as much information as possible for Chief Davis.

"Young lady, I do not make a habit of staring at men who happen to sit down next to me in this establishment."

"Oh, you old biddy, don't get your feathers in a ruffle. Even I know that you look at everything in pants anywhere near you. Tell her what you saw," Charlie said with unmasked irritation in his voice.

"Sir, I am highly offended," Miss Althea sniffed.

"Doesn't make a goldanged bit of difference. Tell her. Now!"

"He had dirty-blond hair, not too long. He was wearing a blue tee shirt with some kind of logo on the front. Holey blue dungarees. Dirty black boots." Miss Althea put her mouth right next to Charlie's ear. "Are you happy now, you old coot?"

"Too bad you weren't paying any attention to him." Charlie chuckled.

"Thank you both. Breakfast is on me. It won't take long." Kat raced back to the kitchen, put their orders in, and called Chief Davis with Miss Althea's description. Between that and the motorcycle and helmet information, Chief Davis thought they had a good jump on finding him.

Miss Althea and Charlie finished their breakfasts without speaking to one another. "Thank you for making up for your ineptness by buying my breakfast," Miss Althea said softly as she stood to leave. "As for you, I don't know how you can stand yourself," she scolded Charlie, then left.

"Ain't she a dilly? Sorry you aren't having a good day. It'll get better, Kitty. Just hang in there. C'mon, Sheba, it's time for us to go. See ya tomorrow."

Thank goodness Chase couldn't stay for breakfast. She was positive Dirk knew it was her. Seeing him in the flesh in Whistler's was shocking enough; it was the wink that had completely unnerved her. He knew where she worked. Did he know where she lived too?

Kat called Emma on her break to tell her to be extra vigilant. Timmy had been invited to spend the afternoon at the Merricks so he could see Trevor before they left for Boston. She couldn't refuse the request, although she repeated the warning for Emma to watch for Dirk.

****

Kat pushed food around on her plate. Emma hadn't seen Dirk. They wouldn't be safe until the police had him in custody. Timmy told her all about Trevor's vacation. "He gets to fly on a big airplane and see his grandpa and grandma. He's so lucky. Mom, when can I see Pop Pop again? I really miss him."

"I know. We both do. We can't see him right now."

A roar echoed down the street. She raced to the window. The rider wore a neon-green helmet. Just what she needed—another motorcyclist to torment her.

Emma allayed her fears saying, "It was Johnny Butler from two blocks down the street. He's showing off the motorcycle he got for his birthday yesterday."

"Mom, I want a motorcycle when I'm old enough to have a license," Timmy announced. "Dr. Chase told me he'd teach me how to ride—if it's okay with you."

"He told you what?"

"He said when I was older, I could learn to ride on his. But only if I have your permission," Timmy explained.

"You do not have my permission. No motorcycles. Absolutely not. Not ever."

"Why, Mom…"

"This discussion is closed. I said no."

After Timmy went to bed, Kat called Chase.

"Hello."

"Who do you think you are telling *my* son that you would teach him to ride a motorcycle?" Kat almost screamed.

"Hello to you too. Katrina, that is *not* exactly what I told him. He and Trevor were talking about how much fun they could have if they both had a motorcycle when they start to drive. I told them it was important to learn the right way to ride and I'd be happy to help them *if* you said Timmy could," Chase explained.

"You what?" Her voice was instantly at top volume

again. "I don't want my son riding motorcycles with *anyone*."

"Calm down. A motorcycle is pretty fascinating to little boys...bigger ones too. I was trying to help, not make you upset," Chase spoke quietly.

"Keep your suggestions to yourself. I don't need *another* motorcycle-riding Romeo in my life." She hit the *End* button on her phone and paced around the living room.

Emma put down her knitting. "Did something happen while Timmy was playing with Trevor today?"

"I can't believe Chase could be so heartless."

"I don't believe he is. What did he do?" Emma asked quietly.

"He offered to teach my son to ride a motorcycle. You heard Timmy at supper. How could he?"

"Katrina, he doesn't know," Emma said softly.

"Know what?"

"That the evil you're facing rides a motorcycle. Remember, you haven't shared anything about Dirk with him. You're upset, but Chase doesn't understand what he did wrong."

"Oh, no. Emma, you're right." Kat stopped pacing and sat down. "Chase probably thinks I'm some kind of lunatic. Dirk is scaring the wits out of me. I've been on edge since seeing him this morning."

There was a soft knock at the door. Kat looked out the peep hole. She slowly unlocked and opened the door. Chase came in.

"I know it's late, but I couldn't leave town on such a sour note." Chase looked at Kat.

"I'm embarrassed. I've had a very rough day, and you got the brunt of all my built-up anger. I apologize. I was wrong to unload it on you," Kat said blinking back tears.

"I know you said I can't help, but this behavior isn't like you. What's happening? Sometimes it helps to talk, even if I can't fix it."

Kat turned her back on Chase. "Please, just leave. Go on your trip. I made this mess. It's my responsibility to clear it away."

"Are you sure?"

"Please…"

"I'm going, but I'm not happy about it. Emma, Mom will know how to get in touch with me. Please let me know if I need to come back early. I care deeply for you, Katrina Russell. Even if you don't want me to and won't let me help you." Chase kissed her shoulder and quietly left.

"It took everything I have to not butt in. Now, I can't wait any longer." Emma planted herself in front of Katrina. "Chase cares for you. I love you. You can't do this alone. You need help."

"I have the police involved."

"And they're doing everything they can, but they don't care for you like we do. You need us—me, Chase, Claire, Trevor, Timmy—all of us," Emma insisted.

"You all care for Katrina Russell without knowing who she really is. And when you find out…" She began sobbing.

Emma hugged her, then clasped her hands over Katrina's. "Dear Lord, we are fighting an evil man. We all need your love to protect us, to shield us through this battle. Amen."

Emma checked all the doors and turned off lights.

Chapter Fifteen

"Ms. Russell, I need you to come with me, please," the patrolman said very soberly.

Kat put down her order pad, removed her apron, and followed the officer outside to the parking area in the alley behind Whistler's.

Her car's driver's side window was smashed in. Safety glass littered the seat and floorboard. The patrolman had interrupted someone trying to hot wire it. When the police car neared the parking area, the suspect jumped out of the vehicle and onto a nearby motorcycle. He wore a red helmet. The officer never saw his face and lost him when he left the alley and cut through the block on a sidewalk back to Main Street.

"It had to be Dirk Crowe. But why steal my car?"

"Well, he would know the car since you haven't changed license plates yet," the patrolman scolded. "Has this always been your car or was it his? Could there be something of his hidden in the car?"

"It's always been my car. Dirk drove it sometimes, but it's my car. He hasn't driven it for almost six years. I haven't found anything he left in it. He figured out that I worked here yesterday. I guess it was just a matter of time before he found my car."

"The window will need to be replaced. Is there anyone who could lend you a car while yours is being repaired?"

Kat told Muriel there was an emergency and she'd be back shortly. The officer accompanied her to a garage for repairs to be scheduled, then took her home. Emma loaned her the car without hesitation. She said Claire would be happy to take her wherever she needed to go while Katrina's was being repaired.

"What on earth happened?" Muriel greeted Kat at the back door. "Someone said your car had been vandalized. In thirty years, we've never had any problems with people parking back there."

"Don't worry. It was just a window. Nothing was taken. They weren't successful hot wiring it." Kat tried to brush off the episode.

"Susie and Doris checked their vehicles right after you left. No one else seems to have been hit. I just don't understand it." Muriel walked away shaking her head.

****

Timmy was in bed. Kat needed to talk to Pop. He would know the right thing to say to calm her down and might know where to look for something hidden in her car.

"Hello…" A groggy voice answered the phone. It was only eight o'clock, nine o'clock in Philly. "Russell Residence."

"Hi, Jocie, I need to talk to Pop."

No response.

"Please, Jocelyn. It's really important. Is Pop there?"

"No. He's not."

"Where is he? Is he still at the shop? When will he be home?"

"It's none of your business."

"Why does this have to be a battle?"

153

"Don't you want to tell me what's wrong?"

"No. I need to talk to him. You can't help me. When are you expecting him?"

"Some of his army buddies are in town. They're having kind of a reunion dinner and boys' night out. I don't know when he'll be home." Jocelyn hung up.

At least Pop's feeling well enough to get out with friends. That's a good sign. Jocelyn might even give him her message.

****

No obvious new terror today, but waiting for danger to step out of the shadows ate holes in Kat's soul. After Timmy was down for the night, she paced the living room like a caged tiger.

Emma looked up from her knitting and asked, "Would you like to learn to knit? It would be something to take your mind off things. Chief Davis knows his job. If Dirk shows up again, he'll take care of us. Please, sit down with me." She patted the sofa beside her.

Mom had taught Kat how to knit when she was seven, but she hadn't picked up any needles in over ten years. She intently watched Emma's motions.

"I think you're right. I need something to keep me busy, or I will go even crazier than I already am. Would you do a refresher course for me? Maybe I could manage some scarves for Christmas. I always seem to work better when I have a deadline in mind. That's a good long way off."

"I'd love to help you remember how. I have some scrap yarn for practicing. When you get the hang of it again, I'll take you to Knitting Pretty to look at some of Elsie's beautiful stuff." Emma got up and dug around in a basket behind her chair, coming out with two knitting needles and a skein of dark brown yarn.

Kat carefully mimicked every knitting move Emma made, even the special trick for the end of a row. Emma was right; her fingers remembered the comforting rhythm of knitting.

"I'm afraid this wouldn't work very well." Kat held up her test swatch at the end of the evening—one end was twice as wide as the other.

"That's perfectly natural. Once you get back in rhythm and relax a little, both sides will match up. You just need a little more practice," Emma assured her.

Practice wasn't the only thing she needed to loosen those too tight stitches. At least the evening had flown by when she had tangled skeins to sort out instead of her unraveling life.

****

Who was the man sitting at the counter? Where did she know him from? He definitely wasn't one of her regulars. He looked up from the menu. She gasped. Mr. Casterelli from Philly. The creepy man who came to Pop's asking all kinds of questions immediately after Dirk went to prison and who reappeared after the parole. Kat was about to ask Susie to take his order when their eyes met. Too late.

Casually approaching him, Kat asked, "What would you like for lunch today?"

"Miss Russell, it is imperative that we talk somewhere privately. I have it on good authority Dirk Crowe is headed to Wisconsin, if he's not already here," Mr. Casterelli said quietly.

"Your warning is too late. He broke into my car and tried to hot wire it. I don't believe there is anything else for us to discuss."

"I'd rather not talk here. Do you have a break so we could go somewhere near by?"

"No. I'm not comfortable going anywhere alone with you. You need to eat and leave."

"Unfortunately, you do have to talk with me." Mr. Casterelli flashed a Federal DEA badge discreetly. "When do you get off work?"

"Five o'clock," Kat said softly. Then she gave him directions to Emma's house. He left without ordering anything. He'd meet her at nine. She didn't want to see him until her son was soundly asleep.

Kat immediately called Emma. She promised to fill in all the details after Timmy was in bed. It was good Emma would be there. She didn't want to be alone with Mr. Casterelli, even if he really was a DEA agent. He'd never flashed the badge in past meetings.

One o'clock. Two. Three thirty. Four forty-five. Finally, at five o'clock, Kat hung up her apron. The trip home seemed longer than usual.

Emma met her at the kitchen door. Timmy hugged his mom. When he returned to the battle on the living room floor, Emma whispered, "Is this something to do with Dirk?"

"Yes, I'm pretty sure it is," Kat replied.

Most of the supper conversation was about how much Timmy missed Trevor. Kat kept checking the clock over the dining room table. Twice she got up to compare it to the clock on the kitchen stove. Emma reminded Timmy to tell his mom about the special outing they had planned for tomorrow to the museum over at the university and lunch at the drive in.

"Sounds like you're going to be having lots of fun

while I'm at work tomorrow. I'm glad Susie can pick me up in the morning. Your Nana certainly takes good care of you."

"I know. I have the best Nana in the world."

"If you're going to have such a busy day, you'd better get into the bathtub and to bed. You want to be ready for your trip," Kat coaxed him upstairs.

The warm bubble bath was just the thing to relax Timmy. He went right to sleep. Good. Sometimes things worked out like they needed to.

Kat told Emma about Mr. Casterelli's visit to Whistler's and the ones in Philadelphia. "He knew Dirk was coming here and said he'd explain everything tonight."

A knock. Right on time. Kat answered the door. "Thank you for meeting with me Miss R..." Seeing Emma on the sofa, he quickly added, "This must be a *totally* private discussion."

"Emma Ritterskamp is my landlady. More than that, she's my very dear friend. There is nothing you're going to say that Emma can't hear. I won't talk to you without her," Kat said in a tone that left no doubt about her resolve.

"Very well," Mr. Casterelli began. "I'll get right to it. Dirk Crowe served time on federal drug charges related to cocaine and heroin distribution. How much did you know about his dealing and the organization he worked for?"

Maybe having Emma hear all this first from someone else was not such a good idea. Kat trembled. "I didn't know he was a dealer until I had been living with him for over a month. I only knew he liked to party and always seemed to have money, but I had no idea how he made it. I worked every day. I thought Dirk did too. I never met any of his associates, except Marco Pasos, who was dating my coworker, Nancy Raymond."

Mr. Casterelli removed his glasses and stared directly at Kat. "So you lived with him but had no knowledge of his business dealings? That seems highly unlikely. Forgive my skepticism, but you moved out of his apartment only a few days before he was arrested. Did he tell you the drug bust was planned?"

"No. I do not lie nor appreciate your implication that I do." Anger's heat rocketed across her cheeks. Her hands clenched into fists. "Dirk Crowe savagely beat me on two occasions—the last time was the night I moved out. I feared for my life and for the safety of my unborn child. That was why I left. Besides, how could Dirk have known he was about to be arrested?"

"The answer to that question is why I'm here," Mr. Casterelli continued. "Dirk Crowe agreed to turn state's evidence against one of the major drug distribution kingpins in Philadelphia and South Jersey. As part of the agreement, my agency supplied him with the drugs and money to make him a large enough player to get the attention of the Scacchi syndicate. In return, Mr. Crowe provided the DEA with details on the organization's structure above the street dealers. Just taking low level dealers off the street has very little impact on the flow of illegal drugs. We're interested in the organization members who keep it all running, the brains of the syndicate so to speak.

"Mr. Crowe anonymously helped us identify three midlevel members of the Scacchi syndicate who were later convicted. When he was at risk of being discovered, we arrested and convicted him so he would be safe. Once he was in prison, we discovered cocaine with a street value of half a million dollars and $250,000 in cash had disappeared shortly before his arrest and were never accounted for."

"So, you think Dirk still has the missing cocaine and cash? After almost six years in prison? What does any of this have to do with me?"

"We believe Mr. Crowe hid the missing drugs and money in your car. We searched his apartment, motorcycle, and personal possessions after he was incarcerated. That was the only place we haven't looked. We are concerned the Scacchis suspect he may have cooperated with us to get an early parole."

"Life and death, that's what Dirk kept saying to me." Kat shook her head.

"That would explain why he tried to steal your car," Emma interjected.

"Yes, it would," Mr. Casterelli agreed.

"Why didn't you retrieve the evidence while Dirk was still in prison?"

"We didn't know how deeply you were involved. Your vehicle was only serviced by your family members, so we couldn't be sure they would cooperate if we tried to remove the items without your knowledge."

"I'm sure you're right. Fine, impound my car or whatever it is you need to do. It's in the garage being repaired," Kat volunteered. "I want this whole mess to be over and done. I need Dirk Crowe permanently out of my life. The car is a small price to pay to make it happen. It's at Gilman Brothers Garage."

"Impounding your car would get the missing items

back. It would not, however, guarantee we recapture Dirk Crowe. He must go back to prison. Now would be the ideal time for the retrieval, while it's being repaired. I'll contact local law enforcement to assist us. You'll be eligible for a substantial reward once this is resolved."

"Chief Davis knows about Dirk and the danger Katrina is in. I'm sure he'll be happy to help," Emma said.

"Thank you. I'm aware of his involvement. But we won't seize your vehicle. We think it would be more dangerous for you and your son, if you no longer have the car." Mr. Casterelli put down his pen and looked directly at Kat. "Miss Russell…"

Emma interrupted, "Mr. Casterelli, for Katrina's continued safety, please refer to her as Mrs. Russell. Everyone in Lansdale knows her as Mrs. Russell. I think it's the least you can do since it sounds like you're about to ask her for a big sacrifice."

"I apologize. Mrs. Ritterskamp is correct. I have to ask you to take a major risk, Mrs. Russell. We want you to continue driving your car every day. More importantly, we'd like you to leave it parked in the driveway here, instead of in the garage."

"I can't do that. It will put Emma and my son even more at risk. Just take the car." Kat choked the words out. "I will not risk my family. I don't care about any reward."

"We will have undercover DEA agents keeping your house, car, and family under close surveillance. We're already working with state and local law enforcement to coordinate this effort. I'll give you my personal cell phone number and be available any time you need me—day or night. I know we're asking a lot, but if we don't find Dirk Crowe soon, the Scacchi Syndicate will. They can't be far behind us. They don't know your role in all this either. Believe me, you want to have him securely incarcerated by the government and back in Pennsylvania before they figure out where Crowe is. When we recover our property and capture him, we'll all leave Wisconsin. I know it's a lot to ask. But we haven't come up with another way to do this." Mr. Casterelli straightforwardly stated his case.

"I think we have to do as Mr. Casterelli asked. It sounds like they have added lots of extra security to help," Emma said hopefully. "We must have faith it will work out."

Kat spoke with tear-filled eyes. "I'm not sure my faith is strong enough, Emma. I'm not worried about us. I'm concerned about you, and now, the Merricks. What if Dirk's been watching us, waiting for an opportunity to spring?"

"Mrs. Russell, we're hoping he will spring. We want him to know where you live. I promise that I will keep you, your son, Mrs. Ritterskamp, and your friends safe. Will you help us?" Mr. Casterelli repeated his request.

"I don't want to, but I will. Tell me exactly what you want me to do." Kat put her head in her hands as she listened to Mr. Casterelli lay out the details of the whole plan.

On the way out the door, Mr. Casterelli said, "One more thing: it is imperative that you do not share the details of my visit with anyone else. I know you want to tell your friends, but my experience is that the more people who are involved, the more likely it is Dirk Crowe will also learn what's planned. This has to be secret. I wasn't happy about having Mrs. Ritterskamp here, but I'm sure we can count on both of you to be silent." He gave his card, with three different emergency numbers on it, to them both and quietly left.

"Emma, I hope we did the right thing. Thank you for being with me. I couldn't have done this alone. I hope Mr. Casterelli can really keep everyone safe, especially since we can't warn them. I'm so sorry for bringing this evil to your doorstep. All because I was a headstrong, sad, little girl who had lost faith in everyone and everything when she lost her mom. I'm so sorry."

"Nonsense. God will take care of us. He brought you to me because He knew exactly where you needed to be. We're not the only ones who know about this plan. He knows too. He will not fail us."

"I know when the truth comes out, everyone will be very disappointed in me."

"I think you've been remarkably brave, my dear. I'm not sure I could have taken such a risk, fleeing a dangerous felon, traveling somewhere new with my young son in tow."

"Timmy thinks he's on a grand adventure. It's such a relief to tell you. There's a lot more to the story, but I haven't the strength to explain it all right now."

"Come on, my dear, it's late, and you have to go to work in the morning. Let's go to bed."

"Emma, thank you. You are my rock. You don't judge me, just love me. Thank you."

Chapter Sixteen

Timmy excitedly explained all about their museum visit over supper, pizza that Kat picked up on the way home. "Mom, it was so cool. We went down in a lead mine and even rode a little train. There's all kinds of old-timey stuff from pioneer days. We were there for hours and hours. Nana didn't even complain once about getting tired."

"Thank you, Emma. Maybe when Trevor and Dr. Chase get home, we can all go back one day. What do you think?" Kat suggested.

"It would be super, Mom. Today I got to eat out three times. Breakfast at Whistler's. The best hot dog and French fries with a milk shake at the drive in, and Nana said I didn't spill even a crumb in her car. Now pizza for supper. Quack. Quack. Quack." He stuffed the last of the pizza slice in his mouth.

"Okay, lucky duck. I think it's time you washed some of your mining experience off and crawled in bed."

"Will do, Mom." He ran over and hugged Emma. "Thanks, Nana. Today I wasn't lonely even a bit." He ran upstairs to get his bath.

"I'll be back after I get him snug in bed."

"I'll get things thrown away. A day without dishes! Yea!" Emma laughed.

Kat picked up her lopsided knitting and unraveled

every stitch.

"What's wrong, my dear?" Emma asked looking up from her project.

"It's a mess. I need to start over to see if I can get the tension more consistent."

"Well, they say practice makes perfect. Personally, I don't like to make practice swatches. I'd rather jump needles first into a real project. Maybe you should get some yarn to make the scarves you want to give as gifts."

"Good idea. I might as well have a real project in progress. Emma, do you think Dirk's still here? I haven't seen him in days."

"I don't know him, but from what you've said, I don't think he would ride all the way from Pennsylvania and turn around after only a couple of frightening encounters. Especially if he knows Philadelphia drug dealers have questions for him."

"My mind knows you're right. My heart's hoping you're not. I would feel better if I could talk to Pop. Oh, I forgot to charge my phone."

"Use my phone. I have unlimited long distance on my landline," Emma volunteered.

"Good idea. Thanks."

Jocelyn answered on the first ring. "Russell Residence."

"Hi, Jocie."

"Oh, it's you. Don't you know how late it is? Now what's wrong?"

"I'm sorry. Has Dirk been around lately?"

"Haven't seen him. Why would I?" Jocelyn snarled.

"No reason."

"What did you want? Calling to upset your father about something you think I did to you?"

"No. What did you do to me? I just miss Pop and you."

Jocelyn snorted. "I'll just bet you do."

"You can believe me or not. I do. Jocie, what happened to us?"

"What do you mean *us*?"

"You and me, our relationship. When Mom was still alive, you were like an aunt to me. You kept me sane when we lost her. Then, when you married Pop, it was like you became a total stranger. Suddenly, we seemed to be in competition with each other, and Pop was the prize. Why don't you still love me?"

Jocelyn didn't respond immediately. Her voice wavered. "So much like Renata...I think you have a little girl's rosy memories. Things haven't changed on my side." She took a deep breath and her voice got stronger. "You're feeling guilty and trying to make me responsible for your problems. I'm not the one who made the horrible choices that broke her father's heart."

Kat wiped away the tear that spilled down her cheek. "Jocie, I'm sorry. I'd give anything to change the past."

Jocelyn hung up without saying goodbye. Kat sat staring at the phone. Emma got up from the sofa and hugged her.

"It sounds like you were talking to Jocelyn, and it could have gone better. I'm sorry," Emma said softly.

"She has a right to be upset with me, but how are we ever going to have a good relationship, if she won't forget my past mistakes?"

"Pray that God touches her heart, so she can hear

165

you with love."

"How can I do that when I'm not sure I still believe in God? How do I know He's there and He cares about me?"

"Open your heart. He's there waiting to love you and help you. I know it's true. I'm praying that in time, so will you." Emma hugged her again. Kat walked upstairs to her room.

She lay in bed and stared at the ceiling for several hours. When sleep finally came, motorcycles and pain filled her nightmares. She woke suddenly, gasping for air. Tears ran down her cheeks, pooling in her ears. In the nightmare, Dirk had kidnapped Timmy to force her to see him. If it were true, then the waiting would be over. One way or the other, it would be resolved.

Kat was still awake when Timmy came bounding in to tell her it was time to get ready for Sunday School. Dirk-deprived of sleep again, her reflection was ashen, but she was going to church, no matter how she looked or felt. She needed to be closer to divine protection.

As Kat left the young adult Sunday School classroom, Joan Schneider whispered over her shoulder to her friends, "Looks like she hasn't lassoed him yet. Still no ring." Joan laughed and then said to Kat, "Who are you trying to impress? Your lover isn't even here today? He should see how bad you look. Isn't your plan to hook him working?" Before Kat could think of a response, Joan was gone. Just as well. Silence was the best response to hatefulness. She would never be that mean to anyone—even Joan.

****

Timmy moped around the yard after Sunday dinner. It was a beautiful day. Kat coaxed him outside, even pushed him on the swings. He missed Trevor.

"Honey, let's call Pop Pop. We'll surprise him," Kat suggested. She'd find out if Jocelyn had told him about her call yesterday.

"Hey, Pop Pop. This is your grandson, Timmy!" he giggled.

"Timmy? I used to have a relative named Timmy," Jim Russell teased.

"Pop Pop, you remember me."

"Now I do." They talked and laughed for almost ten minutes. Then Timmy said, "I think my mom, your daughter, wants to talk to you too, if you remember her." He burst into laughter as he handed the phone to his mother and retreated to the swing set.

"Hey, Pop. Quite a conversation you two were having," she started. They talked for almost five minutes. Pop hadn't mentioned her call yesterday.

"Honey, we haven't seen hide nor hair of the scum bucket. Maybe he finally gave up and went to terrorize someone else," Pop said optimistically.

She involuntarily sighed.

"Kat, is he there?" Pop could read her so well.

"I wasn't sure I was going to tell you, but I can't lie. He's been here a week."

"Call the cops."

"I did immediately. I have all kinds of protection. And none of it has been able to capture him."

"If the scumbag is there, then come back home."

"I thought about it, Pop, but I think it'd be more dangerous to be alone on the road than to stay where we are."

"You're right. I know you are, but... Do I need to come out there?"

"No, you don't. I have people looking after me. I know it's not the same as having you here, but I don't need you to try and travel when you're just now well enough to go to work. We'll be fine."

"Stay in touch. I worry less if I hear from you regularly."

I've been trying to call regularly. I just don't always get through. "I will. I love you, Pop."

"I love you, baby girl. Very, very much. Hug that grandson of mine. We'll talk soon."

Talking with Pop always helped. His calming love emanating from the phone wrapped around her. Everything would work out. If she kept saying it, it might come true.

****

"Hey, Kat, do you have relatives visiting?" Doris asked Monday morning.

"What are you talking about?" Kat asked.

"I waited on two guys today who sound just like you. They must be from Philly," Susie explained. "They sure aren't locals."

"Never seen them before; glad they seem to be good tippers." Kat quickly finished clearing the table in front of her and escaped to the back of the diner.

Mr. Casterelli's word was good. He'd brought help, but didn't he realize how much they would stick out in Lansdale? *It's not good if people are noticing them. All that needs to happen is for someone to tell Dirk he sounds like the other strangers in town. Then the cat will be totally out of the bag.* Then this stress would be for nothing. Unfortunately, with all the protection readily at hand, she heard no motorcycles. Where was Dirk? Invisible. Like he knew she wasn't alone anymore.

****

About noon, Gilman's Garage called to say the car was repaired. Mr. Casterelli left her a message sometime in the afternoon saying their property had been recovered from under the lining of the back seat. Susie followed Kat home after work to return Emma's car, then took her to the garage to pick up Thelma. Pop's Rainy Day Fund paid the insurance deductible. Thankfully.

The first stop after picking up the car was the driver's license station to get her Wisconsin driver's license and new plates. Better late than never. It wouldn't keep Dirk away, but it was a clear sign she'd made up her mind to stay in Lansdale come what may. At least to herself.

****

Kat was wide awake at two a.m. when a motorcycle pulled into the driveway behind her car. A red-helmeted driver looked at her standing in the second-floor window and waved. He boldly went to the driver's side and tried to open the back door. She threw on her slippers and robe. This mess had to end now.

Kat softly closed the front door. Dirk smirked. "Well, I see you couldn't pass up an opportunity to show me how glad you are to see me."

"What do you want?"

"Got your keys?"

"No." She noticed a patrol car turn onto her street. "But I could go in the house and get them. Wait right here."

Dirk saw the police car. He leapt onto his bike. "Nice try. I won't forget you tried to trap me." The

169

motorcycle was gone before the patrol car reached the house. Kat flagged him down and sent him in pursuit.

Shaken, she called Mr. Casterelli, who answered on the first ring. Talking to him calmed her down, but she sat the rest of the night in the old rocking chair in the corner of her room.

He knew exactly where I was and keeps getting more daring. He got a kick out of terrifying me. He wanted me to know he's here; to be afraid of him; to worry about what he's going to do next. Well, it's working—I am.

The alarm went off. Kat crawled in the shower wishing for a miracle. Why was she the only one seeing him? How did he slip away from the police and the Feds? If he hadn't broken into her car, no one would even believe he existed. No one except Mr. Casterelli and Emma.

Kat met a patrol car coming down the street on the way to work. Another one was parked in the Whistler's lot next to her usual parking space. Chief Davis obviously took the threat seriously.

Before she went into the diner, she called the garage and left a message for Pop. Why hadn't she thought of that earlier? She could hear his voice on the machine and assure him that she was okay, but not be put in the position of having to lie to her father about her safety. Or having to talk to Jocelyn.

Each time she waited on strangers, she wondered if they were DEA agents on special duty to protect them or Syndicate members searching for Dirk—and maybe her.

****

Emma invited Claire to dinner.

"Chase said the conference was excellent. Lots of new techniques. Trevor is enjoying getting to know his Michaels grandparents better. They've been swimming, clamming, and hiking at their cottage on Cape Cod. All the right things to tire out a rambunctious six-year-old," Claire reported the news from the travelers.

"I'm sure the Michaelses love having Trevor with them. They must be proud of how Libby's little boy is growing up," Emma said from the kitchen.

"Yes, he looks more like Libby than Chase. I'm sure they're reminded of her. It's a shame they're so far away and have missed a lot of Trevor's growing up. Libby's father recently retired, so they hope to have more time for traveling now."

"I miss Trevor. It's pretty boring without him to play with," Timmy chimed in and then quickly added, "Sorry, Nana. I like being with you, but it isn't the same as playing with Trevor."

Emma chuckled. "I know, I'm not too good at getting down on the floor with race cars. But I can beat you at the ladder game."

"Awww, Nana, did you have to remind me?" Timmy giggled.

"Trevor told me he misses you too. He's gathering all kinds of things to bring back for you," Claire told Timmy. "And Chase misses you, Katrina. He said he hopes that your problems have worked out by the time he comes home, whatever that means."

"Thanks for the message." After the blessing, Kat asked, "If it isn't too difficult for you, I'd love to know more about Chase's father."

"I love to talk about my Walter. It seems like I only lost him yesterday, but it's been twenty-five years.

Walter Chase Merrick was the classic high school heartthrob. Chase was named after him. He has his father's chestnut-brown curls and twinkling deep-blue eyes. And the exact same crooked smile. Walter played football, baseball, and basketball—in those days, if you were athletic, and Walter was, you didn't just concentrate on one sport—you played them all.

"We started dating when I was in the eighth grade, ignoring my father's concerns about me dating someone eight years older than me. We got married two days after my high school graduation. Walter worked in a small appliance repair shop that he bought when the owner retired.

"Chase was born on our first anniversary. Walter was a great dad, always taking Chase with him, even when he was an infant. He was so proud of him. He wanted to have a houseful of children, but it was not to be."

"Then you weren't married long?"

"Only six years and a few days, one year longer than we had dated. Walter worked long hours, like lots of small businessmen do. He didn't finish up until midnight that night. The police believe he fell asleep at the wheel in a spot with a shoulder too narrow for him to get the car under control before it flipped and threw him out the front window. He died at the scene." Claire teared up and briefly closed her eyes.

Kat reached over and patted her hand. "I'm so sorry for your loss. I didn't mean to bring up sad memories. I just want to know more about Chase. You and I've had so little opportunity to talk."

"I understand. I'm pleased you want to know about him. I hope it's a positive sign of things to come."

Kat signaled for Timmy to join her in the kitchen. "We'll do the dishes, Emma. You and Claire haven't had any time to visit. I've been monopolizing the conversation. I won't take 'no' for an answer. Sit and enjoy your coffee."

After Claire went home and Timmy was in bed, Kat asked, "Emma, how did you know Godfrey was *The One* for you? Do you mind telling me?"

"Not at all. I'm fond of reminiscing about when our love was young—and so were we. I'd known Godfrey my whole life since we lived in the same village. He was older. I didn't think he even knew my name until the day he asked my father for permission to walk me home from church. It was a different time, much more formal. From that moment on, we were officially courting. Honestly, I didn't realize how much I loved him until we'd been married for five years and he had a near fatal accident."

"You married him without knowing you loved him?"

"As I said, things were done differently then. Godfrey was a kind, patient man who my father respected. I knew Papa would never knowingly match me with someone who'd do me harm. That was enough. The love came later. When it did, it was deep, satisfying, and forever. I never thought I'd be facing the future without him."

"It had to be hard to lose him."

"I didn't expect to be the one left behind. I'd always had more ailments than he did. Then suddenly, I was alone. Claire Merrick was my lifesaver. She'd been living a widow's life for a long time, and she made it her business to help me find my way in a new situation.

I don't know what I'd have done without her."

"Thanks for sharing with me. I'm sorry you were left alone."

"But I'm not. I have you and Timmy, at least for the moment. When you marry Chase, I'm sure God will provide a new companion for me."

"We haven't even been on a date yet. *If* I marry Chase one day, you will continue to be an important part of our lives. If they find Dirk and permanently remove him from my life, I might be able to move forward with Chase, but I still have doubts."

"About Chase or about yourself?"

"I think it's me. I'm amazed that Chase is so sure about us. He tells me my past doesn't matter, but I have to be sure. I'm lucky. He already treats Timmy as if he is his own son. Did you know Timmy's been asking me to work on getting him a dad—so he can learn secret man things that a mom wouldn't know how to teach him?"

Emma laughed. "Actually, I did. Timmy asked me if I knew any special prayers to help you fall in love so he could have a dad like Trevor does."

"Oh, no. I guess he's really serious."

"The only recommendation that I can make is for you to pray about your doubts and your hopes. God is always waiting to hear from your heart. He will listen. He will help."

"Thanks. I'm beginning to feel like you are the special angel God sent to keep me sane and on the right path. I don't know what else you could be." She hugged Emma and said good night.

Chapter Seventeen

It had been a long day at work. Kat slowly pulled in the empty driveway. No car at the curb. She walked in the kitchen. Emma answered the unasked question, "No word yet. I guess we should go ahead and eat dinner while we wait to hear from our travelers."

"Mom, do you think they'll come over tonight?" Timmy whined.

"I'm pretty sure they will. They were supposed to get in this morning, and it was perfect flying weather," Kat said.

About six thirty, there was a knock at the door. Timmy leapt up from the sofa and opened the door to Chase, Trevor, and Claire. He hugged his best friend like he hadn't seen him in a year.

"I hope you don't mind us crashing in uninvited," Claire said. "We stopped and bought ice cream to celebrate the return of our intrepid travelers."

Emma chuckled. "You may not have been specifically invited, but you were definitely expected." She and Claire went to the kitchen to find spoons and bowls. Timmy and Trevor both talked at once about all that had happened while they'd been apart.

"I hope you've missed me," Chase said as he held both Katrina's hands in his. "I sure have been lonely without you. Trevor was homesick—even at his adoring grandparents' home where he was being spoiled rotten—he kept talking about getting back to all of you here."

"Chase, I did miss you both." Kat kissed his cheek and took him by the hand leading him to the dining room table where ice cream dipping was in full swing.

There was lots of laughter as Trevor described going clamming for the first time and his first impression of the Atlantic Ocean. Timmy happily volunteered he'd been to the shore to see the ocean lots of times with his Pop Pop.

As soon as the last bite of ice cream was gone, Timmy and Trevor went upstairs for some play time. Emma and Claire sat in the living room visiting over their coffees. Chase volunteered that he and Katrina would clean up the ice cream dishes.

"I'm glad you volunteered for KP. It's nice to have time alone together in our usual spot."

"I'm glad you want to be alone with me." Chase picked up the dish towel. "I'll dry."

For a few minutes, neither spoke. She just enjoyed standing beside Chase and breathing in his unique scent. There weren't many dishes. When they were finished, he said, "Want to stand and talk for a minute?"

Katrina put down the dishcloth and without thinking leaned toward Chase. He put his arm around her waist and bent down to kiss her cheek. Then he tipped her head back and sweetly, gently kissed her, for the first time, on her lush full lips. She responded by putting her arms around his neck and returning his kiss with the same sweet feeling.

"Oh, I'm sorry. It's not a good idea for us to do this." She tried to slip out of his embrace, but he held her in place.

"Au contraire. I think it is an excellent idea. I've wanted to do that almost since the first time I looked up to see you pouring my coffee. You weren't my waitress, but I noticed you. I startled myself when I realized how attracted to you I was, right from the very beginning. I don't think you understand how much you've affected me. Even Libby's mom noticed something was different about me. She guessed that I had someone special in my life again."

"What do you mean?" Katrina asked, getting comfortable in Chase's embrace.

"The morning we were leaving to come home, Trevor was out with Libby's dad for one last shell-seeking foray. Liz and I were having our coffee on the deck listening to the waves roll onto the shore. From out of the blue, she said, 'I'm glad, it's time.' When I asked what she meant, she said, 'Libby has been gone for over six years. Trevor needs a mom. I'm thrilled to see that sparkle in your eyes again. You look like you did when Libby first brought you home. I imagine she must be an amazing woman to reach your heart after all this time.'

"She continued with, 'Chase, Libby would want you to be happy. She wouldn't want you to be alone, without a mom for Trevor. If you were to marry again, I would take it as a tribute to your happiness with Libby. Please don't hesitate to embrace this gift of a second chance on Libby's account, or on ours. You will always be part of our family, regardless of who you marry.' I needed to hear that. I hadn't realized until Liz said it that I was waiting for their permission to be happy again, to be with someone new. Someone not Libby.

"Katrina, you make me happy. Liz is right. You put

the sparkle back in my life. More than anything I want the opportunity to make you feel the same as I do. I want us to be together."

She hugged him. "Chase, I didn't come to Lansdale looking for love. I was drawn to the place where I'd created my happiest memories growing up. Finding you here complicated things. Nothing from my past has been resolved yet. I can't make any commitments. I don't know what's going to happen tomorrow, much less far into the future. Until I get my past settled, we have no real chance at true happiness. Will you wait a little longer?"

"I will wait for you as long as it takes. If I had even a shred of doubt about what you mean to me, being away from you made me sure. I love you. I love every single thing about you. I want you to believe that completely. You are loved and you are not alone," Chase assured her. "Is there anything I can do to remove what's haunting you? I'll stand by you, no matter what the problem is."

The moment of intimate conversation was shattered as two boys came racing into the kitchen at full speed. "Dad, Gran said we need to go home now. Can't we play just a little longer? Please, Dad," Trevor pleaded.

"Mom, it's early. Can't Trevor stay, please? Nana said it is up to you two," Timmy added.

Their parents looked at one another and burst out laughing as they nodded in unison. The boys ran back out the door with bug jars. Hand in hand, Chase and Katrina joined Emma and Claire outside on the patio. The crickets chirped in the distance. Soon, two very excited boys were stalking blinking lightning bugs across the backyard.

Life was very good. Sitting there, watching this tranquil scene while holding the hand of the man who loved her, Katrina had to believe it would all work out. For a brief moment she could almost forget danger was still near and her heart feared it was drawing closer.

It was too much. A tear slid down her cheek. Chase reached over and brushed it away. She closed her eyes and shook her head. She couldn't look at the concern she knew would be in his eyes. He said nothing. He held her hand. Her lifeline to a happy future. If he held on, could he pull her out of the past in one piece? She could only hope.

****

There was a bigger than usual crowd in the diner Saturday morning as the Dairy Days parade goers stopped for breakfast before and after the festivities. Chase had arranged for Trevor and Timmy to ride in the parade in an ambulance. Kat managed to get outside just in time to see them roll by Whistler's waving. They even got to flash the lights and periodically run the siren.

In the crush of the crowd, Kat got bumped so hard she almost fell. When she turned to excuse herself, she stared into steely-gray orbs of pure evil. She closed her eyes not wanting to believe what she saw. She forced herself to open them. Dirk was gone. Again.

When Kat went back in Whistler's, Charlie Bishop was at the counter. She shook off her fear and began reciting the specials of the day. Charlie stopped her. "I thought when your fella got back, he'd bring the angels with him, but they're still gone. Are you okay?"

"No. But I will be."

Charlie placed his order, then he said, "Kitty, evil can only have its way if you stop battling. Keep fighting. Sheba and I are in your corner."

Kat leaned over the counter and kissed Charlie's cheek. "Then how can I lose?"

****

At dinner, Timmy gave a full report on his parade experience. Then he announced that he was going to drive an ambulance when he grew up because it was the most exciting job anyone could have.

After Timmy said his prayers, he took her hand and said seriously, "Mom, remember when we talked about me needing a dad?"

"Yes, so he could teach you man secrets, right?"

"Well...there's a simple way to fix everything. Trevor and I heard Nana and Gran saying that you and Dr. Chase might get married someday. That would be perfect. I could learn dad stuff from Dr. Chase and Trevor could learn mom stuff from you. Then we'd be better than best friends. We'd be brothers. What do you think of marrying Dr. Chase, for me?"

Kat forced herself to breathe. "It's very rude to eavesdrop. Getting married is a major step. It's one for Dr. Chase and me to decide, not you and Trevor or Gran and Nana. Do you understand?"

"Yeah, Mom, I get it. But just think, then I'd have Nana and Gran, plus a dad and a brother. I'd like that," Timmy said with an impish grin. "All I'm asking is for you to think about it, Mom. Okay?"

"I'll consider your request."

Kat was about to turn out her light when she heard a motorcycle in the distance. She ran to the window. Red helmet. Dirk. He didn't stop but drove up and down streets all over the neighborhood—knowing he would disturb her. Terrorize her. She called Mr. Casterelli. A patrol car silently passed in front of the house about twenty minutes later. No more motorcycles were heard.

****

Sunday dinner after church was at Emma's. The boys wasted no time bolting out the door to play on the swing set as soon as the last morsel was off their plates. Katrina and Chase took their posts at the kitchen sink.

This was such a little thing, to stand side by side doing dishes, but a normal thing, a we-could-be-together-forever kind of thing.

"My parents always did dishes together. Mom washed and Pop dried. We didn't have an automatic dishwasher until after Pop married Jocelyn. Mom never asked me to help. It was like she wanted that time alone with Pop. Their heads would be bent toward one another in quiet conversation, and I'd hear laughter coming from the kitchen. Sometimes they'd stay in the kitchen after dishes were done, just leaning against the counter talking to one another. Often, Pop's arm would be over Mom's shoulder or around her waist as they stood together. They looked so happy, no—more than that—truly contented. Somehow, seeing them doing that little everyday chore together made me certain of the love between them. It's my fondest childhood memory."

"I think sometimes parents crave time alone together, even at the expense of dishpan hands, no matter how much they love their children. Want to stay and talk for a minute?"

As they sat down at the kitchen table, Chase's

pager went off. He phoned the hospital.

"I understand. I'm on my way. I'll be less than ten minutes." Chase hung up. "Sorry, Katrina, there's been a multi-car accident down by the river. Three ambulances are headed to the Emergency Department. They need me at the hospital. I'll take Mom and Trevor home and go over there."

"Go ahead. I'll take your mom and Trevor home, if you can't get back." She gave Chase a hug, then went out to let everyone know he had left.

After a supper of leftovers, Kat took Claire and Trevor home. Timmy rode with her to squeeze out a few more minutes with his friend. No sign of Chase yet. It must have been a really bad accident.

****

Chase came in for breakfast and decaf coffee about nine a.m. He'd been at the hospital all night. There were eighteen people injured. Fortunately, no one died, but several of them were in critical condition. He had operated on a seven-year-old girl. "She may have to be airlifted yet, but she seems to be stable now."

"It's good to see you. I'm sure you're beat. When do you have to be back to work?"

"Evening shift. After I get some sleep."

On her lunch break, Kat went across the courthouse square, not to Knitting Pretty, but to the five and dime store. She found some inexpensive acrylic yarn. She'd start with something cheap and washable for the boys' scarves. When she'd perfected her knitting, she'd go to Elsie's for something special for Chase's gift.

Kat stepped off the curb. A motorcycle sped around the corner. Its rider touched her arm with his hand before she jumped back on the sidewalk to avoid being run over. Pennsylvania plates. Red helmet. The driver laughed and waved as he raced out of sight.

Mr. Milton, the banker, rushed to her side. "Are you okay, Kat? He should lose his license for that. He didn't even check to see if you were all right. It looked like he was aiming for you." He led her to a nearby bench to sit down. "Do you want me to walk you back to the diner?"

Kat shook her head in disbelief. Dirk. She was the target. "Thank you, Mr. Milton. It just frightened me. I need to sit for a moment to collect my wits. I can get back to the diner on my own. Thank you."

Ten minutes later, she walked into Whistler's. News of the near miss hit-and-run had raced there ahead of her. Muriel, Susie, and Doris all ran over to make sure she had not been injured.

"Please, I'm okay. It was just some careless guy who apparently didn't see me. I wasn't paying enough attention when I stepped off the curb. Don't worry. Really, I'm fine. We all need to get back to work," Kat insisted.

"Mr. Milton said he ran right at you. Are you sure you're not hurt? Do you want to go home?" Muriel asked.

"No, please. I didn't get a scratch. I'd rather finish my shift than leave everyone shorthanded."

Kat stepped to the back of the diner and called Mr. Casterelli to let him know about the near miss. He'd already heard about it from the agent who had been monitoring her from a block away. The man hadn't realized what Dirk intended to do soon enough to warn her, but he did run the plates and verified that it was Dirk's motorcycle. As if there were any doubt.

"It was definitely him. No one else has that evil laugh. How could he come so close to me without any warning? I thought you had people protecting me. I hope you're doing a better job protecting my family and friends."

"This tells us how desperate he is to get to you. He means business. You're right. We failed. We're stepping up our surveillance. In the future, my people will follow you more closely. This won't happen again," Mr. Casterelli promised.

"Thank you, but I don't think you can completely guarantee my safety, can you? Please make sure my son, Mrs. Ritterskamp, and the Merricks are safe. I only agreed to this charade because of your assurances," Kat said, worry overtaking the anger in her voice.

She hung up, raised her eyes above, and said aloud, "Dear God, please bring this to a resolution soon. Thank you for keeping me out of harm's way today. Please keep your protective love around all of us. Amen."

News traveled quickly in the small town. Almost everyone who came into the diner knew about the reckless motorcyclist with out of state plates. Chase would hear too.

Once Timmy was in bed, Kat pulled out her new yarn and started knitting a bright purple scarf as a surprise for him. Emma put down her knitting. "I didn't say anything earlier because I didn't want to frighten Timmy. Was that really an accident this morning?"

She tried to sound calm. "No, it wasn't. It was Dirk. I notified Mr. Casterelli. He'd heard about it before I called. I'm trying hard not to be scared. Dirk must be watching me constantly. I had only been away from the diner about ten minutes. Mr. Casterelli's people weren't following closely enough today. He swears it won't happen again, but I think he was surprised Dirk would do something so bold in the middle of the day right downtown. He doesn't realize that Dirk's brain doesn't work like a sane person's."

A knock at the door caused them to gasp in unison. Cautiously, Emma looked through the peep hole, then smiled and unlocked the door. Chase. Until she exhaled, Kat hadn't realized she'd been holding her breath since she heard the knock.

"Katrina, are you okay? I know what happened, but this is the first time I could get away from the hospital." Chase rushed in and wrapped his strong arms around her.

"I wasn't hurt. I'm all right." The tears welling up in her eyes denied the truth of her statement. "You could've just called to check on me."

"No, I couldn't. I had to see you for myself. I had to hold you."

"You shouldn't be here. Did you see anyone when you came in?"

"No. Why? What's going on? Was it a random accident or something else? Please, I can't help you if I don't know what's happening."

Emma spoke up, "Katrina isn't at liberty to discuss this, as much as I'm sure she'd like to. Timmy's father is in Lansdale. He's threatening her. It's a complicated issue. The authorities are working together to protect all of us from this evil man."

"Darling, how come you're trying to face this alone?" Chase hugged her again.

"I haven't been alone. Emma has been with me. I

didn't want to put you in a more dangerous position than you already are just because you're around me. Dirk Crowe is unpredictable and violent. They need to capture him soon. My nerves can't take much more of this."

"I have to get back to the hospital, but I'll return in a couple of hours to spend the night when my shift is over," Chase said with concern.

"That's silly. Emma hasn't any extra space."

"I'll sleep on the sofa."

"Chase, you need to be with Claire and Trevor. They need you too. The authorities are keeping Emma's house under close surveillance. Please, go back to work. Sleep in your own bed tonight. Stay with your family. Keep them safe. Please," she pleaded.

"All right. I'm leaving. Emma, double lock everything as soon as I'm out the door. I'm not happy about this, but it appears I have no choice." Chase kissed Kat's cheek and gave Emma a hug before he left.

"Should we have told him anything?"

"We did the right thing. He wasn't going to leave without some explanation," Emma said. "We both need some sleep. Everything is locked up tight. We're good until morning. Don't worry. Keep praying. We will all be okay."

Chapter Eighteen

A scream woke Kat. Her scream. Her arms were protectively wrapped around her middle. Emma, brows furrowed with worry, stood over her, gently touching her shoulder. "Katrina, wake up. You're having a nightmare. It's me, Emma. Don't be afraid."

Kat slowly worked herself into a sitting position and tried to believe the person before her was real. Emma. Not Dirk. "I'd hoped telling Chase about Dirk would purge the demon, but it's having the opposite effect." She stopped, realizing she'd just said that aloud and Emma was still at her side.

"Do you want to talk about it? Would it help?" Emma asked softly.

"What time is it? Do I need to get ready for work?"

"It's two a.m., much too early to get up. I heard your screams from downstairs. Your room's right above mine. I checked—Timmy isn't awake. Do you think you can go back to sleep? Or would you rather I stayed with you a while longer?" Emma asked, her voice brimming with love and concern.

"Thank you for waking me. I was reliving my last night with Dirk, and more. It was as terrifying as it was the first time. It seemed so real. You don't have to stay with me. Please, go back to bed. I'll try to not disturb you anymore."

Emma reluctantly left. Kat sat in bed, afraid to turn

out the light. She didn't want to return to Dirk's apartment, to that night replayed in excruciating detail. Her fingers ached. Her ribs hurt. As if it had all just happened—tonight—in this room.

Nightmare Dirk stormed into the apartment, furious and high. He ranted, called her every foul name he could think of, said he'd never loved her. He was only looking for sex. He didn't believe her baby was his. She was a whore. Those words stung almost more than the physical blows he'd dealt her over and over again. How could she protect the baby? Get out of his reach? When would he stop?

The physical pain hadn't made her cry out. She hadn't screamed that night. She wouldn't give Dirk the satisfaction of knowing how badly he had hurt her. This time Dirk didn't leave when he finished the beating. Instead, he loomed over her, taunting her—about Chase. It was as if he had been listening to their intimate conversations.

Nightmare Dirk screamed, "What kind of idiot are you? Do you really believe a man like Chase Merrick, a doctor to boot, wants to spend the rest of his life with a tramp?" He stormed around the bedroom ranting. Kat curled up on the floor nursing her wounds. "His first wife was an elegant lady from a fine Boston family. Why would he want some lowlife who'd lived with me, slept with me, and liked sex? What do you have to say for yourself?" He kicked her again, battering her with more profanity.

"Chase loves me. He doesn't care about my past. He loves my son too, the son you never wanted. He's a good man. He wants to marry me," she sobbed.

Nightmare Dirk laughed. It was a harsh, guttural

laugh. His tone dripped with sarcasm. "Right. I'm sure. Why would he want to marry another man's castoff and be a father to her bastard? Just wait. When he knows the whole truth, he'll just enjoy your many sexual pleasures—you are still a beautiful woman—then dump you and your snot-nosed brat. He doesn't love you. He just wants to get you in his bed. You'll see, I'm right. You aren't worthy of his love or anyone else's. You're the used-up mother of a bastard. He could do so much better."

She screamed, "You don't know. Chase loves me. I'm not worthless. You're wrong." That was the moment Emma woke her. Sobbing and trembling, she replayed the nightmare, again and again, in an endless loop of torment.

Dirk doesn't know Chase. She'd let her doubts spew out of Dirk's mouth. He was pure evil. He couldn't be right about Chase. He simply couldn't be.

Kat finally fell into a fitful sleep with the lights still on. At four a.m. her alarm jolted her fully awake. Time for work. If only the soap and water could wash away the memories of the nightmare and remove the dark circles under her eyes. Her reflection in the bathroom mirror was of a frightened woman who had been crying all night. Nothing could hide the evidence of the night of terror.

Thankfully, Emma and Timmy wouldn't see her this way. They were both still asleep. She left Emma a note on the kitchen table: *Dear Emma, Thank you for your love and concern last night. I am so lucky to have you in my life. Katrina*

Kat's shift went by quickly. Chase came across the diner, coffee to-go cup in hand, just to say he'd check

189

in on her later and squeeze her hand. She was relieved he didn't have time to sit down for breakfast. She didn't want Chase to worry, and she was sure he would if he knew she couldn't talk without crying.

Emma wanted to help, but Katrina wouldn't talk about the nightmare. She pretended everything was okay, that Dirk couldn't hurt her or the people she loved. She knew it was foolish, but if she was honest with herself about the situation, she would curl into a fetal position and never leave the bed.

She couldn't hold her breath—paralyzed with fear—until Dirk was caught. She wouldn't let him rob her of happiness. Ever again.

****

Irene was late getting to work. Timmy had already eaten and had his bath by the time Kat got home.

"Mom, you're finally here. I missed you so much today." Timmy raced to embrace her when she walked in the door. He always knew when she needed a hug. Such a precious child.

As she ate the reheated supper, Timmy chattered about his afternoon play date with Trevor at the Merricks' house.

"Now, big guy, it's way past your bedtime." Kat led him to the steps.

"Mom, I think Trevor and I met a friend of yours today. He said we could have a ride on his motorcycle anytime. It was really cool, even bigger than Dr. Chase's. Could we ride it the next time we see him? Is it okay with you?"

Her legs turned to mush. She abruptly sat on the stairs to keep from falling down. She struggled to take a deep breath and pushed down the bile rising in her throat. *Don't let him hear the fear in my voice.* She pulled Timmy onto her lap. "Where did you meet this friend of mine?"

"We were playing in Trevor's backyard. He rode his motorcycle through the back alley and came to the fence to talk to us. He seemed nice, even if he was kinda odd."

"What made him odd?" she asked quietly, almost calmly.

"He kept saying something about how I'd turned out pretty well, all things considered. What does that mean, Mom? Did he know me when I was really little?"

"No. He's never met you. Do you remember what I said about talking to strangers?" She held both his hands in her own, struggling to control the panic that engulfed her—wave after wave.

"But he's not a stranger. He said he's a really good friend of yours. He knew we moved here from Philadelphia and all about Pop Pop and Jocie. Wasn't it okay to talk to someone who knows all about me? How can he be a stranger?" Timmy cocked his head.

"No, it isn't okay. Sometimes bad people find out things about you so they can hurt you. He isn't a good man. Please, don't talk to him or anyone you don't know. He isn't a friend of mine. He's a mean person and did bad things. If he comes around again, don't stop. Run to an adult you know. Don't let him talk to Trevor or touch either of you. Promise me, okay?" She could no longer keep the tremor out of her voice.

"Gee, Mom. You're scaring me, but okay. I won't talk to him anymore. I guess that means I can't ride on his cool motorcycle either, huh?" Disappointment coated each word.

"It's good to be afraid of bad people. No, you can't ride or do anything else with him, okay? I'm serious. He isn't my friend, and he isn't yours." Kat struggled to speak without crying.

"Mom, are you sure he's a stranger? He looked kinda familiar to me."

Kat gasped. "No. No."

"Haven't I seen him before? In Philadelphia?"

If she started lying to him now, she'd lose all his trust. Forever. Kat took a deep breath and slowly exhaled. "Yes, honey. You have seen him before, but only once."

"Was he the man who hurt you and made Pop Pop go to the hospital?" Tears welled up in Timmy's eyes.

"Yes. You saw him that day. I'm so sorry." Kat hugged her son harder.

"I heard Jocie talking on the phone. Now I remember that she was talking about him, and I think about me. Is he related to us?"

What could she say? She kissed the top of Timmy's head.

"Did that man go to prison?"

"Yes. He did."

"Is he my dad?"

"Oh, Timmy. I didn't want you to ever know. I'm so sorry. You are the most important person in my life. You are the one good thing that came from him. Yes, he's your dad." Tears gushed down her cheeks.

"Don't be sad, Mom. I won't take a ride with the bad man. I won't talk to him ever. Even though he's really my dad. I promise, cross my heart." He hugged her.

"I'm sorry, honey. I love you so much."

Kat held him tightly and such a long time that he finally said, "Mom, you're choking me." Then he wriggled around until he could slip out of her arms and escape to his bedroom.

Timmy said his prayers and crawled into bed without another word about his discovery.

"Do you want to talk anymore about what happened today?"

"No, Mom. I think I want to sleep on it first. Thanks for telling me. I needed to know. I love you."

"I love you." Kat kissed him and left his room—her heart in a million pieces. Her past foolish behavior haunted her son now. Why did he ever have to remember?

****

After Timmy was in bed, Kat called Mr. Casterelli. Once again, no one in law enforcement had seen Dirk. How could she have agreed to put her son at risk? And now, Trevor too. Kat sounded harsh, but she was furious. These DEA agents didn't seem very competent. Not from where she sat.

Emma's landline rang. It was Chase. "Is Timmy all right?"

"Yes. Is Trevor?"

"Yes, was the man on the motorcycle Timmy's dad?"

"Yes. It was Dirk Crowe. I'm more frightened than ever. None of the authorities who are supposed to be monitoring him saw anything. How can one man in a small town become invisible almost at will?"

"I don't know. I gave Trevor the stranger danger speech again. He seemed to think he was okay because he wasn't alone. I had to explain someone bad could hurt both of them. There isn't necessarily safety in numbers." Chase sounded exasperated.

"I never would have let them play together if I'd known this would happen. I'm so sorry to drag Trevor into the middle of this."

"You never told me his father rode a motorcycle. Is that why you were upset with me when I offered to teach Timmy how to ride?"

For a minute, no one spoke. Then she broke down sobbing. "Yes, it was. I know you're not like him at all. I'm sorry. Now, I have an even bigger problem. Chase, Timmy didn't know who his father was until earlier this evening. He pieced it all together, and I couldn't lie to him. I'm doubly worried for him and for Trevor, and I'm worried something could happen to you. Dirk targets the people around me. I should have thought it out more before I agreed to do it. Forgive me for putting you in the middle of all this."

"Katrina, what did you agree to do?"

"It's complicated. I can't say anything more right now. I'm sorry."

"You can always talk to me. I'm good at keeping secrets. I'm here to help you. We can talk tomorrow. This situation is fraying everyone's nerves. Good night." Chase hung up.

She paced across the living room. Tears freely flowed down her cheeks.

"Please be very careful, Emma. Leave the doors locked, even when you're in the house, and run the garage door down as soon as you leave the house and as soon as you are back in. Mr. Casterelli said they'll add another agent to watch Chase's house from the alley. Dirk's playing a game—daring them to catch him. I'm afraid the next time he'll hurt someone. And I'm worried Timmy will be drawn to him now that he knows Dirk is his father. That could have disastrous consequences."

"I understand."

"I didn't handle Timmy's questions well. I'm at a loss about what to do. How can I cope?"

"Have faith, dear. Pray."

Chapter Nineteen

Buzz. Buzz. Buzz. Kat walked over from the rocking chair to turn off the alarm. Wide awake since Dirk slunk back into her dreams at two a.m. This time he boasted about his son Timmy and how he would never let him be another man's child. No matter what he had to do to prevent it. It was as if he had been sitting on the stairs next to Timmy when he learned the truth about Dirk. She made herself wake up so he couldn't continue terrorizing her. It would be an extra long shift today. Too long for her faint, still slipping grasp on sanity.

The drawn face in the mirror clearly showed she hadn't slept, especially the dark circles under her eyes. Her usual smile was nowhere to be found. If this continued, she definitely would have to buy some makeup. Gran would've said Kat looked like something dragged in from the alley. She would have been right.

****

Kat had Miss Shumacher's pot of tea waiting at her spot when the unsmiling woman reached the counter. "Good morning. Are you having your usual today?" She tried to sound more cheerful than she felt.

"Well, don't you look a sight this morning," Miss Shumacher said harshly. "Look like you've been out cattin' around all night instead resting up for work. That's what's wrong with young people today! No work ethic."

"For your information, Althea Shumacher, she was not, as you so rudely said, 'cattin' around.' She was here working double shifts," Chase announced as he sat down. "Some people have more problems to deal with than you do. Where's your Christian charity?"

"Well, I never..." Miss Shumacher sounded incredulous. "Of course, my usual. Quickly. I have things to do today."

Kat mouthed "thank you" to Chase and went to the back to put in both their orders. *Miss Althea certainly is a piece of work. Initially, she couldn't tell me from Vicky, but let me lose some sleep, and she jumps right on it.*

After the morning rush, Muriel came to her. "Kat, are you feeling well? You look like you've been pulled backward through a knothole."

"I'm sorry, Muriel. Not sleeping well. I'll be fine after a cup of coffee. Then I'll be ready for the lunch crowd. You're sweet to worry about me," Kat assured her employer. The coffee helped.

Irene called in. After checking with Emma, Kat volunteered to work late. She called Mr. Casterelli to insist an agent stay parked outside Emma's in plain view. Muriel said she wasn't sure Kat needed to work another long shift. But she insisted. She remembered Susie's first-day advice and didn't sit down. She kept moving. Even when every muscle in her body screamed to stop.

The lunch crowd bled over into the dinner one. Soon, it was time to close for the day. There were a couple of late, lingering tables. It was ten o'clock before she got home. She hoped being totally exhausted would induce sleep.

"I was ready to send out scouts to find you, my dear," Emma greeted her at the door. "I put Timmy to bed about thirty minutes ago, but he said he was staying awake to kiss you good night."

"Thanks, Emma. I'll stick my head in to see him before I go to bed. I don't know what I would do without you."

"I'm glad I can help. Oh, I almost forgot. Chase called twice for you. He's worried, thought you looked extra tired this morning. I can see why."

"Thanks, Emma. It's kind of late now. I'll talk to him when he comes in the diner in the morning. I appreciate you taking the messages. I have got to sleep tonight, or I'll drop." She went upstairs.

Timmy was awake when she crept into his room.

"Hey, my little man, it's way past time for you to be asleep." She pushed the blond curls off his forehead.

"I'm thinking. Mom, I don't need a dad anymore," he said softly.

"I thought you wanted a dad to teach you man secrets."

"I don't want to ever have a dad, if it's *HIM*." Tears ran down the child's cheeks.

"Don't worry, honey. Dirk Crowe will never really be your dad."

"But you told me he was. Wasn't that true?"

"He is your biological father. He hasn't the right to be called your dad."

"What's the difference? I don't understand."

"Everyone who is born needs two things—a woman to be the mother and a man to be the father—it takes both of them to make a baby."

"I know, remember, Trevor told me."

"Oh, I'd forgotten. Once the baby is born, the man who helps the mom feed and care for the baby, who plays games with him, takes the baby places, hugs and kisses him, becomes the baby's dad."

"Like Pop Pop was for you."

"Exactly."

"Dr. Chase is a good dad for Trevor, isn't he?"

"Yes, I think so."

"Trevor is such a lucky duck."

"He is, but I promise, someday you'll have a real dad who loves you and loves me. I'll marry that man, and we'll be a family. Do you understand?" she gently asked her son.

"I think so. I'm glad the bad man won't be my real dad. I wouldn't want a dad who would hurt you. Not ever. I'm a lucky duck too. I have you for my mom. Thanks for explaining. I think I can sleep now." Timmy sat up and hugged her.

"Good night. I love you."

"Love you."

He lay down. He looked so angelic—blond curls spread halo-like on his pillow. He needed a haircut. He wasn't a baby anymore, as he was always quick to remind her.

Timmy was the only reason she kept going when all she wanted to do was to curl into the fetal position and forget the rest of the world until this was all over.

After a hot shower, she read until her eyes could no longer focus. She finally turned off the bedside lamp a few minutes after midnight.

Right on schedule, Dirk made his appearance at two a.m. This time he was not beating her, only taunting her. Saying no one would ever love her once they knew the whole truth about Timmy. Why would Dr. Merrick want a woman like Kat to be the mother to his son?

The alarm buzzed. She was still awake. What if Dirk was right and Chase didn't love her once he knew the truth? That evil man had to get out of her nightmares, out of her head, and out of Wisconsin. She couldn't keep going much longer.

****

Chase took his usual seat at the end of the counter. Worry etched deep lines across Katrina's face, accented by the dark circles under her eyes. That man's menacing was clearly taking its toll.

I know she's worried about her ex-husband...and all of us. But I have the feeling something else is going on. How can I make her understand I'd do anything I possibly can to help?

"How's my favorite server this morning?" Chase asked in an overly cheerful tone.

Katrina managed a weak smile. "Not so great, as I am sure you can see. But don't worry. As Gran used to say, this too shall pass. What can I get you?"

"My usual breakfast and coffee, please."

When Kat brought his check, Chase suggested, "What if I pick Timmy up tomorrow morning for brunch with the family? We're headed out to explore some caves. He could come with us and spend the night. On Sunday, he could go home with you after church and dinner. It's at our house this week."

"Chase, that would be wonderful. He'd love going spelunking. What a marvelous adventure. He'll be so excited. What time should he be ready tomorrow morning?"

"I'll pick him up at eight thirty. We'll see you here for brunch. Hope you get some sleep tonight. Take care of yourself." Chase squeezed her hand, then left.

Irene's mom was back in the hospital, and Kat volunteered to work through supper. Phyllis could close alone.

Susie came up to Kat about one o'clock. "Look, girl, I know you're beat. You've covered for me lots of times. Rich went back to work this morning. Why don't I cover Irene's shift tonight? Go home and sleep."

Kat started to protest, but the slightest breeze would probably knock her over. "Thank you. You're right."

Emma and Timmy were delighted to see her home in time for supper. She couldn't have commented on the conversation at the table. She nodded and ate. Timmy hopped up when everyone was done and volunteered to do dishes with Nana.

Kat sat down on the couch and leafed through a magazine. When dishes were finished, Emma came in with a small hot-pink gift bag and handed it to her. "What's the occasion?" Kat asked.

"I saw this today, and it screamed Katrina to me. You'll see why when you open it."

The bag had lavender-scented bubble bath, soap, and lotion with a CD called *Sounds to Relax By* that had nature sounds like waves, rain, and birds along with peaceful classical music—at least that was what the cover said. It was packaged as the ultimate relaxation kit complete with chamomile tea "to help you sleep."

"If this doesn't do it, nothing will. Thank you, Emma. You are so good to me."

"Mom, you mean you *want* to go to sleep? That's pretty weird," Timmy interjected.

"Go on upstairs and get in the tub. A CD player is on the shelf in your sitting room. Fill a hot tub and put on the music. I'll put water on for tea and bring it up when I hear you in your room," Emma instructed. "Timmy and I can make sure he gets to bed on time."

Kat didn't argue. The lavender scent calmed her as she soaked in the tub, tension seeping away. The music *was* peaceful. It seemed to live up to the album cover claims.

Knock. Knock. "Katrina, are you okay?" It was Emma.

Kat's head lolled to one side on the inflatable pillow. Stone cold water. The music had stopped. "I fell asleep in the tub. Thanks for checking on me. I'll be out in a minute."

When Kat got to her bedroom, she saw the pot of tea and cup that Emma left her with a little note saying *Enjoy, go back to sleep. Blessings, Emma.*

How wonderful to be cared for so well. How lucky they were to find Gran's dear friend.

After she finished the soothing, hot tea, Kat brushed her teeth and settled under the covers hoping to fall back asleep. An hour later, the arms of Morpheus still did not hold her. She got out of bed and began reading until she couldn't focus her eyes any longer. Still sleep would not come. When her clock blinked two thirty, she lay back down. She'd made it past two a.m. Maybe there would be no nightmare tonight.

Chapter Twenty

A little after nine, a party of five was seated in Katrina's area. Emma joined Claire, Trevor, Timmy, and Chase for brunch. Katrina walked up to the table. "This looks like a very hungry crew."

"Hi! I sure am. We have to tank up so we won't run out of energy in the caves today." Timmy grinned at his mom. "Two chocolate chip pancakes with two pieces of bacon. And, Mom, could I have a little extra whipping cream on top, please," he ordered enthusiastically.

Trevor's order was exactly what Timmy ordered. No surprise there. Those two were truly two peas in a pod. Claire and Emma had a little lighter fare, spinach and feta omelets, and Chase had his usual.

Claire and Emma were going to a class at Knitting Pretty while the boys were off exploring the cave out on the Schuster farm about ten miles from town. Timmy was thrilled to be included in the father-son adventure.

Chase bought breakfast for the whole crew. On the back of the ticket, he wrote: *I'll be thinking of you all day. Hope you will be thinking of me too.*

About three o'clock, Emma and Claire stopped by after their knitting class for some homemade blueberry pie and a cup of coffee. They had some new yarn from one of the local spinners who raised sheep and alpacas. Emma had skeins of a natural dark brown alpaca. Claire had some mixed Merino wool dyed in shades of blue. They both had new sweater patterns to try with the homespun.

At dinner time, the boys and Chase stopped for burgers and milkshakes. They were a little scruffy looking after spending the day running through caves. They'd enjoyed a picnic lunch in the early afternoon and were starving according to Timmy and Trevor. It sounded like the day had been a perfect adventure for two little boys and one big boy.

For the second time, Chase left money for the bill and tip on the table. His note on the back of the ticket said: *Thanks for sharing Timmy with me today. He's a great kid. Looking forward to seeing you tomorrow.* She handed the money and the check to Muriel at the cash register.

"I almost hate putting these love letters on the spindle," Muriel said laughing. "I have the feeling I may be looking for another waitress in the not-too-distant future. The new one is really good, but I think she's going to be under a doctor's intensive care very soon." Muriel's eyes twinkled. Her face crinkled into a broad smile.

Kat smiled and went back to work. *It seems like everyone is certain Chase and I will be married, everyone but me. It's too soon. There is so much Chase doesn't know yet.*

Emma was still awake when Kat got home. They sat down to cookies and milk before going to bed. "Thanks for waiting up for me. Did you have a good day?"

"My dear, it was lovely. When you have the time, I'll show you the new patterns we got in class today.

You may want to use the scarf one for Chase—it's very masculine looking, not at all frilly," Emma said cheerfully.

"It was so kind of Chase to include Timmy in their Saturday outing. He's such a good dad. Timmy always loved tagging along with Pop. Even going to the hardware store with his grandpa seemed to delight him. He misses having regular adult male contact."

"I know Claire worried about Chase not having enough male influences when he was growing up. Maybe that's why he goes out of his way to include Timmy," Emma suggested. "Of course, maybe he's just trying to get in good with him because he loves Timmy's mother."

Kat's ears grew warm. "I believe Chase does love my son. But getting a good father for Timmy isn't enough. If I marry him, it has to be because he loves me completely. I have to be worthy of his love. He doesn't know everything about my past. Neither do you, Emma."

"My dear, I believe I know more than you give me credit for. Like the fact that you and Dirk Crowe were never married, even though he is Timmy's father."

"I never told you I wasn't married. I've been so ashamed. Everyone feels sorry for me being a divorced, single mom, when I'm really an unwed mother. I've made a string of bad choices with forever consequences. I never intended to deceive anyone. I just wasn't ready to dump out all my dirty laundry for everyone to pass judgment on."

"My dear, you never once said to me that Dirk Crowe was your husband. You have always carefully referred to him only as Timmy's father and ignored any references to him being your husband or ex-husband."

"Emma, are you ashamed of me? Embarrassed to have me living with you? Chase doesn't know I've never been married. How am I going to tell him?"

"You are shortchanging me and Chase. Most of all you're not giving yourself any slack. Why don't you think about all the good that has happened since your arrival here? Stop worrying about the past long enough to love yourself half as much as we do," Emma gently chided her. "Once Dirk Crowe is gone, you'll be able to marry the man you're meant to be with."

"You're right. Dirk is terrifying. He's driving me crazy."

"I believe Dirk Crowe will be captured soon. Then Chase will leave no doubt in your mind about how he feels. Come on. We need to go to bed. Morning will be here all too quickly."

At two a.m., Nightmare Dirk Crowe tried to slink back into her dreams. Dream Katrina (yes, Katrina, not Kat) stood in front of a large, red brick house with her arms folded across her chest in a defiant stance. When he tried to come into the yard, she said, "Get out! You're not welcome here." To her surprise, he shrugged his shoulders, got on his motorcycle, and left.

She slept the whole night through. Nightmare Dirk Crowe seemed to be finally gone for good. If only real life would follow suit. Soon.

The boys were already in Children's Church when Katrina joined Chase in the young adults class. His face lit up with a broad smile when she came through the doorway. He stood when she came across the room and pulled her into a brief hug. "Glad to see you. You look well rested this morning."

"I've slept the whole night. I'm back on track." She smiled.

Dinner included a detailed review of spelunking at Schuster's cave, wading in the creek, and spending the night together. The boys were like twins separated at birth—finishing each other's sentences and breaking out in childish laughter at a shared joke no one else could understand.

"Emma, you and Mom are the dynamic duo of Sunday dinners. If I'm not careful, I'm going to start gaining weight. You two spoil all of us," Chase said as he pushed away from the dinner table.

"I love cooking for an appreciative audience," Emma said. "I'm glad Timmy and Katrina moved in so I didn't forget how to cook. It isn't much fun to fix meals for only one person."

"I know exactly what you mean," Claire chimed in. "When I lived alone, I ate a lot of sandwiches and soup because it didn't seem worth the effort to cook an entire meal. It's nice for two old women, like us, to still be needed. Besides, I'll always cook for anyone who cleans up for me. I can't stand doing dishes," she added with a twinkle in her eyes.

"I think that's our cue," Kat said as she took a load of dirty dishes to the kitchen, followed closely by Chase with an armload too.

As Chase picked up the dish towel, he said, "I love Sunday dinner. This is a very nice habit. If I were a little kitten, I'd be purring very contentedly and loudly."

"I know exactly what you're talking about." Katrina made a purring sound and began washing dishes. "I like our life here in Lansdale."

"Boy, am I glad to hear you say that. I wasn't sure where things with us were going in the middle of the week."

"Dad, we need you to come back in the living room," Trevor called out.

Trevor stood in the middle of the floor with his hands behind his back. "Come on, Dad. Sit right here in the big chair."

"What's the occasion?" Chase asked as he sat down.

"It's Father's Day!" Trevor shouted gleefully and plopped a not-perfectly-wrapped gift in Chase's lap. "Open it."

Chase picked up the gift and held it to his ear. "I don't hear anything. It's kind of heavy."

"Just open it!" Trevor insisted.

Chase opened the package. It was a paper weight made from clay with the words "*World's Best Dad*" printed on it. "I love it. I have the perfect spot for it on my desk." Trevor beamed. Chase hugged him.

Timmy waited off to the side watching the father-son embrace. He brushed a tear away, then spoke. "Dr. Chase, I know I'm not your son, but I have a present for you too."

Trevor pulled his friend over to his dad. "Wait 'til you see what Timmy made! It's way cool!"

Timmy handed Chase a box sloppily wrapped in the comics page of the paper. He unwrapped it. "Timmy, you're an artist. This looks exactly like the ambulance that you and Trevor rode in for the parade. Wow! You're right, Trevor, it's way cool!"

"I'm glad you could tell what it was." Timmy grinned. "Do you have a perfect spot for it on your desk too?"

"You bet I do!" Chase pulled both boys into a hug. "I'm the luckiest dad I know. Thank you both."

The boys raced outside to the sandbox. At the door, they turned and shouted in unison, "Happy Father's Day!"

Emma and Claire took their coffees to the patio leaving Katrina and Chase alone to finish the kitchen chores. Tears streamed down Katrina's face.

Chase put down his towel and took her wet hands in his. "Hey, no crying unless they're happy tears! That's the rule here."

"Timmy wants a good dad so much. It's worse since he learned about Dirk. He wants a good dad like Trevor has."

"Why don't we give him what he wants?"

"If only everything were that easy. Dirk is still at large. I've made commitments to help him be captured. He knows where I work and live. We probably shouldn't even be coming here. It puts all of you more at risk. I don't know what I was thinking, other than that I want Timmy to be able to see Trevor. To have a normal friendship."

"Who have you made commitments to? Why?"

"I can't disclose that information. I would tell you if I could."

"Other people's demands don't matter. Don't you want to be with me? Why would you put our chance for happiness on hold for that beast?" Chase shook his head.

"I'm sorry to interrupt." Timmy stood just inside the kitchen door. "Mom, I don't feel good. I lost my happy. I need to go home."

Katrina knelt in front of her son. "How long have you been standing there?"

Timmy shrugged his shoulders.

"It doesn't matter. You don't need to apologize. Dr. Chase and I are finished with the dishes. Did you tell Trevor you were leaving?"

He nodded.

"Sorry, Chase, but we need to go home."

"I understand. I'll bring Emma back a little later so you two can be alone."

Katrina and Timmy left the kitchen hand in hand.

As she pulled in the driveway, Timmy asked, "Did the bad man ever get a Father's Day present from me?"

"No. It was very sweet of you to make a present for Dr. Chase. He couldn't love you any more if you were Trevor's brother from birth. We're both lucky to have him in our lives."

"I don't understand, Mom. If that's true, why can't he be my real dad? You love him, don't you?"

She hesitated a moment. "Yes. I do love him. But there are other issues."

"You mean the bad man could still hurt us."

"I hope not."

"Being a grown-up is always complicated, isn't it, Mom?"

She hugged him—*if you only knew*—"Let's go in and call Pop Pop."

They walked into the kitchen. Kat handed the phone to her son. Timmy hit the "1" on his mother's speed dial. "Hi, Jocie. It's me, Timmy. May I please speak to Pop Pop?...Oh, when will he be home?...Please tell him I called to tell my grandpa Happy Father's Day...Yea, she's right here." He put his hand over the microphone and said, "Pop Pop's out. She wants to talk to you."

Kat took the phone. "Why don't you go outside? I'll be right out to push you on the swing."

"Hi, Jocie. Where's Pop?"

"Why? Are you going to tell him something else that will upset him?"

"No, what do you mean?"

"You couldn't wait to spill the beans about your scumbag lover showing up in Wisconsin. Haven't you caused enough worry for your father? Do you want him to end up back in the hospital?"

"I didn't blurt it out. Pop asked a direct question, and I answered it. I do not lie to my father."

"So what else did you tell him?"

"Nothing."

"He told me you wanted to come home."

There was no point in correcting Jocelyn. "We talked briefly about that possibility. I believe it's safer for us to stay put here," Kat calmly explained.

"Safer. And your *only* option," Jocelyn fired back.

"What do you mean? Pop told me we could always come home."

"You took my money. That was one of the conditions, remember?"

Kat didn't respond.

"If you even *think* about moving back here, I'll make your life miserable."

Kat bit her tongue. Like Jocelyn hadn't already done that—for years. "Jocelyn, I just want to talk to Pop to wish him Happy Father's Day. When will he be home?"

"Too late to talk to you."

Dial tone. Jocelyn had hung up.

Kat went outside and joined her son in the afternoon sunshine. "Honey, did Jocie tell you when Pop Pop would be home?"

"Yes, really late. He and Uncle John went to see a Phillies double header. I bet if I'd been there, they would have taken me too. Mom, how much longer are we going to be on this adventure?"

"I'm not sure. How about I push you on the swing for a while?"

"Great idea."

The rest of the afternoon was spent playing outside on the swing set, a little whiffle ball batting practice, and blowing bubbles. After his bath, she pulled out his favorite story book. They took turns reading aloud on alternating pages. She wasn't sure how much he was reading and how much he had memorized. It didn't matter. They snuggled together in his bed just being a normal mom with her little boy.

After prayers, she tucked Timmy in and kissed him good night. Before she turned out the light, he said, "Thanks, Mom."

"For what?"

"My happy came back."

"I think mine did too. I love you, little man." She smiled with tear-filled eyes.

"Love you."

Chapter Twenty-One

Before she left for work, Kat called the garage to leave Pop a belated Happy Father's Day message. She hadn't gotten a call back last night. She doubted Jocelyn even gave him the message.

Gone to the Shore. Was it almost the Fourth of July? Pop had reminded her about the trip the last time they talked. Their annual vacation. No way to leave a message at the garage. Pop was old school. No cell phone. She had no idea what Jocelyn's number was, like she'd take any calls from Kat.

****

Susie brought Chase his coffee. "Oh, good morning, Susie. Is Katrina okay?"

"Yep, Doc. She asked for the back this morning. It's no problem for me, so we switched. Doris is on vacation all week, so we're really hoppin'. What'll it be?"

Chase put in his order and scanned the restaurant looking for Katrina. *Her snake of an ex-husband needs to crawl out of her life. The sooner, the better. And whatever else is eating at her needs to be resolved. If only she'd let me help.*

Susie passed Kat at the kitchen window saying, "Doc asked about you, just so you know." Kat turned from the window balancing a full tray and nearly ran into Chase.

"Yes, Doc did ask about you," Chase said smiling, noticing the worry in her face. "What's happened? Was Timmy okay after you went home last night? I thought that would help both of you."

"I'm okay and Timmy's better. He's homesick for Philly. Truth be told, so am I. Chase, I'm sorry, I'm really swamped. Can we talk later?" She started around him. "You can call me tonight."

"Sure, I will. Take care of yourself." Chase left for the hospital. *There is something else she hasn't told me. How can I get her to trust me enough to let me help?*

****

A motorcycle in the driveway. A red helmet on the seat. Someone was sitting in the shadows on the front porch swing. *Take a breath, Kat.* She pulled out her phone to call 911, then the man rose and walked toward her.

"Chase." She exhaled. "Is something wrong?"

He reached for her hand. "Yes, something major. The woman I love went out of her way to avoid me this morning. I thought we were getting to the crux of the matter yesterday before Timmy needed to go home. Something is not right. We need to talk."

She anxiously looked around. "Let's go in the house."

Emma was fixing dinner, and Timmy was playing on the living room floor. He jumped up to hug his mom.

"Hi ya, Dr. Chase."

"Hi, Timmy. Looks like you're having fun."

"Yep."

"Mind if I borrow your mom for a little bit?"

"Sure, Dr. Chase, where are you going?"

214

"Just out for a little drive and a bite to eat."

Kat quickly changed clothes and told Emma she was going with Chase. She wasn't certain exactly what he had in mind or when they'd be back.

Chase motioned for Katrina to get on behind him on the motorcycle. Tears filled her eyes. "No way."

"Oh, yeah, sorry, this Romeo forgot." He got off the bike.

"Not the least bit funny. I'll go with you. If we take my car. You drive since you know where we're going."

"I'd be happy to."

Chase drove to the Purple Cow Drive-In on the edge of town. He parked on the far side of the lot, next to a lonely picnic table. They walked over to the window to place their order, then back to the picnic table.

Katrina shook her head. "I'm sorry, I've made such a mess of things—my life, my son's life, and now, I've put you and your family in danger. Timmy loves it here, but he's so homesick that he asked me when our adventure would be over. When we left home, I told him we were going on an adventure to make it more exciting than scary. I had no idea how all this would unfold. It would be better for you to forget all about me. I'm beginning to believe Dirk Crowe is going to plague me forever."

"Too late. You made me fall in love with you, so now you're stuck with me. When your issues are resolved, I hope we'll be together. Permanently. You are staying in Lansdale, aren't you?" Chase smiled, hoping to ease the tension between them.

The loudspeaker on the pole beside them announced "*Order 63 Ready for pickup.*" Chase said,

"That's us. I'll go get the order. Stay right here. I'll only be a minute."

Immediately after Chase left, a shadow fell across the picnic table from behind her. She shuddered. *His* cologne. She tried to get up from the table looking frantically toward the window where Chase waited in line to pick up their food. A hand clamped on her shoulder and forced her back into a sitting position.

"Isn't this a cozy little scene. Out on a date?" Dirk's voice oozed hatefulness.

"Get out. I'll scream," she struggled to whisper.

"Don't worry. I'm leaving. After you give me your car keys."

She started to check her pockets, then remembered that Chase had the keys. "He drove."

"Then I guess you'll have to introduce us. I need those keys." The glint in Dirk's eyes burned holes in her skin. She itched. She couldn't look away.

What was taking Chase so long? Finally, he started toward their table. "Dirk, let me go get the keys. You don't need to talk to him."

"Not on your life. Stay right where you are. You're not getting away from me this time." Dirk dug nicotine-yellowed fingernails into her shoulder inflaming the old injury, riveting her in place.

Chase approached the table slowly. He put down the sacks and drinks. "Who are you?"

"The better question is who are you?" Dirk snarled. "The latest guy enjoying her bed? She's quite a little wild cat, isn't she?"

"Don't say another word. Get out of here." Chase strode closer to him.

Dirk let go. Kat collapsed with her head on the

table, her shoulder throbbing. He backed away from the table two steps. "No one will be hurt. I only want the car keys. No big deal."

"She's already hurt." Chase sat next to Katrina on the bench. "This is Dirk, right?"

"You win a prize, Sherlock. The keys." Dirk took a step toward Chase.

"No."

"You have no business in the middle of this. It's between us." He swung around and glared at Kat. "Tell him what happens when I'm not happy. The keys now or there will be hell to pay."

"Chase, please, give him what he wants. I don't want to be hurt more or for you to be."

"At least someone around here has sense." Dirk held out his hand.

Flashing red lights lit the sky behind Dirk's head. She quickly looked away, hoping he hadn't seen them.

Chase ignored the outstretched palm. "It's easy for you to beat a woman half your size into submission." He stood. "I am not half your size. And you have no idea what happens when *I'm* not happy."

Dirk reached toward him. "I'm not leaving without those keys." Then he saw the flashing lights. He ran into the woods shouting over his shoulder, "This isn't over."

Two patrol cars raced past. One car went to block Dirk's exit from the other side of the woods. The second car stopped to question them. One of the officers followed Dirk on foot down the path into the woods.

Chase explained that he'd seen Dirk when he got to the window to pick up their food. He had the clerk call

911 and hand the phone to him. He asked for a silent approach, hoping this time they would capture Crowe. The dispatcher said all available resources were on their way to participate in the manhunt. This was the best opportunity to capture Crowe they'd had in three weeks.

Katrina tried to eat but was afraid it would come back up. She sipped on her milkshake staring intently into the woods as if she were willing the authorities to find Dirk.

"Katrina, I haven't heard the motorcycle leave. Have you?"

"No, but I never heard him come either. He had a hold of me before I had time to react to smelling his cologne."

"Why did he want your car? What's going on?"

"It's my mess, Chase. I need to fix it."

"Was he going to take you with him? What did he say to you before I got here?"

"Nothing. Nothing at all. If I'd had the keys, you never would have met. Please, just let it go."

Chief Davis pulled his patrol car into the parking lot next to their table. "No one has seen him yet, but we have the area surrounded. They're loading his motorcycle on a trailer and taking it to the impound lot. Maybe we'll be able to catch him if he's on foot."

"Are you certain he's still in the woods?" Katrina asked fearfully.

"We were here quickly. There were agents in place on the other side of the woods before the patrol car approached you. He has to still be in there," Chief Davis surmised.

Chase didn't press her for more details. He reached

over to hold her hand. She shook her head. They walked back to the car. Katrina grimaced when she tried to fasten her seat belt.

"He's hurt you. Let's stop in the Emergency Room."

"No. I just want to go home. I'll be okay after a warm shower."

Awkward silence filled the close space inside the car. Chase parked in Emma's driveway and got out. She stayed in her seat so long that he opened the passenger door.

"Are you going to be all right? Are we?"

"I don't know how to answer those questions. I have no idea what is going to come out of all of this."

"That's not very encouraging. What do you want to have happen? How would you write the ending to this story?"

"Chase, I want you to step back and let me get through this. Then we can talk about endings."

"Or new beginnings?" he asked hopefully.

"Yes, if we can wait to finish this conversation until a less eventful day. I'm totally exhausted."

She slowly got out of the car. Chase walked by her side to the porch.

"Katrina, I just have one more question. I'd like an honest answer."

"What?"

"How did your ex-husband know where to find you and his son?"

She took a deep breath. Then another. "He's not my ex-husband." She turned toward the door.

"He's what? Is that why you told him where to find you? Why would you want to be with someone who hurts you?"

Katrina whirled around. S L A P. "You are an idiot. I never wanted to see that animal again. I came halfway across the country to escape him. I was trying to keep my son safe. Get away from me." She pulled open the door and dashed inside.

The motorcycle revved up. She shuddered involuntarily. She leaned against the door unable to stop the burst of tears rolling down her face and dripping off her chin.

Emma got off the sofa and walked toward her. "My dear, is everything all right? From the look on your face, I don't believe those are happy tears."

Katrina fell into Emma's embrace with heaving sobs. "Where's Timmy?"

"He's in bed."

"Dirk found us. Chase managed to alert the authorities. Dirk told Chase the foulest things about me, all true but horrid. I thought they were going to come to blows, but the police arrived and he got away. They're hunting for him in the woods behind the Purple Cow, and they've impounded his motorcycle."

"I'm sure that was traumatic. But surely, not worthy of all those tears. Are you in pain? You're holding your arm like you've hurt your shoulder again," Emma asked.

"I'm not crying from the pain. Or even Dirk meeting Chase. Emma, I lost it, completely. I don't understand how he could think that. I couldn't stop myself. He'll never forgive me."

"Katrina, Chase is a man of strong faith. I'm sure there is nothing you could do that he wouldn't forgive."

"I slapped him. Hard."

"Why would you attack Chase?"

"I'm not sure I know exactly. He asked questions I couldn't answer. He doesn't understand why I can't commit to him yet. The final straw was he accused me of telling Dirk where to find us because I wanted to be back with him for some reason."

"I know you did not tell that beast where you were. You've made every effort to keep Timmy and yourself safe. Katrina, who did tell him where you were?"

"I'm afraid that's part of the reason I slapped Chase. I'm angry at myself for not asking the question when Dirk first showed up here. The only people who knew where we were going are you, Pop, Jocie, and my Uncle John. No one else."

"I know you don't want to hear this, but doesn't it have to be someone in your family?"

"If that's true, I won't be able to go home, and if Chase doesn't want me to stay here, then what?"

"We won't solve it tonight. Timmy is tucked in. You need to go to bed too." Emma kissed her cheek. "I know it looks bleak, but this is going to work out. I can feel it in my heart. That evil man will be captured, and you will make up with Chase. Go to bed, dear. My love and prayers go with you."

Timmy was sound asleep and didn't stir when she kissed him and said good night.

As Kat closed her eyes, she heard the sound of a motorcycle in the distance. It couldn't be Dirk. His bike was in the impound lot. But he was still out there. Looking for her. Nothing had changed, except that now he knew who Chase was and had a score to settle with him.

Chapter Twenty-Two

Chase stood on the porch trying to figure out what had just happened. He couldn't believe it. Katrina had slapped him. The lingering stinging in his cheek proved it. Why? What was the real reason for the assault? What was she not telling? She said he wasn't her ex. *Is she still married to that cretin?* He hated to walk away without any explanation, but it seemed to be the best option at this moment.

Chase got on the motorcycle and drove slowly home. He'd have to address this in the morning. Or maybe not. He couldn't force Katrina to tell him the truth if she was more afraid of something or someone else than she was of losing him.

****

How could it be four a.m. so soon? Dirk was back in her nightmares. The shower couldn't wash away the evidence of a too little sleep night. The reinjured shoulder throbbed. Doris was off all week. She had to go in and help Susie with the morning rush. She stuck the shoulder immobilizer in her purse. If it got too bad, she'd strap it on. She'd go to the urgent care clinic when her shift was over.

Chase came in for a to-go coffee and breakfast sandwich. She was afraid she'd still be able to see the outline of her handprint on his cheek. He paid Muriel at the register and left. He never looked in her direction.

At all. She couldn't blame him.
****

Dr. Merrick spoke to the shirtless man sitting on the exam table. "Mr. Miller, it looks like a hairline fracture of your forearm. Nothing shows yet on the x-ray. The MRI confirmed it. Sorry for the delay in getting it done. We had to contact the insurance manager at your employer to get approval. It's getting harder and harder to get more expensive services done."

"Sure hurts like the dickens."

"It's going to for several weeks. I need you to wear this compression sleeve and do not lift with this arm for about a month. You should ice it down if the pain is too much. I'll give you a higher dose of ibuprofen to take if the basic one doesn't help. How long are you in town?"

"Oh, I'm probably leaving tomorrow. I was just here fishing, and if I can't use my arm, I can't fish."

"You are supposed to check in with your insurance manager when you get home. They'll probably have another MRI done in a month or so to be sure you're healing properly."

"Thanks, Doc."

The nurse came in to help the patient get his shirt back on. After Mr. Miller left, Chase pulled up his chart on the computer. Why would a fishing trip injury be filed under worker's comp? He was from Philadelphia. Where was a spot around here so exceptional that you would travel to Wisconsin for fishing?
****

Kat made it through the morning without the sling. Shortly after she put it on, Muriel called Irene to come in early so Kat could get her shoulder checked. She drove one-handed to the clinic. Dr. Raymond was working today. She specifically requested to see him.

Kat tried to get comfortable on the exam table. The door opened. "Good morning, Mrs. Russell. What seems to be the problem this morning?" the doctor asked, not looking up from the paperwork on his clipboard.

Kat gasped. "I asked for Dr. Raymond."

"I'm caught up and he's not. Should I move on to my next patient?" Dr. Merrick stared at her.

"No. I'm sorry. I just thought it might be awkward for us to see one another so soon after last night."

"You were right. It is incredibly awkward." He frowned when he saw the sling. "You didn't tell me the truth. You weren't all right last night. And since you had a sling already, I'm guessing this isn't the first time he did this to you."

"You're right on both counts. I can't raise my arm above my head. It pops and clicks when I move it. Last time my shoulder was dislocated, I couldn't move it at all."

Chase carefully examined her, constantly asking what movement hurt running through a complete range of motion exercises. "It's not dislocated. You've strained the muscle this time. Ibuprofen and ice will help deaden any pain. Don't lift or reach and be careful with your sleeping position. You should wear the immobilizer as much as possible. No driving."

"I can manage driving one-handed. I did it all the way from Philadelphia to Lansdale."

"I'm telling you the normal precautions. You're the patient. You can choose to heed my advice or not."

"I'm not trying to be difficult, Chase. I was simply letting you know I understand what needs to be done. I wouldn't have come in at all if Muriel hadn't insisted," she explained.

"I heard that they didn't capture Dirk Crowe last night."

"I know."

"Katrina, who were the agents who participated in the manhunt last night?"

"I'm not sure who you mean." She wouldn't look at him.

"Chief Davis referenced them being in place prior to the patrol cars coming over to us. Remember?"

"Did you ask him?"

"I'm asking you. You are right in the middle of this in some way that you won't trust me enough to tell me about. What is going on?"

Katrina took a deep breath. "They're Feds, DEA agents."

"And what's your connection to Drug Enforcement? Are you an agent?"

She laughed weakly. "Nothing like that."

"Katrina, we have a lot to discuss. You're right about me not really knowing you. I've learned some new things recently. But you're still keeping secrets. Why are you reluctant to move forward in our relationship…"

Chase was interrupted by a knock at the exam room door. A nurse stuck her head in the room. "Dr. Merrick, we've got an eight-year-old who fell out of a tree. Some serious bleeding."

"I'm sorry. I need to go. The nurse will complete your discharge." Chase left the room.

****

Emma and Timmy huddled around Kat when she

came in wearing the immobilizing sling. Emma was the first to speak. "Katrina, looks like you were injured last night."

Timmy asked, "What happened, Mom? How did you get hurt?"

She didn't want to frighten either of them. "When Dr. Chase took me to eat last night, we ran into Dirk Crowe. There was an altercation, and I reinjured my shoulder. Dr. Chase fixed me up after work today. It's not as bad as last time. I'll probably only be in the sling about a week."

Timmy shook his head. "Mom, aren't they ever going to send the bad man back to prison?"

"They will when they catch him. Don't worry. It will all be okay."

Timmy muttered something she couldn't understand and sat down to play on the floor.

The clinic nurse called just before dinner to tell Kat she needed to log onto the patient portal and look at the exercise sheet posted there. She instructed her to be diligent about doing the stretches and to use ice and ibuprofen for the pain. If she had any questions, she could call the nurse back.

A call from the nurse. Not from Chase. Instructions on the patient portal. Not from Chase. Was this abrupt change to his bedside manner an indicator of things to come?

After supper, Timmy curled up on the sofa, leaned against his mom, and asked her to read the little bear stories to him so he could be brave like the stuffed animal who always helped his owner be. Soon, he fell asleep nestled against her.

Timmy got his bath, into his pajamas, and to bed

without any fuss. In fact, he barely spoke. His prayers were short: bless Mom, Nana, the Merricks, Pop Pop, and Jocie.

She bent to kiss him good night and saw a big tear rolling down his cheek. "Hey, my little man. They'll catch the bad man soon. No more tears. We're going to be okay."

"Mom, will I be a bad man when I grow up because my dad was?" Timmy asked sadly.

"Honey, people don't have to turn out like their parents. Just keep being good, like you are now."

"Will Trevor still be my best friend when he finds out the bad man was my dad? Will he still like me?"

"Trevor will still be your best friend because he loves you. He doesn't care who your father was. That's how it is when you love someone. The most important thing is the person they are—not who their parents are, or where they live, or the clothes they wear. The person you are today doesn't change because of Dirk Crowe."

"I need a dad, but I want a good one. Good night, Mom. I love you."

"I'll work on that, Timmy. I promise. I love you. Good night."

****

For three nights in a row, Kat tossed and turned most of the night. The authorities had not recaptured Dirk Crowe yet. No one had seen him since he fled into the woods behind the Purple Cow. Of course, that wasn't a reliable indicator of anything. How many times had she seen him and no one else had? Had he given up terrorizing her? Did he realize the DEA was in Lansdale? Or were the Syndicate people? Walking away would definitely be out of character for him.

Maybe meeting Chase was too much. Dirk had to realize that she wasn't as vulnerable and alone as he thought. Or was he lying low because he was planning something far more evil than what he had done so far?

Chase hadn't been in the diner since Tuesday. It was so out of character that people were asking about him. She couldn't help. She didn't know why he was missing. If she was the reason, she didn't want that widely known. It was too embarrassing. He hadn't given her a chance to apologize.

Muriel had Susie's son, Todd, come in to help her carry trays and bus tables. With Doris on vacation it was a challenge to cover without him.

Timmy greeted his mom at the door. "Guess what. We're going to the movies tomorrow."

"Who is we?" she asked tiredly.

"Trevor and Gran and Nana and Dr. Chase and you and me."

"I work until two thirty."

"I know. We're going to the four-thirty movie and then to Ray's Pizza for supper. It's okay, isn't it? Nana and Gran thought it was a great idea."

"Okay. Guess it's all settled."

****

The movie was a big hit with everyone. Lots of silly jokes for the boys and a positive overall message. There was lots of laughter that spilled over to dinner. They looked like a normal family enjoying a night out until you looked closer. There was no doubt that Trevor and Timmy were still besties. Why couldn't adults be as forgiving as kids?

Katrina had hoped for some handholding in the dark while eating popcorn. It was a little juvenile, but she craved a romantic gesture. Chase didn't sit next to her. The boys separated them, and Claire and Emma sat on the other side of Chase. He hadn't even reached across the top of the seats to touch her. And he didn't fuss about her paying for their tickets. Pretty reserved behavior for a man who declared how much he cared for her only two weeks after their first meeting.

Was she being punished for not embracing his attentions early on? Or was it because of the secrets lingering between them? Had she damaged their relationship irreparably with her impulsive violence?

Dirk was still out there. Kat couldn't commit yet. And Chase was reluctant to be alone with her. They'd never resolve their issues if they didn't talk. That was a frightening prospect. And totally unexpected. Sunday dinner with the Merricks. Doing dishes. And talking to Chase. Most of all talking. They had a lot to discuss. This uncomfortable limbo couldn't continue. She was tired of peeling pieces of eggshell off her feet.

After a "good morning" which Chase said to each person as they came in the Sunday School classroom, there was no conversation between them. KP duty couldn't come quickly enough. No one seemed to notice the two unsmiling people in the back row.

Reverend Cox's message was on the importance of forgiveness. *How timely.* She'd never heard before that you had to forgive others for God to forgive you. She had a long list of people she needed to forgive. And a lot to be forgiven for. Would Chase ever realize how necessary her secrets had been?

He sat next to her through the service but never once looked in her direction. She shivered involuntarily.

"I guess you know we're all going out to lunch today," Emma said cheerfully after they got in the car.

"No. I didn't know." Kat spat the words out. "Where are we going?"

"There's a new buffet over in Carlinville. Chase is treating us all to lunch there. Claire told me in Sunday School."

Kat didn't say another word during the twenty-minute ride to the restaurant. Timmy entertained them with a new song he learned that day.

Kat and Timmy got in line. So many choices. So little room on his plate...and in his stomach! She helped him make the best selections for an almost balanced meal. She stuck with a garden salad and grilled chicken breast. Claire helped Trevor with his plate. Emma and Chase brought up the rear. When they sat down, Chase ended up on the opposite end of the table from her. So much for a hushed conversation over dinner.

They all filed out of the restaurant after eating and into the parking lot. Chase leaned against the driver's door of his car, waiting for his passengers to say their goodbyes. This was ridiculous. Kat marched over and stood defiantly in front of him. Claire and Trevor got in the car.

"We have to talk, Dr. Merrick. We can't keep acting like two twelve-year-olds who had a puppy love spat. I'm sorry I slapped you. I've never done anything like that before in my life. If you can't get past what I had to do to keep my son and myself safe from that cretin, then I have no reason to remain in Wisconsin. When my father gets home from vacation, I'll be making arrangements for us to return to Philadelphia. I have trusted you more than any man in my life except my father. And I'm sure now that I love you. I know—too little, too late—but I do." Kat started to walk away.

Chase put his hand on her good shoulder and turned her back to face him. "You're right. We're not twelve. Your past doesn't matter, except that you haven't shared all of it. Why do you continue keeping secrets from me?"

"Can't you understand the danger is still out there? He hasn't been captured. He could be anywhere."

"All the more reason you shouldn't be alone. Do you know yet how he found you? Why he came here?"

"No. I won't until I can talk to Pop. He's still out of reach. This is all one giant mess."

Angry tears poured down her cheeks. She pulled herself out of his grip and strode to the car where Emma and Timmy waited inside.

"Mom, why are you crying? Did Dr. Chase hurt you?" Timmy hollered from the back seat.

"No, honey. Dr. Chase didn't do anything wrong."

The afternoon was very quiet. Timmy played on the swing set. Kat watched from the patio. How had she let everything good disintegrate because of Dirk? Hadn't he robbed her of enough happiness?

After a soup and sandwich supper and a little playtime, Timmy volunteered to go take his bath. He told her he was worn out. She understood the feeling.

She tucked him in and kissed his forehead. "I love you, my little man."

"I love you, Mom. Don't worry. I like Dr. Chase, but if you don't want him to be my good dad, I'll be okay. You don't have to marry him. We'll find someone else to be your husband and my good dad,"

Timmy said earnestly.

Kat blinked back tears. "Thanks, honey."

"You know, I think Trevor will be my best friend forever, don't you?"

"I certainly hope so." She kissed him again, then turned out the light.

Chapter Twenty-Three

Kat got to the diner just after Susie. A few minutes later, Susie called for her to come to the front window. Doris was out on the sidewalk wrapped up in all of six-foot-four, dark-haired, hunky Jason Demming. She knocked on the front door to be let in as Jason drove away blowing her kisses until he was out of sight.

Susie unlocked the front door. "Really, Doris, don't you think it's a little early for such public displays of affection? I guess Jason went on vacation with you?"

"No. And no," Doris said with a mischievous twinkle in her eyes.

"Then he must have really missed you to bring you to work at five in the morning," Kat observed.

"He didn't miss me." Doris smiled.

"Okay, what's the deal?" Susie sounded a little aggravated.

"He was with me."

"I thought you just said he didn't go on vacation with you," Kat said.

"We weren't on vacation. We were on our honeymoon!" Doris laughed and held her left hand out with a big diamond and thick gold band on it.

Her coworkers embraced her. "No wonder he was blowing kisses to you." Susie shook her head.

"How wonderful. But who will tell me who's date-worthy anymore?" Kat teased.

"I don't think you'll need my help on that front. I'm pretty sure you'll be under medical care very soon. I guess we better stop lollygagging and get ready to open."

Kat was surprised and pleased to see Dr. Merrick come in the front door and sit in his usual place. Chase told Doris he'd never seen her looking happier.

She said, "You ought to come on in, Doc. The water's fine in the marital pool."

"I'd love to—if I could find someone who wanted to swim with me." Chase looked right at Kat.

"You shouldn't have to look too far." Susie nudged her coworker.

Kat's ears burned. "Doesn't anyone have work to do?" Why did Chase pretend nothing had happened over the past week?

"That's my cue. Got a busy day." Chase grabbed his lab coat to leave.

Kat handed him the check. "We still need to talk. I'm off Thursday. What's your schedule?"

"I'll have to check. You're right. It's past time we got this ironed out. I'll let you know tomorrow."

"Have a good day."

The day was filled with hugs and good wishes as the regulars learned Doris' news. Miss Althea's comment was, "It's time you became an honest woman." Doris only laughed.

Jason came in for lunch. He turned bright red when Walt came out of the kitchen to congratulate him and told him lunch was on Whistler's. Doris assured Muriel that she wasn't losing any help, just gaining a waitress-in-law.

Kat shared Doris and Jason's news at dinner.

Emma remembered seeing them together in church. "They make a lovely couple."

"Mom, does Doris have any little boys?"

"No. She doesn't. Why?"

"I just wondered if her little boy was getting a dad when she got married." Timmy pushed the peas around on his plate.

"Little boys aren't the only reason people get married."

"But it's a pretty good reason. Don't you think, Mom?"

"I think my little boy is going to help me with dishes so his Nana can have a break!"

Mother and son tackled the cleanup amid lots of gentle teasing and giggles. They had lived with Pop, and now with Emma. They'd never been in their own home, their own two parent family. It would be different. Maybe that's why it seemed so alluring to her son.

Timmy knelt back down after finishing his prayers to add, "And, God, please make Mom fall in love with Dr. Chase. He's a good dad to Trevor, and I want him to be mine too."

"Honey, you seem to change your mind pretty often about who would be a good dad. I don't think you need to call in God about something like this," she chided her son.

"Yes, I do, Mom. I need a miracle." He smiled impishly and kissed his mother good night.

Pop would be home tomorrow, even though the shop wouldn't open until later in the week. He always liked a little time at home to putter in the yard and maybe see a day Phillies game. She'd call him as soon as she got home.

Kat enjoyed knitting at Emma's side. She could even visit without losing her place on the pattern. The bright purple scarf turned out beautifully. Now she was working on Trevor's in his favorite color, bright orange.

****

Chase confirmed he was available Thursday evening. They planned to have a no-kids dinner so they'd have plenty of time to talk uninterrupted. You couldn't really call it a date. It was more of a reconciliation negotiation on neutral territory. Kat called it progress.

****

After a delicious bowl of her world-famous vegetable soup and hot cheddar biscuits, Emma began clearing the table. "Say, do I have a helper who'd like to dry dishes? There's still some leftover apple crisp for dessert after we finish."

"I'm on it, Nana." Timmy leapt up and started carrying bowls into the kitchen.

Emma said, "I have all the help I need, if you'd like to go outside and make a phone call."

"You're the best. Thanks." Kat walked outside and hit "1" on her cell phone.

Jocelyn answered. Darn.

"Hi, Jocie. Is Pop around?"

"I guess the peace and quiet is over. Couldn't you wait until we'd been home a couple of days?" Jocelyn said testily.

"Is Pop there?"

"He's in the kitchen helping me put away groceries. I'll have him call you." She hung up.

What the heck was that? Kat hit "1" again.

Jocelyn answered, "You can't take a hint, can you?"

Kat heard Pop ask, "Who are you talking to?"

"Please, Jocie. I'm going to keep calling until I get to talk to my father."

Pop got on the line. "My baby girl. We sure missed you and my grandson at the Shore. Is everything okay? I didn't want to be gone right now, but Jocelyn convinced me to go. We'd paid for the house back in January. Nonrefundable."

"Luckily, I called the garage and got the reminder you were out. I made a guess that you might get home today. It's not an emergency, but I have some news."

"I was worried while we were gone, but I didn't see any messages here when we got back, so I figured no news was good news. I'm afraid if you tried to call Jocelyn's cell, it wouldn't have helped. She left it on the kitchen table."

How convenient.

"Did they catch the scumbag?"

"Not yet. He hasn't bothered us since last Tuesday, but no one can find him. They impounded his motorcycle, so I don't know how he's getting around. The worst thing that happened this week is that Timmy met Dirk and figured out he was his father. He's been upset about having a bad man as his dad. We're working through it, but it's been kind of rough."

Kat hesitated a moment. "Pop, do you know who told Dirk where to find us?"

"I didn't tell anyone. I know John didn't. He didn't even tell your aunt. Jocie wouldn't. She knows how dangerous Crowe is."

"Someone had to have told him. He had no reason

237

to break parole and drive all the way to Lansdale, Wisconsin, unless he knew exactly where we were."

"I wish I was there to hug you both. Next time I want to talk to that grandson of mine. You tell him he's a lot more Russell than Crowe. He shouldn't worry about it. I'll get to the bottom of this and let you know what I hear. Goodbye."

After Timmy was in bed, Kat called Nancy Raymond before going back downstairs. Nancy immediately apologized for Dirk using her phone to find Kat's number. She didn't know he was out of prison until he appeared at her door. In her surprised state she just gave him the phone. She tried to call and say she was sorry, but Kat had blocked her number.

Dirk grilled Nancy trying to find out where they were, but finally he believed she didn't know and left her alone. Nancy had no idea how he found her. Once again, Nancy seemed clueless to the danger she had put Kat in. She left the call block on. Some friends were better off being past friends.

Kat went downstairs to join Emma knitting. There was something peaceful about the repetitive process that helped her think and calmed her.

"Did you have a good chat with your father?" Emma asked.

"Yes. It was great to hear his voice. He doesn't believe anyone consciously told Dirk where to find us. I wish he was right, but I don't think he can possibly be."

"My nightly prayer is that this is wrapped up soon. Dirk Crowe is wearing you out," Emma said.

"I had some good news today. Chase was back in the diner yesterday morning. I've apologized for the slap, and he agreed we need time to talk together. Could

I impose on you to babysit on Thursday night? Chase and I are planning to go to dinner. Without our boys—if you and Claire are willing to be our sitters."

"My dear, I'd be delighted. Your instincts are right. You two won't get anything resolved if you don't have some uninterrupted face-to-face time. Maybe Claire and I can take the boys out to dinner too, as a special treat. I'll check with her tomorrow. I think this is a great start toward reconciliation. You two are meant to be together. I'm sure of it." Emma wrapped up her work and put it in the knitting project bag. "Now, this old woman needs to get to bed."

"I'm right behind you."

Emma went to her room, and Kat turned out the lights in the living room and walked upstairs.

****

What was that noise? Her phone.

"Is Pop all right, Jocie?"

No response.

"Why did you call me?"

No response.

"Talk to me," Kat demanded.

"How did you know it was me?" a slurred voice finally asked.

"You show up on caller ID."

"But how did you know?"

"What are you talking about? You've been drinking."

"Yes. Yes, I have… He doesn't know."

"Pop doesn't know what?"

"Don't play games with me. You're waiting to tell him until you can drop a bomb on me, aren't you?"

"Jocie, what did you call to tell me? It's after

midnight."

"He was going to hurt Jim. Don't you understand?"

She *did* know. "It was you who told Dirk where to find us?"

Jocelyn sobbed incoherently.

"Do you hate me so much? He's still here and he wants to kill me."

Jocelyn's voice was soft but understandable, "No. I've never hated you. I had to choose."

"Telling where I was or he'd hurt Pop?"

"Dirk was in my living room. He had his arm around my neck. He said if I didn't tell him where you were, he would go to the garage and beat the answer out of Jim. I knew your father would die before he would give you up. I never thought the scumbag would leave Philly. I thought once he knew you were gone he'd just leave. Not go after you all the way to Wisconsin."

I'd have made the same choice. "Why didn't you warn me?"

"I couldn't. I was afraid you'd tell Jim what I'd done. He'd never understand. All I wanted was to be alone with my husband."

"You got that when you drove us out of the house. I wish you had just called the cops."

"Me too." The phone went dead.

Jocelyn.

Could she ever forgive this? Now Kat was certain there was no going home. Not to live in the same house with her. Even if she confessed to Pop and they stayed married. What would Kat do if Pop asked her if she thought Jocelyn told Dirk? She couldn't lie to her father. There was nothing to worry about. Pop would never believe his wife was capable of that kind of betrayal—of them both. Kat wouldn't have thought it either—if she hadn't heard the confession from Jocelyn's own lips. Emma was right. Her own family had dispatched danger to her doorstep.

****

Chase waved from the cash register. He only had time for a to-go cup of coffee and breakfast sandwich. That was fine. They'd have plenty of time to talk it all out tomorrow. And now she knew what to tell him when he asked how Dirk knew where they were.

Chapter Twenty-Four

Kat planned to sleep in Thursday morning, but Timmy bounded into her room at seven thirty a.m. At least, it was better than her usual waking hour.

"Mom, it's time to get out of bed so we can have lots of fun today."

"I hope you're this excited about getting up early when school starts in the fall. Let me get a shower, then we can have the treat I picked up for breakfast."

"I know, chocolate iced long johns from the bakery. Yummy! Hurry, Mom, I don't know how long I can wait to start eating."

The day was sunny and warm enough for shorts and flip-flops. Happily, she left the immobilizer on the dresser. Her shoulder seemed to be back to normal. Kat ran the brush through her hair. This style was quicker and easier to care for, but she missed the peaceful motion of brushing and braiding her waist-length hair. It needed to grow faster. She'd never cut it again.

Timmy and Emma were in the kitchen. Both were patiently waiting before biting into the tasty bakery treats in front of them. Kat poured an aromatic cup of coffee for herself, then refilled Emma's cup, before sitting down.

Delicious. The chocolate flavor flooded her mouth. They tasted even better than they had smelled in the bakery. What a sweet start to her day off.

Kat made her list of errands. Timmy, not wanting to miss out on spending a whole day with his mom, planned to go with her. The list was short: the drug store, dry cleaners, and the bank. Emma asked them to add a stop at the farmer's market to their errands. Chase told her they'd probably drive to a neighboring town for their famous prime rib for dinner. He planned to pick her up at five thirty.

At the farmer's market, Timmy tasted all the delicious samples. Kat's artistic side loved the colorful displays. Green peppers and cucumbers. Orange carrots with fresh green tops. Deep red beets. It was a good thing Emma's list had been specific or she would have bought at least one of everything. The aroma of fresh baked breads and pies wafted through the air. You could probably gain weight by just breathing in deeply.

To Timmy's delight, their last stop was for a lunch of fast-food burgers and fries with a chocolate milk shake. Kat opted for some fries and a diet soda, saving her appetite for dinner.

As soon as they got home, Timmy made a beeline for the swing set. Kat took the book she was halfway through reading and plopped down on the chaise lounge close enough to keep an eye on him.

He hollered, "Mom, look what I can do!"

She looked up to see her son balancing precariously on the top cross bar of the swing set. "You're too high. Get down now!" she called as she raced across the yard, trying to get to him before he attempted whatever daredevil trick he was planning.

Reluctantly, he crawled off the cross bar and into the tower. "Awww, Mom. You never let me have any fun."

"Thank you. I want you to have fun, but I don't want anything bad to happen. It only takes a second for an accident to send you to the ground. You could break your arm or worse."

"I'd be okay. Dr. Chase would fix me right up." He grinned at his mom.

"Let's not give him any business today, okay?" She walked back over to the chaise lounge and picked up her book.

She turned to one side to get out of the looming shadow. That smell. A scream stuck in her throat. Dirk Crowe towered over her. She quickly looked to the swing set.

How did he get in? All the doors were locked. No. The gate by the garage was wide open. She hadn't heard him. Apparently, he hadn't found a replacement motorcycle. If she hadn't heard him, neither had anyone else.

A wicked smile crossed Dirk's face. His steely-gray eyes leered at her. "Hey, Kat. I was going to tell you the other night, before we were so rudely interrupted, you look better than ever. A little meat on your bones suits you fine. You've become quite the foxy lady. Guess your lover boy is at the hospital. Saw the old lady leave earlier." He let loose an eerie, braying laugh. "Holler for the brat to come over here."

"Please, Dirk, no. I'll give you whatever you want. I'll go with you. Just don't hurt Timmy. Please."

"Call him. I'm not going to say it again." Dirk grabbed her arm. "I won't hurt him. I promise. C'mon, Kat. Don't make this harder than it needs to be. I don't want to harm you, but you know, I will. Remember, I don't like to be pushed." He twisted her arm behind her back—again—pulling her to a standing position.

"Honey, please come over here," she called, her voice wavering from pain and nauseating fear.

"Mom, I'm being careful. I'm not doing anything dangerous."

"I need you now, please."

Timmy came out of the tower and bounded over. "Why do you need me, Mom?" Then he recognized Dirk. "I know you. You're the bad man. Let go of my mom." He hit Dirk and tried to pry his hand off her arm.

"So I'm the bad man. You little snot-nosed kid." Dirk let go of Kat long enough to cut Timmy's lip with a slap across the face. He was bleeding, but still flailing his arms wildly at his mom's captor.

"Call him off, Kat, or I'll really hurt him," Dirk barked at her.

"Timmy, I'm okay. Please stop, honey. I don't want him to hit you again. Come over to my side."

"Mom, this is the guy. This is the bad man who tried to get Trevor and me to go on his motorcycle. The one who was my dad. Why is he here?"

"I don't know, honey." Kat pulled Timmy to her with her free arm. She kissed the top of his head and hugged him. "Dirk, what do you want?"

"You don't know? I don't believe it." Dirk brayed. The harsh, ugly sound frightened her even more. "Maybe I'm only here to spend a little quality time with my son, to see how he's getting along. Can't have some doctor stealing my kid, can I?"

"No one wants to spend any time with you," Kat hissed, glaring at Dirk.

"I'm here to ask his mother why she would take

my stash and keep it for herself. I waited almost six years to get back what's mine and you picked this time to leave Philly."

"I left Philadelphia because you caused Pop's heart attack. I didn't want him to have another one, and I didn't want Timmy to meet you. Ever." Kat held her son tighter.

"Well, that didn't work out too well, did it. Luckily, your darling stepmother was more than willing to tell me where to find you. She practically drew me a map. I think she believed I was just going to walk away, stupid woman. Looks like the little guy is growing up just fine. Maybe I'll take him back to Philly with me. He needs a strong male influence—a little time to bond with his old dad."

Timmy sobbed. "Mom?"

"You'd have to kill me first. Sperm donors don't have parental rights."

"That's rich. I have the right to do whatever I want. I'm the one in control here." Dirk twisted Kat's arm at a sharper angle.

"Stop hurting my mom. I don't want you for a dad. You're bad and mean," Timmy cried.

"You've sure done a number on him, Kat. Get over it, kid. I don't intend to be permanently saddled with a brat like you. I never did. I need to get in your mom's car. I've been trying to do that ever since I got to this burg. Sure are a lot of cops around for it being such a podunk little town. Get the keys." Dirk let go of her but grabbed Timmy's arm.

"Mom, run away. I'll fight him. Run, Mom, run," Timmy hollered and tried to hit Dirk.

"Shut up or I'll knock your brains out." Dirk jerked

him roughly.

"Honey, don't make him angry. I'll be right back." She turned to Dirk. "If you so much as breathe hard on him, you'll never get my keys or *anything* from me. Are we clear?" Kat said fiercely. Dirk nodded. "My keys are upstairs. It'll take a minute." She ran into the house.

Kat dialed 911 as soon as she got to Emma's landline. Thankfully, they picked up on the first ring. She blurted out the address, who she was, and said she was in danger from Dirk Crowe. Then she hung up and ran upstairs for her keys.

When Kat got back to the patio, Timmy was sitting on the edge of the chaise lounge quietly crying. Dirk paced back and forth in front of him.

"We're all going to the car—together." Dirk pulled Timmy behind him, just out of Kat's reach. "Coming, my beloved?"

At the car, he yelled, "The keys! Now!" He tightened his grip on Timmy. A siren split the air. "Cops? What a stupid thing to do. You're staying here. He's coming with me as insurance. The keys, Kat." Dirk slapped her with his free hand. Blood gushed out of her nose. She backed away from him.

Kat hurled the keys at Dirk's head with all the force she could summon. He released his grip on Timmy to catch the keys. She yelled, "Run!" She stumbled backward and landed hard, flat on her back.

Timmy ducked under their captor's outreached arm, but Dirk grabbed the back of the boy's shirt and flung him to the ground. Kat struggled to a sitting position but couldn't see past Dirk to know if her son was okay.

Dirk's face flamed with fury. "We're not through."

The sirens got louder. He jumped behind the wheel and peeled out of the driveway headed in the opposite direction of the sirens.

He was gone. They had to capture him this time. "Thank you, Jesus," she cried out loud putting her head in her hands sobbing. Then she saw a crumpled heap on the far side of the driveway. Timmy.

She ran to his side and gently rolled him over. Blood gushed out of the gash on his head and from his split lip. She cradled him close to her. Frozen. Unable to think. She wrapped him in her arms, struggled to her feet, and turned toward the house. She had to get help.

Emma's car pulled in the driveway. She stepped out of the vehicle. "Katrina, what's happened?"

"Thank God you're here. We need to call for an ambulance. Dirk hurt him."

"It will be faster to just go." Emma helped Katrina into the back seat with Timmy wrapped in her arms and gave her a handkerchief to hold against the gaping wound.

The receptionist in the Emergency Room waved them immediately through the double doors to the back, where two nurses took Timmy into an exam room, trailed by Katrina.

The door opened. Chase. "What do we have here?" His voice broke when he recognized the patient. "What happened?"

"It's all my fault. Dirk showed up at the house. He wanted my car. He was trying to kidnap Timmy to take as insurance that he would get out of town. I threw the keys at him, and he slammed Timmy to the ground. He must have hit the edge of the driveway. He hasn't said anything. He's barely breathing. Will he be all right?"

She sobbed.

Chase checked Timmy's pupils and listened to his faint heartbeat. "Katrina, we need to get a look inside his head. A CT scan will show if there's internal bleeding. You can walk with the stretcher back to Radiology."

Zombie-like, Katrina stayed at Timmy's side, never releasing his hand until they took him into the radiology scan room. She collapsed into a waiting room chair and looked up to see Emma. "He'll be all right, Katrina. Have faith."

"I can't lose my son. I fled Philadelphia to keep him safe. But I couldn't outrun pure evil. What am I going to do, Emma?"

Her friend sat down next to her and folded her hands around Katrina's shaking ones. "Dear God, please guide Chase as he cares for Timmy. Please restore him to his mother. Amen."

Katrina joined aloud in the Amen and continued sending frantic, constant prayers of her own upward. She was a sight. One flip-flop. One bare foot. Timmy's and her own blood covered her tee shirt and cutoffs.

Chase came out of the scan room. "Katrina, Timmy is bleeding just under his skull. He has a large clot that needs to be surgically removed as soon as possible. The closest chopper to airlift him to the pediatric hospital in Madison can't be here for at least an hour. Dr. Hill is here. He's done this procedure numerous times on adults. He'll need your permission to do the surgery."

"Chase, I don't want Timmy in any other surgeon's hands. Didn't you just get back from the pediatric trauma conference? Could Dr. Hill be there to help you?" Katrina pleaded.

"This is the procedure I've just reviewed. After the last couple of weeks, I didn't know if you wanted me to care for your son."

"I have complete faith in you. Please," Katrina said softly.

The nurse stepped forward with the necessary consents. Chase asked her to prep the patient for surgery. Then he turned to Katrina. "This is going to take at least three hours, possibly as long as five, depending on what we find. You have time to go home and change, maybe get a bite to eat. I'll come to you as soon as the surgery is over. I promise."

"I couldn't eat. I won't leave him. Please, just point me to the surgical waiting room," Katrina insisted. She kissed her son's forehead before they wheeled him out of sight.

Claire met them in the waiting room. "Katrina, Claire is here to stay with you. I'll go home and pack you a bag. I'll be back soon." Emma hugged Claire saying, "Thanks for coming. I don't want her to be alone. We're all the family she has here."

Katrina was vaguely aware of Emma leaving. She held Claire's hand without talking. Suddenly she said, "I have to talk to Pop. He needs to know about Timmy. I want to hear his voice. He always knows what to say to calm me down. My phone is in my purse—on the kitchen counter."

Claire held out her cell phone. "Use mine."

Katrina called Pop's number. After ten rings, a groggy Jocelyn answered the phone. "Russell residence, who's calling, please?" Apparently she was in the middle of an afternoon nap.

"Jocie, it's Kat. I need to talk to Pop. This is an

emergency. Please put him on the phone."

"Calling to rat me out? Already? He's not home."

"What? No. It has nothing to do with you. I need Pop. Please tell him to call me as soon as he gets home," Katrina begged.

"Sure. I'll ask him." Jocelyn hung up without saying goodbye.

Tears filled Katrina's eyes. She handed the phone back to Claire. "I don't think she'll tell him I called."

"Why don't you call your dad at work?" Claire handed the phone back to her.

"Thank you. I'm not thinking clearly, or I would've started there." Katrina punched in the number for the shop.

"Russell Motors, this is John. How may I help you?"

"Uncle John, this is Kat." She broke down crying.

"Honey, what's wrong? Are you okay?"

"I am. Timmy's not. I need to talk to Pop."

"He headed home for a bite to eat and a nap. He'll be back later tonight. You can probably catch him at home in a few minutes."

"I doubt it. That's where I started. Jocie hung up on me."

"I promise, he'll get this message. What's happened to Timmy?"

Katrina brought her uncle up to date on Dirk's attempted kidnapping and Timmy's injury. She left out the part about the man she loved holding her son's life in his hands. When she hung up, she was much better.

"Thanks. Uncle John will get a message to Pop." She handed the phone back to Claire. "How long has it been? Shouldn't Timmy be out of surgery soon?"

"Time always drags when you're anxious for news. It's only been a little over an hour. We still have some waiting to do."

"I'm back," Emma called cheerily as she crossed the waiting room. "I hope I brought everything you need."

Katrina took her overnight bag and purse into the restroom. She washed and changed clothes. Her nose was no longer bleeding. Her reflection was a major improvement. No blood.

She dropped to her knees on the cold tile floor and closed her eyes. She prayed out loud, "Thank you, God, for Emma and Claire. Please continue to guide Chase's skilled hands and restore Timmy's health. Please let Pop know I love him and need him. And please put Dirk Crowe out of my life forever."

Katrina glanced at the surgical monitor board as she crossed the waiting room. Every patient had their own privacy code so their family could track their progress from pre-op to the operating room to recovery to post-op. She double checked the slip of paper, TR555. Timmy's privacy code had just moved out of the operating room.

"According to the board, Timmy's in recovery. We should see Chase soon."

"Your wish is my command," Chase said bowing to her, garbed in surgical scrubs from cap to shoe covers.

"How did he do? Can I see him yet? Were you able to get the whole clot?" Katrina fired questions at Chase without giving him time to respond.

"Okay. One question at a time. He tolerated surgery very well. Dr. Hill and I successfully removed the entire clot. I can't take everyone to the recovery room, but I can take you. Mom and Emma can go ahead to his post-op room, 227. He'll be up there in about thirty minutes."

Chase led her to the recovery area. "He's going to look pale. He got eighteen stitches in the gash at the front of his head. The craniotomy stitch line is across the back. He'll look a little rough. I want you to be prepared."

The Recovery Room wasn't a room, but a small partitioned-off area. Chase drew the curtain at the end of the bed aside.

"My poor sweet baby. He's naked without his curls and so white. He looks totally worn out. Is he really all right? When will he wake up?"

"He's progressing exactly as we hoped he would. Dr. Hill was glad we didn't send him to Madison since it was time critical," Chase assured her. "Look, he's stirring."

"Mom? Is he gone? Are you okay?" Timmy said groggily.

Katrina sat in the chair at his bedside. "I'm fine now that you're awake. I haven't seen Dirk since he peeled out of the driveway."

Chase stepped to Katrina's side. "Dirk Crowe came into the emergency room by ambulance shortly after you brought Timmy in. He'd been in a car accident."

"Thank goodness he's finally in custody."

"There was no need to arrest him. He was dead on arrival," Chase said.

Katrina gasped. "Timmy, we're finally safe. The bad man will never bother us again."

"Hooray," Timmy exclaimed. "I can get a good

dad."

"Sure, honey, but first we need to get you healed and back home. When you fell, you split your head open. Dr. Chase and Dr. Hill operated on you. You've got a buzz cut and eighteen stitches in the front of your head and more in the back." She leaned over and kissed his cheek.

Timmy reached up and carefully felt his stitch lines. "Cool. I wanted a buzz cut. And stitches too!"

"Thank you, Chase. My little man is back. Please thank Dr. Hill for me. And thank you, God, for giving Chase the skill and guidance to save Timmy's life. Amen." Timmy and Chase joined in the "Amen."

Chase reached into his scrub jacket pocket and handed Katrina a small plastic bag.

"Timmy's curls. You know this mother's heart." She hugged him.

It was six o'clock by the time Timmy was released to his room. He could move his arms, fingers, toes, and legs on request, and his pupils responded to the flashlight appropriately. Shortly after he got to his bed, the nurse came into his room with a scoop of ice chips in a cup.

"Ice? I need real food. I'm so hungry," Timmy complained.

"If you can keep the ice down, I'll get you some clear broth and apple juice. You don't want to get sick to your stomach and pull out your stitches," the nurse explained.

"Okay. Tomorrow can I have pancakes and bacon for breakfast?" Timmy asked hopefully.

"If you keep improving, I think Dr. Merrick will allow that. Here he is. You can ask him yourself."

Chase came to the bedside laughing. "Timmy, are you giving Mrs. Myers a hard time? You must be feeling better."

"I'm sorry, Dr. Chase. I didn't mean to be bad. I don't want to starve. I'm a growing boy, and I need to eat."

"Don't worry. I'll make sure they feed you. You're definitely on the road to recovery." Chase pulled Timmy's chart up on the bedside computer to show everyone a photograph of the clot they'd removed. He turned to Katrina. "I'm sure you don't want to go out of town for dinner tonight. Could I at least buy you a sandwich at the grill downstairs?"

"Honestly, Chase, I'm not sure I can eat yet. I'm trying to process all this. Could I have a rain check for after Timmy gets home?"

"You bet. I want to have your full attention when we go out," Chase agreed.

"Go out? I didn't think this was a date, just an opportunity to talk."

"It was. Now it's a date. We haven't had one yet, and I think it's past time." Chase winked at her. He checked Timmy once more and hugged Katrina.

Emma and Claire said their goodbyes leaving one very tired little boy and his totally exhausted mom alone.

For a long time, neither of them spoke. Katrina thought her son had fallen asleep. She stood up to pull the covers around his shoulders and was surprised to hear him singing softly to himself.

"My little man, you need to go to sleep. What were you singing?"

Timmy didn't respond immediately, then he softly

said, " 'Jesus Loves Me.' You know, He's strong, Mom. He protected me from my bad dad."

"Yes, I know he did. Aren't you a lucky duck?"

"You are too, Mom, 'cause we have each other."

"Quack, quack," his mother said as tears spilled down her cheeks.

Chapter Twenty-Five

A riff of music played from deep inside Claire's purse.

"Chase, can you get that? It's probably a wrong number," his mom called from the kitchen.

Chase answered, "Hello, this is Claire Merrick's phone."

The voice on the other end hesitated, then said, "I'm sorry. I must have called the wrong number. I'm looking for Kat Russell. My apologies."

"Wait. Don't hang up," Chase said. He saw the caller ID said Russell Garage. "Excuse me, sir, but are you Katrina's Pop?"

"Yes. I'm Jim Russell. Who am I talking to?"

"This is Dr. Chase Merrick. I'm your grandson's surgeon. Katrina borrowed my mom's cell phone to call you."

"I really want to talk to my baby girl. Is she there?" Jim asked.

"No, sir. She's staying at the hospital with Timmy. I'm certain she's asleep by now. They both had a pretty rough day. She has her cell phone with her now. Timmy is doing quite well. He was alert and joking with the nurses when I left. He cut his head in a fall and had a blood clot under the skull. It could have been much worse."

"That evil animal. I should have taken care of him

before they ever had to leave here."

"Personally, I'm glad they came to Wisconsin," Chase said cheerfully.

"I'm thankful Kat thought to call John at the shop. We found your mother's number from our caller ID here. Excuse me for being so direct, but from your comments, Dr. Merrick, I'm fairly certain that you are much more than Timmy's surgeon. What exactly are your intentions regarding my daughter?"

Chase laughed. "A valid observation, sir. Your daughter is very aware of my intentions. I assure you they are honorable and long term. The whole Crowe incident has kind of put our plans on hold. But I'd like you to get the whole story from her."

"Maybe with that cretin gone, things will get back on track. Hope my Kat has landed on her feet again. I'll mention you the next time I talk to her. Would you ask her to phone me at the shop in the morning? That way I won't call at the wrong time and mess up Timmy's care. A pleasure to meet you, Doc. Hope we have more to talk about soon."

Chase assured him that he would pass along the message. Claire was at his side when he hung up. "Was that Katrina's father?"

"Sure was. His brother let him know about her call, even though the wife must not have." Chase shook his head. "I don't understand how she can come between a father and daughter, especially when Katrina was clearly in trouble."

"I can't answer that. I'm just thankful I gave Katrina my phone to make those calls. And that she thought to talk with her uncle. What wonderful news to give her in the morning." Claire kissed Chase's cheek.

"I'm going to bed, son, and you had better too. You've had a full day. Morning will be here long before we're ready to roll out of bed."

"I'll be up in a few minutes." Chase sat in the quiet, dark living room thinking about Katrina. *Maybe now she'll be ready to take the next steps and tell me everything.* He hoped so.

****

Chase made rounds about seven o'clock. He left Timmy's room as his last stop, so he could linger there. "Good morning. How are my best patient and his lovely mother doing this morning?"

"I'm fairly certain the doctor slept better than the mom did. Luckily, I was so exhausted I didn't notice how uncomfortable this recliner was until about an hour ago. Now I'm a little stiff and sore," Katrina responded.

Chase checked Timmy's e-chart and did a physical exam.

"Am I okay, Dr. Chase?" Timmy asked softly.

"Yes, you are. Your stitches will come out in a week or so. All things considered, you'll be fine if you do exactly what your mom tells you."

"I will. I promise," Timmy said solemnly.

"Katrina, a call came in last night on Mom's phone. It was your father."

Katrina's eyes glistened.

"He had Mom's number from when you called the shop yesterday. He wants you to call him there today. He said he could tell I was more than just Timmy's surgeon and wanted to know what my intentions were."

"What did you tell him?"

"That he needed to talk with you. And you and I need to have an uninterrupted conversation like we were supposed to have last night," Chase said smiling. "We still have a number of loose ends to tie up."

"You're right. We need to reschedule dinner. I'd like to call Pop now though. I need to make sure he's all right," Katrina said.

Timmy chimed in, "I want to talk to Pop Pop too."

Katrina carefully dialed the number for the shop. Pop answered, "Russell Garage, how may I help you?"

"Hi, Pop."

"My little Kat. John, it's my baby girl," her father hollered with his voice choking. "It's so good to hear you. Honey, I know we have a lot to talk about. I have to apologize for letting my wife put you through hell for so long. I was there, and I completely missed it. A father is supposed to protect his child. Can you ever forgive me for being so blind?"

"Pop, the hell is in the past. I always knew you loved me even when Jocelyn was at her worst. I've already forgiven you ten times over."

"Mom, please, I need to talk to Pop Pop," Timmy insisted.

"Just a minute. Here's our impatient patient. We can talk more after you two are done." Katrina handed the phone to her son.

"Pop Pop, is it really you? I'm in the hospital. I was in a fight with my bad dad, and I cut my head open. Dr. Chase had to operate on me. I've got stitches in the front and the back, and I have the coolest buzz cut ever." Timmy rattled on a good five minutes about everything that had happened. When Katrina asked for the phone back, he added, "Pop Pop, my mom still needs to find me a good dad. Can you do anything about that? I really have to get some help."

Jim chuckled. "I'll see what I can do. Let me talk to your mom."

"Sorry about that, Pop. Ever since he found out Dirk was his father, he's been on a mission."

"I think the boy will be fine. He talked a long time, hardly had to take a breath. I know it's none of my business, but are you considering Dr. Merrick for Timmy's job opening?"

Heat raced across Katrina's cheeks. "Um, Pop. I don't think now is the time to discuss this. It's complicated and not resolved yet."

"You mean the good doctor is nearby?"

"Exactly. I wanted to find out how you are. This has been a crazy couple of days."

"I understand. Honey, I know that the move to Wisconsin was your opportunity for a fresh start, but was it truly your idea? Jocelyn said it was your choice, but given everything else I've learned in the past twenty-four hours, I don't believe her."

"After your heart attack, I agreed with Jocelyn that you needed less drama around you."

"She had erased all the caller ID information after you called yesterday—apparently not for the first time. If you hadn't called the shop and talked to John, I wouldn't have known about any of this. I stayed with John and Judy last night. I was too angry to face her," Pop said sadly. "I have to decide if I can ever forgive her for this episode and for things I'm just learning about that have happened since I married her. I'm not sure I can still be her husband after this."

And he doesn't know the whole truth yet. "Pop, I know that your marriage is none of my business, but I believe Jocelyn does love you. She's so insecure. It wasn't easy, but I've forgiven her for everything. I pray you can too. If you don't deal with it, it will eat you up inside. I don't want to be the reason you leave Jocelyn and are alone. I have made my peace with the past—all of it. I want to leave it behind me and move forward," she gently pleaded.

"You are your mother's daughter, the same kind heart and gentle persuasion that Renata had. I'll think about what you've said. If you can forgive Jocelyn after everything you've suffered at her hands, I'll have to consider it."

"Thanks, you won't regret it. And then you can both come to Wisconsin to see us."

"Just to see you or for some other reason?" he teased.

"That remains to be seen."

"Do me a favor. Make some time to talk to the doctor. He seems to think you two have things to talk about. I think he's probably right. I want you to be happy."

"Thanks, Pop. We'll talk soon."

"Maybe we'll both have some good news to share. Goodbye, baby girl. I love you."

"Love you. Goodbye."

Chase stepped closer. "If he continues to make such good progress, Timmy can go home in the morning. I'd like to make sure he tolerates the meds and can eat normally. Do you have time to have dinner with me tonight to finish our discussion?"

"It's so soon. I hate to leave Timmy alone," Katrina insisted.

"I'm sure Emma or Mom and Trevor would keep him company, or we could make it after visiting hours.

I hear my family in the hall. We can ask them now."

When Trevor entered the room, Katrina began laughing. "Two peas in a pod!"

Trevor's blond curls were completely gone. Claire trailed behind him. "Sorry, Chase, but he insisted if Timmy was going to have a buzz cut, so was he."

Claire said they'd come back in the evening for Katrina and Chase to have dinner. Chase left to go to the clinic.

Chief Davis called Kat's cell phone. He confirmed that Dirk had taken Campbell Curve too fast and been thrown from the vehicle because he wasn't wearing his seat belt. He'd broken his neck. Her car was towed to the police garage, but the chief was pretty sure it was totaled since it caught on fire after it rolled.

Chase had only been gone about twenty minutes when there was another knock at the door. Muriel and Walt Whistler came in hand in hand. "Kat, are you both okay, honey?"

Kat explained what had happened. Muriel told her to take off until Monday. Irene had volunteered to cover for her to repay all the times she'd covered for Irene.

"Muriel and Walt, I am so sorry that my lingering personal problems have caused such havoc at Whistler's. I'm lucky to work for you and to have such wonderful coworkers. Thank you."

"Everyone has problems, girl. I'm just glad we were there for you," Muriel said.

Walt never said a word but wrapped her in a bear hug before leaving. Thanks to their continued kindness, she wouldn't have to leave her traumatized son until Monday.

****

Chase picked Katrina up at the hospital at six o'clock. Emma came back to keep Claire company. Trevor brought a checkerboard to challenge the recovering patient to a game or two.

Chase pulled up in front of a nondescript brick building with a parking lot full of pickup trucks. "Where are we?" Katrina asked.

"The place that serves the best prime rib in the state. Let's go in." Chase opened his car door and walked around to help Katrina out of the car.

He led her through the darkish bar with a juke box crooning an old Hank song and into a small dining room with red and white checkered tablecloths.

A man with menus in hand came across the room. "Good evening, Doc. Your table is ready in the alcove. Follow me." They walked behind him to the back of the dining room and down a short hall where a table for two was set. Chase pulled out Katrina's chair, and she sat down.

"Call me impressed. A private dining room. You were serious about an uninterrupted discussion," Katrina said with a smile. She glanced at the menu. "The prime rib sounds wonderful after two days of not much to eat and hospital food at that."

Chase placed their order and poured them each a glass of wine from the open bottle on the table. "Now, we won't be bothered for a bit."

"Me first," Katrina began. "Again, I'm sorry for the slap. I've never done anything like that in my life. I just couldn't believe you thought I would put my son and myself in danger by telling Dirk where we were. And I was angry at myself that I hadn't thought to ask the question earlier about how he found us. Please forgive me."

"Of course, I forgive you. I was caught off guard. I didn't think you would intentionally put yourself in danger. I hadn't realized you were still married to that abuser."

"Dirk did beat me. The last time was the night Timmy was born. I told you he wasn't my ex-husband. That was the truth. He never married me." She couldn't look at him.

"That's the secret? Why didn't you tell me? Did you think I was a prude? You can't continue to feel guilty for the choices you made as a sixteen-year-old girl, even if they have lifelong consequences. Knowing about your past doesn't change how I feel. I love you."

"It's good to hear you still love me. If that's true, why were you avoiding me?"

"Once I realized this was something more than threats and harassment by Dirk Crowe, whatever his relationship with you was, it gave me pause. When I learned federal agents were in Lansdale, I thought they had to be connected to either your or Dirk's appearance here. You confirmed they were DEA agents. I couldn't believe you were Dirk's co-conspirator in the drug trade, but I wasn't certain how involved you were or in what. My imagination was on overload.

"Were you a material witness who would be whisked away into witness protection when this was over? Were you an agent who was sent to lure Crowe into a trap and apprehend him? For all I knew, you'd return to Philadelphia for your next case after he was apprehended. There are TV shows and movies based on the idea of a single mother or everyday housewife secretly being a federal agent. They always seem a little incredible but...after all, you kept insisting I didn't really know you, and you wouldn't commit to a relationship. The slap, which was totally out of character for you, didn't help at all. I decided to do as you asked. I stepped back to think about this whole relationship."

"I told you I love you. I hoped it wasn't too late."

"I know you said that, but... Chalk our behavior up to excessive stress on both sides. This situation would shake the foundation of any relationship. We need to recognize that's what happened. We should be able to put it behind us, if it's over—if no second shoe is waiting to drop."

"There isn't anything else. No more secrets. I promise. We're such an unlikely pair. An unwed mother with a GED who waits tables for a living and a well-respected, widowed, physician dad."

"Katrina, unlikely or not, I believe we are supposed to be together. To someday be a family. Don't doubt yourself. I hope you can find it in your heart to put all of this behind us and love me for the rest of our lives."

"Does this mean you know I trust you and don't want to disappoint you? Have you completely forgiven me for not explaining my past immediately?"

"A hundred times over. You are totally forgiven. Please tell me you'll marry me."

"I can't make wedding plans yet. I have to decide how to deal with the person who told Dirk where I was."

"You know?"

"Yes, it was my father's wife, Jocelyn. She called me earlier this week in the middle of the night with a drunken confession."

"Why would she hurt you? What did your father say?"

"He doesn't know. She said she had to choose between Pop being hurt and revealing where I was. She didn't feel like she had any choice. Dirk confirmed she told him where I was, but it's just the last thing in a litany of her jealous, hateful behavior over the past ten years. She has acted like Pop's love was finite and if he loved me, he wouldn't have enough left for her."

"Some people are very insecure, especially if they are thrust into parenting someone else's child."

"That's Jocelyn. Thirteen is a very awkward age for any girl, and an especially bad time to lose her mother. Pop didn't help when he was always saying I looked just like Mom. You could see Jocelyn bristle every time he said it. He didn't seem aware of how much it bothered her.

"Honestly, I didn't help the relationship. I was moody and thundered around slamming doors and being disrespectful. Once or twice, I'm ashamed to say, I got right in Jocelyn's face and told her I didn't have to do what she said because she wasn't my *real* mom."

"I'm sure it was a difficult situation for all three of you."

"When I was sixteen, Jocelyn lied to Pop and drove me out of the house and into Dirk Crowe's clutches." She blinked back tears.

"Didn't your father know she was lying?"

"Pop was afraid of being alone and terribly disappointed in me. He didn't seem to know what to do, except to believe her."

"Then they took you back in when Timmy was born?"

"Yes, the very night. Dirk beat me and left me unconscious. After I managed to get home, Jocelyn tried to turn me away. Pop made sure I got to the hospital. Timmy was born later that day, two months early." She stopped and took a deep breath.

"Sounds like this betrayal was keeping in character for her."

"The final straw was that she gave me money to leave Philadelphia after Dirk caused Pop's heart attack. She didn't want Pop to know about it, and I cashed her check. I know I have to forgive her for everything—especially putting everyone in danger by revealing we were here—and I'm trying. I told Pop I already had. He'll be devastated when he finds out what she's done."

"Katrina, your heart is too tender to survive harboring all that darkness. Forgiveness will wash it away. I'm glad you came here. If Jocelyn hadn't driven you away again, I'd never have found you."

Chase reached across the table and gently grasped her hand.

"I know you're right. I feel responsible and want to fix this mess. Pop can't face being alone. Even if it means Jocelyn stays in our lives. There must be something about her I don't understand, something only Pop sees that makes him love her."

"Darling, you are a remarkable force, but I think this can only be fixed by your father and Jocelyn with some divine intervention thrown in."

"Maybe I can point them in the right direction."

"If anyone can, it would be you. You are one stubborn woman." Chase laughed.

Their salads arrived followed by two steaming hunks of perfectly cooked medium rare prime rib with a fluffy, baked potato dripping with butter and topped with a dollop of sour cream. Chase was right. It was the best prime rib she'd ever eaten.

The rest of their dinner conversation centered on the boys, especially on Timmy's recovery.

"This has been a crazy emotional week. I had peace once I knew you were going to be Timmy's surgeon. It wasn't just because I have confidence in your abilities as a surgeon, although I do. It was because I knew that you love Timmy as much as I do." Katrina reached across the table.

"I'm extremely thankful that this time my medical skills could save someone I love. I know Timmy and Trevor became best friends so we would be forced to spend time together for their sakes. Who could ask for better brothers?"

"Speaking of which, we should probably check in on them before visiting hours end," Katrina said.

The boys were playing the tie breaker checkers game to determine the champion for the evening. Emma and Claire had made rows and rows of progress on their prayer shawls. When Trevor jumped across the board with his king, he secured the title.

"So, Dr. Chase, do I get to go home in the morning?" Timmy asked hopefully.

"It looks like it. As long as you don't fall out of bed in the night," Chase said laughing.

"I'll be right here to make sure he stays between the rails," his mother said.

Chapter Twenty-Six

Timmy was released in mid-morning. Emma picked them up. Chase promised to stop and check on him later in the evening.

Mr. Casterelli called Katrina at lunch time to schedule the case wrap-up. They agreed on seven o'clock at Emma's. He arrived promptly.

"Thank you, Miss Russell. Without your assistance we would never have recovered the cocaine and cash. This is your reward."

Katrina almost fainted when she opened the envelope. The check was for twenty-five thousand dollars.

"This is enough to replace my car. I don't know how to thank you." Her hands trembled holding the check.

"Oh, the money's not for your car. That's your percentage of the recovered money. The DEA will replace your vehicle since it was destroyed during one of our operations. It will need to be another of the same model or a vehicle of comparable value," Mr. Casterelli explained and gave her a voucher to purchase her replacement car.

"How ironic. Dirk is providing something for Timmy's future after all. Does this mean you are heading back to Philadelphia, now?"

"Yes. This was my last stop. Are you and your son

planning to stay in Wisconsin?"

"I'd like to. There are some things to work out before my decision is final."

"Best of luck." Mr. Casterelli left.

"I wasn't trying to eavesdrop," Emma began. "I'm glad to hear you'd like to stay. Is one of the things to work out related to a certain doctor?"

"I hope the answer to that question is yes," Chase said as he came in the door Mr. Casterelli had just gone out.

A flash of heat streaked across Kat's cheeks. "The answer is maybe, Dr. Merrick."

Chase smiled. "This girl likes playing hard to get. I am here in an official capacity to follow up on the health of my recently released surgical patient."

"He's in his room." Katrina started upstairs with the doctor close behind her.

Timmy was doing well. Chase said he could resume normal activities—in moderation. The boy was delighted because it meant he could go to Sunday School tomorrow and see his best friend who he hadn't seen all day.

It was pleasant to resume their normal activities too. Katrina sighed contentedly as she and Chase did dishes after Sunday dinner. Chase wanted an answer about their marriage. She couldn't keep him waiting too much longer, but she had to help Pop. He was still living at Uncle John's, and she was certain Jocelyn hadn't told him everything yet.

Before turning out the light that evening, Katrina dug around in her dresser. Where was it? The little white Bible with her name stamped in gold on its front—a gift from Grandpa and Gran for her ninth birthday—the only treasure she had left from them. Chase had made her think about Jocelyn in a different light.

Jocelyn always acted insecure. She'd constantly competed with the ghost of the ideal wife she thought her best friend had been, then saw Renata in Kat's face each day. It was too much stress. Even a secure person would have had a hard time handling the constant pressure.

Pop knew about Jocelyn's insecurities. That's why he backed her, took her side in disagreements. He'd always told Kat that he would love his daughter no matter what. She believed him. He knew she was strong enough to stand her own ground. His second wife needed his constant support more than his only child did.

Reverend Cox's forgiveness sermon echoed in her thoughts. She read the passages from her treasured memento. She had to completely forgive Jocelyn. And Pop. And herself. Chase was right. They couldn't have a future together until she cast off her past.

She crawled into bed and closed her eyes. Demonic laughter echoed through her dreams. Dirk? Why was he back? Nightmare Dirk said, "Just because I can't terrorize you in life doesn't mean I'm gone forever." Nightmare Katrina stood, pointed to the door, and said, "You're wrong. This is over. I'm not letting you rob me of my happiness ever again." He stepped back, gave a mock salute, and faded away. Her heart knew it was for the last time.

****

How could it be four a.m. so soon? Today Kat would have to look the people she had grown to love in the face knowing everyone had heard about Dirk's accident and death *and* that he was somehow connected to her. News like that grew legs immediately and raced through the small community. Emma loaned her the car until Katrina could go shopping to replace hers.

Susie and Doris met her at the door and sandwiched her between them for a long hug.

"We're glad you're here, Kat. And that Timmy's okay." Susie patted her back.

"Thanks for making this easier for me. Looks like we'd better get coffee on." Kat wiped a tear away and readied herself for the day.

Chase grabbed a to-go cup of coffee at the register and talked to Muriel. He waved to her as he left. The roar of his motorcycle made her shudder. Would the noise always have that effect?

Charlie Bishop and Miss Althea were both in their usual spots. No time like the present to share the news. Miss Althea broached the subject before Kat could.

"Young lady, I understand that you have been involved with a hoodlum and it came to a bad end," Miss Althea spit out with more than a smidgen of snarkiness.

"I wanted to talk to you both about that." Kat reached out to hold Charlie's hand.

"I have been hiding from someone who had tried to kill me. He found me and has been terrorizing me for almost a month. He hurt my son." Kat was surprised how even and controlled her voice sounded.

Charlie clasped her hand. "He's the one who scared off the angels, isn't he?"

"Yes," she replied softly.

"But he's gone, and they're not back yet. Why?"

Charlie asked.

"It's complicated."

Miss Althea interrupted, "You old coot and your angels. Let her finish telling us what happened to her hoodlum."

"He's not *my* hoodlum, and he's dead." Kat took a deep breath.

Miss Althea snorted. "I knew there was something not right about her. Knew it from the first minute she came to work."

Charlie turned toward Althea and said, "You need to keep yer yap shut." Then he turned to Kat. "I hope your angels are back soon, Kitty. I miss them."

As customers came in throughout the day, they took her association with Dirk in stride. Most of them expressed relief that she and her son were all right now. Kat remembered Emma saying everyone had mourned with Chase when he lost Libby. Life in a small town. The Scripture was right—neighbors loving one another as they love themselves.

****

Kat called Pop at Uncle John's after dinner and filled him in on all the details about the DEA reward and car voucher.

"Honey, I wish I was there to hug you both."

"Me too."

"Maybe it's time for you to come home. You know you're always welcome here."

She couldn't let it pass. "Pop, I know you love me and want us closer, but *everyone* doesn't feel the same way you do."

"What does that mean?"

"You should probably talk to your wife before you

offer to let us come back."

"I intend to. I'll check with her and John to make certain they didn't let anything slip somewhere that someone could have told Crowe. If Jocelyn says she'll welcome you back, will you come?"

"I'm not sure yet," she said quietly.

"The doctor. Sorry, I'd forgotten. Guess I'm anxious to see you. Are you two making long term plans?"

"Chase would like to, but I'm worried about you. I've put my relationship on hold, hoping I could help yours."

"Jocelyn and I have to work things out between us. We aren't your problem. Don't put your happiness and my grandson's on hold on my account. Promise me you'll move forward whether or not my marriage recovers," Pop insisted.

"But…"

"Please, honey. For me."

"All right. I promise. I'll talk with Chase soon. Will you please give Jocelyn a chance to explain?"

"I guess that's only right. If I expect it of you, how can I do less? I will. I love you, baby girl. Good night."

"Love you, Pop. Goodbye."

****

The next evening, Trevor and Timmy were camping out in the living room when Kat got home. They were eating supper off of paper plates by their campfire of orange and red construction paper with a cast iron pot of beans and franks sitting on it. Their laughter made her smile. Emma and Kat had quiche Lorraine and salads while overseeing the campsite from the dining room table.

Kat answered the door at eight o'clock. Chase with a sleeping bag. She invited him in.

"Trevor, your dad is here."

"Your grandmother said you needed this for your camp out. She was on the phone and asked me to bring it to you," Chase explained to his son.

"Thanks, Dad. See our cool tent." Chase bent down to peek inside the *tent*—one of Emma's old sheets thrown over a clothesline between two of the kitchen chairs.

"Very nice. Looks like it's pretty close quarters in there."

"If you sleep close together, the bears won't bother you," Timmy pronounced with great authority.

"Good to know. Give me a hug, and I'll leave you to your camp out." He bent down and hugged both the boys. Then they pulled the flap down on the tent. Lots of giggling echoed from their temporary abode.

"Want a cup of decaf before you go?" Katrina asked.

"Sure, it's a lovely evening. What about enjoying it on the patio?" Chase suggested. They carried their mugs outside. "Does your father know yet what his wife did?"

"No. It hasn't come up. He did promise me he would talk to Jocelyn and give her a chance to explain herself."

"Sounds like you're making progress."

"Yes. He made me promise I'd listen to the doctor."

"He did. Then don't you think it's time we set the date?"

"For what?" Katrina asked.

"Our wedding."

"Wait a minute. I don't recall saying 'yes' to marrying you. Now that I think about it, I don't recall *getting* a proposal."

Chase immediately got down on one knee. "Katrina Joy Russell, will you marry me?"

She laughed.

"Not exactly the response I'd hoped for, although I do love your laugh—joy seems to bubble out of you. I hope to keep you doing it regularly from now on." Chase hugged her.

"I could tell from the wedding pictures on your mantel, you've already experienced the whole tuxedo renting, bridesmaid dresses, flower girls, big time, all out, matrimonial extravaganza. I never have. I don't know if I want to, but I'm afraid just going to the Justice of the Peace would make me feel like I'd been shortchanged."

"No worries there. We're having a full-blown church wedding with a bride's side and a groom's side," Chase happily pronounced.

"Well, seating will be a trifle one-sided. My side will have Emma, Doris, Susie, and the Whistlers, all of whom could just as easily sit on your side because they knew you first. I may need to rethink this big wedding thing. But I do like the idea of getting married at the church."

"From all this discussion about the wedding ceremony, should I infer that your answer to my proposal is *yes*?" Chase asked.

"When I get an official proposal, with an engagement ring and the works, I'm leaning strongly toward saying 'yes,' " Katrina said smiling.

"You are one demanding woman."

"It's not too late for you to change your mind," she said with a wink.

"Nope. I love you, lady. You're stuck with me. I'll work on that official proposal."

Chase gave her a long, slow kiss and said good night.

****

He's in *his* place. Hallelujah! This was going to be a great day.

"Good morning," Kat said as she poured a cup of black coffee and set it in front of Chase. "Are you having your usual this morning or branching out?"

Chase looked at her for several seconds without speaking. "I don't believe we've met. I'm Chase Merrick. And you are?"

She stepped back from the counter, whirled around, then stepped up with her hand extended and said, "Kat Russell. A pleasure to meet you, Chase Merrick."

"Do you remember what my usual is?" Chase teased.

"Two eggs lightly scrambled, crisp bacon, rye toast, and black coffee." She smiled and went back to put in his order.

On the back of his check, Chase had written, *I've missed you.*

"It's a relief to see the love notes resume. I've been worried about you two," Muriel said as she rang up the sale and put the note on the spindle. "I guess every love story has to have a couple of bumps along the way. Just to keep it interesting."

"It's been plenty interesting so far…oh, my. I didn't mean to say that out loud." Kat quickly retreated to the back of the diner racing the blush running up her neck.

"Good morning, Mr. Charlie. Hi, Sheba," Kat called out as she approached the counter.

"Praise the Lord. The angels have found their way home!" Charlie smiled.

"Amen," Kat said and told Charlie today's specials.

Chapter Twenty-Seven

Before going to bed, Katrina called Jocelyn. This had to get resolved. Now.

"Russell Residence." Jocelyn picked up before Katrina heard it ring.

"Hi, Jocie, it's Kat."

For several seconds, Jocelyn did not respond. Then she said, "Your father isn't in. He doesn't live here any longer." She barely got the words out before she began sobbing.

"Jocie, I called to talk to you, not Pop. I know he's still at Uncle John's. I want to help you."

"What am I going to do? I'm such a ninny. I love Jim too much to lose him."

"Did you tell him that?"

"Of course, and so much more. He's especially upset about how I've treated you and Timmy—forcing you to leave, not wanting you to come back, not telling him about the emergency call. I don't blame him, but I don't know how to fix it. I can't undo what I've done, no matter how much I regret doing it. He'll never forgive me." Jocie's voice was softer and more fragile sounding than Kat had ever heard it.

"I know. Pop told me." Kat took a deep breath. "Jocie, you've been through a lot of pain in the last ten years. It must have been hard to lose your best friend so soon after you lost Frank. When you and Pop first got married, I was glad because you'd been so kind to me through Mom's illness, but somehow it all changed."

"I'm sorry I hurt you, Kat. It's just that your father could never deny you anything; you look too much like Renata. Jim told me he felt like she was still alive every time he looked at you. Something in me snapped. I can't explain it. I was the adult and should have been able to control my emotions, but I couldn't. More importantly, I didn't."

"Jocie, we need to move beyond our history. I have forgiven you for *everything* from that dark time right through to Dirk coming here. I hope *you* can forgive the moody, hateful teenager I was—the one who made terrible choices that affected all our lives so dramatically," Kat said as lovingly as she could.

"You are Renata's daughter to your very soul. I forgive you. If only that was enough. Jim still doesn't know I paid you to leave or that it's my fault Dirk Crowe found you. He could've killed you or Timmy or both of you."

"But he didn't. God kept us protected."

"When Jim finds out the whole truth, he will never forgive me. We won't stay married."

"It's important for you to tell him, not someone else. There can't be any more secrets between you. It's the only way you'll be able to make a fresh start. I want you and Pop to stay together, and to be happily married."

"Do you think he'll come home? Back to me? After he really knows how sick I was? Everything I did?"

"I'm praying he will. I believe you need to *ask* Pop to forgive you. Then ask God to forgive you. It's important to take that first step. I told Pop the same thing."

"I've never been much for religion…"

"Please, for me and *our* new relationship. Make the effort, Jocelyn," Kat pleaded.

"You've grown up. If this is so important to you, I'll try. I want us to have a fresh start—you and I, and Jim and I."

"I love you. Call Pop. You two belong together. I want you *both* in our lives."

"Thank you for being the bigger person and calling me. I would never have had the nerve to call you first. I was afraid you'd hang up when you heard my voice or never have picked up when you saw it was me. I'll call Jim immediately. Please keep praying for me, for us. I hope to call you soon with good news."

"Goodbye."

"Goodbye, Kat." That was the first goodbye Jocelyn had said to her in forever.

Katrina said a prayer for Jocie to be strong enough to tell Pop the truth, and for him to recognize how hard it was for her. And for them to both be forgiven.

****

"Hey, Kat, they need you up at the counter," Doris hollered as she picked up an order at the kitchen window.

Kat picked up a tray and headed to the front. "I'm coming."

She delivered Miss Althea, Charlie, and Chase's food and refilled their coffee and hot water. "Who wanted me up here?" She looked around.

Chase said, "I did."

"Do you need this to-go?" she asked.

Chase shook his head, pulled a small red velvet box from his lab coat, and knelt beside Katrina. He set the box in front of her. "Open it, please."

Katrina could hardly see for the tears in her eyes. Inside the box was an exquisite ruby ring encircled by diamonds. "Chase, it's beautiful. It looks antique."

"It is. I hope you don't mind. It's been worn before." Katrina inhaled sharply. "Don't worry. Libby didn't wear it. Mom did."

"This was your mom's engagement ring?"

"It was her idea to give it to you." Chase slid the ring on her finger and kissed her hand. "Katrina Joy Russell, will you do me the honor of becoming my wife?"

"Yes, a thousand times yes." Tears streamed down her cheeks.

Every patron in the diner stood and applauded, including Timmy, Emma, Trevor, and Claire who came out of hiding in the back.

Timmy and Trevor both let out a whoop and hugged one another. "We're gonna be brothers now," they hollered in unison.

****

The Merricks came to Emma's for a celebratory supper that evening. After dessert Katrina called Pop to tell him the news.

"Sounds like you told the doctor 'yes.' "

"I did. Timmy is so excited about getting a brother and a good dad. In a funny way, Jocelyn is responsible for me finding Chase. If she hadn't insisted we leave, I'd never have met the love of my life. I'm more than happy, Pop. I'm contented, and excited about the future. I hope you can find the same feeling with Jocie again. I want to see you. You remember how to get to Wisconsin, don't you? If you decide to splurge for a plane ticket, I'll drive to Madison or Chicago to pick you up. The train comes from Philly to the Midwest too."

"Okay, okay. I get the message. I need to take a little holiday and visit Wisconsin. I love you. Hug the little guy for me. I've always wanted you to be happy. It sounds like you finally are. Hey, is that future son-in-law of mine nearby?"

"He's standing right here, Pop. Why?"

"Would you, please, put him on the phone?" Pop asked.

Katrina handed the phone to a puzzled Chase. "Dr. Merrick, I know you didn't ask for my permission to marry Kat, but I'm giving it to you. Thanks for making my baby girl and my grandson so happy. I look forward to meeting you and the rest of your family."

"Thank you, sir. Your permission means a lot to both of us." Chase ended the call and handed the phone back to Katrina. "He said I could marry you."

Claire came over and kissed her almost daughter-in-law. "Hope you don't mind getting a used ring. It looks so lovely on your long, slender fingers."

"I don't mind at all. I'm honored that you would share this precious reminder of your Walter with me. Thank you." She kissed the older woman's cheek.

Timmy and Trevor came over to look at the ring. "Mom, did God make you fall in love with Dr. Chase?"

"I think He did. It looks like you two are all right with being brothers."

"Boy, are we ever, even though Trevor's a little older than me. But there's a problem." Timmy wrinkled his brow. "What am I supposed to call Dr. Chase after you marry him?"

Chase stepped to Katrina's side. "I'd be honored if you called me Dad like Trevor does. Would that work?"

"Man, would it ever. Quack! Quack! Quack! We're such lucky ducks. I get a good dad," Timmy said.

"And I get a good mom!" Trevor chimed in.

The boys ran upstairs to play. Claire and Emma sat down at the dining room table with another cup of coffee. Katrina sat on the sofa and patted the cushion beside her. Chase obliged her by sitting next to her.

"I've waited so long for you to say yes that I can hardly believe you did. Don't you think it would be nice for the boys to have a baby sister? One who looks like their mom?" Chase winked at her.

"It's kind of early for family planning."

"As long as it takes you to make up your mind, I thought I'd better start now."

"Good point. I'd love a houseful of healthy, happy kids. Remember, my prophecy said I was going to have ten!"

"Ten seems like a lot, but I'm more than willing to start with one more."

"Quack! Quack!" Katrina said laughing.

****

Miss Althea looked over the ring from every angle, then said, "You know, you don't have to have a man to be happy. I'm living proof of that. Besides, I'm getting too old to keep breaking in new girls here."

Charlie sat down beside Althea. "Well, my little Kitty's going to be a doctor's wife. And just when the angels have come back. I'll miss that voice each morning. Sheba will wonder where you are."

Katrina assured them both that she would still be around a while. When Bobby Murphy came in, Katrina was surprised to see Chase right behind him. "Looks like the gang's all here. I'm buying breakfast for everyone at the counter to celebrate that this beautiful woman said YES!"

Chase got lots of congratulations and pats on the back. Katrina took all the orders and brought Chase his coffee. "I guess in all the excitement this morning, I didn't hear your motorcycle."

"I didn't ride it," Chase replied with a mischievous look in his eyes.

"Is it in the shop?"

"Nope. I sold it. My carefree bachelor days are about to end. My old-ball-and-chain doesn't like motorcycles. I have to straighten up and be a responsible family man."

"Chase, you didn't need to sell it."

"Yes, I did. I should've done it long ago, as soon as I realized what bad memories it dredged up for you. I certainly don't need a vehicle that you won't ride on with me. I don't intend to go anywhere without you!"

"Thank you. No wonder I'm so in love with you."

Susie and Doris came up behind Katrina with trays full of food for the counter patrons. "Boy, she gets engaged and forgets how to work," Susie teased.

"Maybe it's a disease. She should see a doctor," Doris said. "Oh, wait, she is!"

"I'm sorry. Don't mean to be so distracted." Katrina quickly served everyone at the counter.

Chase raised his coffee cup, and the whole counter toasted, "To Katrina," while she stood quietly basking in her husband-to-be's smiling salute.

"I guess I better dust off my 'experienced help wanted' ad," Muriel teased Katrina later in the day. "How much longer do you plan to work?"

"Everyone is assuming that getting married means I'm not going to work. Doris just got married, and she's still working," Katrina protested.

"Right, but I don't have two little boys to chase around the house," Doris explained. "At least not yet."

"Why don't you talk to Doc about it?" Susie suggested. "The way he looks at you, I wouldn't be surprised if he wants you all to himself at breakfast every morning."

Muriel laughed. "My business could take a hit because of this marriage. I hadn't thought of that when I was encouraging the romance to grow."

"I've never even thought about not working. I guess I assumed that I always would. I'll talk with Chase and let you know."

****

That evening, Katrina began, "Muriel asked me if she needed to look for my replacement. I didn't know how to respond. I've been waiting tables since I was sixteen. Not having a job was never an option. What do you think? Should I keep working at Whistler's after we're married?"

"I think you should do whatever makes you happy, as long as I get to stay at your side. Be a full-time mom while the boys are still young enough to appreciate having a mother at home; or go to college and study to take up a completely different profession; or stay at Whistler's and I'll keep coming in for breakfast every morning; or a combination of all of them; or something totally different. It's up to you. So, my love, what do you want to be when you grow up?" Chase asked.

Katrina shivered as goose bumps popped out on her arms. "I've never consciously decided what to do. I waited tables so we could survive. It's never been a question of *if* I worked, but *where*. This is a wonderful, scary, liberating gift—being able to choose my life's path instead of reacting to circumstances. Knowing you'll always have my back, because you have my heart, I believe I can do anything. What *do* I want to be? This will take some reflection and some earnest prayer." Katrina leaned over and kissed Chase. "Timmy would say I'm a lucky duck. I know I'm a truly blessed woman."

****

At the end of the week, Katrina said, "Muriel, please go ahead and post an ad for my position. I won't leave you shorthanded, but I'm not going to keep working after we get married. Not sure what I'll do, but for the first time ever, I have options." She gave Muriel a hug. "This job was a lifeline. Thanks for taking a chance on me. I might never have met Chase, if I hadn't been here. Thanks for everything. I'll be forever grateful."

"I was pretty sure that would be your answer. I posted it yesterday," Muriel said with her eyes twinkling. "I'm glad Whistler's could play a part in the Chase and Katrina Love Story. We've enjoyed seeing it develop. Walt told me the second day you were here that Chase Merrick was going to marry you. Somehow, the old man I'm married to knew how it was all going to play out."

Katrina laughed. "I'm glad he didn't tell me! I'm not sure my nerves would have held up! I'm still reeling from how quickly it happened."

Epilogue

Two Months Later

Emma finished zipping up Katrina's dress. A familiar voice from the back of the room said, "I think I have the perfect accessories for your special day."

Katrina was speechless. Tears filled her eyes. Pop looked dapper in the tuxedo. "Let's try these on." The lustrous pearl necklace felt cool on her neck. The pearl drop earrings glistened just below her ear lobes. "I gave these to your mother on our wedding day. I know she'd want you to wear them today." He kissed her cheek.

"Oh, Pop, they're beautiful. The necklace fits the neckline of my dress as if it were made for it. Thank you so much. I've prayed for this moment, but I can't believe you're really here."

"Someone needed to give you away. It's a father's job. Besides, I had a personal invitation from my soon-to-be son-in-law. I couldn't pass it up."

"Chase called you?"

"He not only called me, he flew us all out here, had a limo pick us up curbside in Chicago, and got us hotel rooms. You're marrying quite a guy."

"All? Who is all?" Uncle John and Aunt Judy came across the room. They embraced her in a three-person hug.

"You're just beautiful, absolutely beautiful," Judy

gushed. "Look, John, isn't she beautiful?"

"She always has been," John said gruffly. "Why would today be any different?" He laughed.

"What a wonderful gift to have you here for my wedding. I can't believe Chase arranged all of this without me knowing."

"There is one other person who hopes to share your joy today," Jocelyn said quietly from across the room. Katrina rushed to her side and locked her in an embrace.

"I'm so glad you and Pop are back together. You couldn't have given me a better wedding gift," Katrina said softly and kissed her stepmother's cheek.

"That forgiveness thing really works."

"Believe me, I know. Love can't thrive without it."

Pop joined his daughter and wife. "Thanks for fighting for our marriage when we couldn't figure out how to go forward. Jocelyn told me *everything*. I'm thankful she was brave enough to tell me the truth. You helped both of us more than you'll ever know. You are as beautiful as your mother was on our day."

"We're both proud of you," Jocelyn said.

"And we're all together to celebrate this occasion as a family." Katrina hugged Jocelyn and Pop. Tears flowed down their cheeks.

She introduced her Philadelphia family to her new Wisconsin family. *This day could not be more perfect than to have the people I love most in the world here when I marry the man I love, who is my world.*

"We'd better get to our seats." Uncle John took Judy in one hand and Jocelyn in the other. "Looks like this show is about to get started."

The organ music began. Jack Coleman, Chase's

best friend from medical school, walked down the wide aisle with Doris Demming on his left arm and Susie Powell on his right arm. When they got to the altar, Emma Ritterskamp followed the same path to the front of the sanctuary with a grandson on each side of her. Then everyone rose and turned to see Katrina Russell, radiantly smiling holding her father's arm.

"It's your party, baby girl. Let's not keep the people waiting," Pop said as they took their first steps down the aisle.

The church was packed. Every seat was taken including overhead in the balcony. Katrina couldn't see Chase until they were almost to the altar. Then he came into sight, standing tall in his tuxedo, looking awestruck. Their eyes met. That look took her breath away. Again.

Reverend Cox asked, "Who gives this woman?"

Pop responded, "Her family and I do," then he slipped into the front pew next to his wife.

Thank goodness for traditional vows. All she had to do was repeat what the pastor said. Chase's "I do" rang out loud and strong as he squeezed her hand. Her "I do" was much louder than she expected it to be. The ceremony was a blur. The deep-blue eyes of the man she loved never left hers. Happiness gushed out of her every pore.

"You may kiss the bride," Reverend Cox said.

Long, slow, and sweet.

"I now present Chase and Katrina Merrick, husband and wife."

Timmy and Trevor ran to stand beside their parents. Reverend Cox said, "And their sons, Timmy and Trevor."

Holding hands the new brothers smiled, bowed, and said in unison, "Quack, quack, quack."

Pop got his wish. His Kat landed on her feet. Again.